By Cynthia Harnett

THE SIGN
OF THE
GREEN FALCON

For a moment Dickon hung in space

THE SIGN
OF THE
GREEN FALCON

Written and illustrated
by

CYNTHIA HARNETT

LERNER PUBLICATIONS COMPANY
MINNEAPOLIS

This edition first published 1984 by
Lerner Publications Company.
All U.S. rights reserved.

No part of this book may be reproduced in any form whatsoever
without permission in writing from the publisher except for
the inclusion of brief quotations in an acknowledged review.

Library of Congress Cataloging in Publication Data

Harnett, Cynthia.
The sign of the Green Falcon.

Reprint. Originally published: Ring out, bow bells!
London: Methuen Children's Books, 1953.
Summary: As apprentice to Dick Whittington, Mayor
of London, Dickon finds himself unwittingly involved in
a plot against King Henry V.
1. London (England)—History—To 1500—Juvenile
fiction. 2. Whittington, Richard, d. 1423—Juvenile
fiction. [1. London (England)—History—To 1500—Fiction.
2. Whittington, Richard, d. 1423—Fiction] I. Title.
PZ7.H228Si 1984   [Fic]   83-24831
ISBN 0-8225-0888-5

Manufactured in the United States of America

1 2 3   4 5 6 7 8 9 10 93 92 91 90 89 88 87   86 85 84

CONTENTS

Looking out over London River

Chapter One

LONDON RIVER

NAN sat on the top of the warehouse steps, her chin in her hands, looking out over London River. Though she was all by herself she did not feel lonely for her brothers were not far away.

Adam, the elder, was in the warehouse just behind her, busily mixing up drugs and spices and concoctions of boiled frogs and other horrible things with which he hoped to make medicines that would cure people's aches and pains.

Dickon, her second brother, was down on the river helping Jenkyn the waterman to ferry passengers across from Bankside. Dickon was crazed about boats. He knew the name of every ship that came up the river and his greatest joy was to board the vessels that brought goods for Grandfather's warehouse and coax the mariners to let him climb the rigging.

Nan had strict orders to bring the boys home punctually for dinner. Master Whittington was coming and Master Whittington was a very great man. True that he was Grandfather's life-long friend and had known them all from babyhood, but that did not alter the fact that he had been three times Mayor of London and was the most important person in the whole city.

However, there was really no hurry. The bells had not yet rung the noon hour. To suit Master Whittington's convenience dinner was to be much later than usual, so Nan settled herself more comfortably upon her perch. It might be dull sitting there alone but it was better than staying indoors and being given dreary household tasks by Aunt Isabel.

In front of her the river shimmered in the sunlight of a bright spring morning. It looked like a big lake shut in on three sides by banks of houses. On the north side the buildings all around her crowded down to the water's edge, ending in a broken line of wharfs and warehouses and a jumble of roofs. Opposite, on the south bank, there were gardens among the houses and a background of tree-tops to mark the open country.

Between the north bank and the south, like a great wall across the river, lay London Bridge which had a street of houses and shops all the way along it, and, into the bargain, a gatehouse and a drawbridge and even a chapel with pinnacles and turrets, all built upon its massive arches and buttresses.

The tide was at the flood and the water lay high against the Bridge, so calm that a second Bankside and a second Bridge were reflected upside down upon its surface. But soon the tide would turn and then the river would rush back seawards through the narrow arches, roaring and groaning like an imprisoned beast, sucking into rapids and whirlpools anything that came in its way.

Nan knew the sound of it well, for their old nurse, Goody Doubleday, lived on the Bridge, and sometimes, for a great treat, she was allowed to stay the night with Goody. She loved to lie cosily in bed listening to the noises that the water made as it gushed underneath the house.

But at this moment everything seemed very quiet. The little ships tied up by the wharfs all lay in idleness, their brightly coloured sails furled. No work was being done, no cargoes loaded or unloaded, for it was Ascension Day, a holy-day, and the few people to be seen were either fishing from the quays or lounging about and gossiping.

Even the clatter of the streets was stilled. She could hear quite clearly little noises which as a rule were lost in the grinding of heavy wheels on cobblestones: there was a solitary horseman clip-clopping along Thames Street, and the doves were cooing in Master Whittington's garden half-way up the hill.

Suddenly from far off a new sound pierced the stillness, the clear shrill note of a trumpet. Nan sat up. She knew where it came from. The King was at the Tower. He had ridden from Westminster this morning after High Mass, attended by a few knights, as simply as he used to ride when he was Prince Hal and lived at Coldharbour, only a bowshot away. Few people knew that he was coming except the Mayor, who met him at Ludgate with Grandfather and one or two of the other Aldermen.

The King was visiting the Tower to see the work going on there. For Henry V was preparing for war. Everybody knew that. From the smithy's furnaces the smoke belched out on every working day and when the wind was in the east the ringing of hammers beating out steel mail could be heard even above the din of London traffic. Carts rumbled through the City carrying hides for leather strappings; and actually on the wharf, quite close to where Nan sat, scores of bowstaves were neatly stacked, unloaded only yesterday from the ships that brought them.

Nan sighed. She wished she were a boy. Boys had all the fun. Screwing up her eyes against the sun she peered across the river. Right over by the south bank she could see Dickon hopping in and out of Jenkyn's boat. He was wearing a saffron tunic that caught the light. Of course he would get his shoes and his hose all dirty and then there would be trouble with Grandfather. She looked round to see if there was some straw lying about with which she could make him clean off the mud before they went home to dinner.

She did not know why she, who was so much younger, should always feel responsible for her brothers. Perhaps it was because they had no father or mother, but all three of them lived with their grandfather, John Sherwood, master grocer, warden of the Grocers' Company, and Alderman of the City of London. They formed a little inner circle of their own within Grandfather's big household. Besides Grandfather and Aunt Isabel, there were two journeyman grocers, three young apprentices, and half a dozen servants, all living in the house, never to mention all the merchants and shopkeepers and sea captains and porters and pedlars who were in and out all day.

It was not so odd that she should fuss about Dickon, for Dickon was the next youngest to herself, and still at school. He was gay and careless, always getting into scrapes and coming to her to get him out of them.

Adam, however, was nearly grown up. He was a steady, studious boy and had already been apprenticed to Grandfather for two years. But Nan knew that Adam was not happy. He wanted to be an apothecary, or, better still, a doctor of some sort —either a physician or a chirurgeon. He was more interested in sick people than in anything else and he spent all his spare time with the monks at St. Bartholomew's Hospital. Grandfather made no difficulty about his becoming an apothecary. All apothecaries were members of the Grocers' Company, because their business was to make medicines from herbs and spices, all of which were sold only by grocers. Therefore Adam was allowed to have his own little corner of the warehouse and look after the spices, some of which came from far-off lands and were worth their weight in gold.

But Grandfather had quite made up his mind that Adam was to be a master grocer and carry on the business. Grandfather had brought them all up ever since their parents died in the last visitation of the plague, when Nan was quite tiny; so of course his word was law.

By this time the boat rowed by Dickon and Jenkyn was on its way back. They carried one passenger, a man in black who in the distance looked like a monk. Instead of steering for Dowgate, the public landing-place, Jenkyn was heading towards Grandfather's special wharf. Looking at the stranger again, Nan saw that he was no monk. On his head was a tall pointed hat and beneath his cloak he wore a surcoat of warm dark red. She wondered who he was and why they were bringing him this way.

As they neared the wharf, Dickon shipped his oars, jumped up and shouted through the hollow of his hands.

'Adam! A-D-A-M!'

Nan scrambled to her feet, determined to be helpful. But before she could clamber down from her perch, the door of the warehouse opened and Adam appeared. He was a tall boy, and his hair, cut to the level of his ears, was smooth and neat, a contrast to Dickon's unruly mop. He looked up at Nan.

'Did someone call?' he inquired. 'Is it time for dinner? I have not heard the noon bells yet.'

At that moment Dickon clambered up the ladder on to the wharf, followed by the stranger, a lean sallow man with a long pointed nose.

'Hey, brother,' cried Dickon. 'Here's a customer for you.'

As Adam turned, the stranger stepped forward and bowed.

'God keep you, young master,' he said. 'I am anxious to

'Hey, brother,' cried Dickon. *'Here's a customer for you'*

buy some turmeric, and I have been told that I should surely find it in the warehouse of John Sherwood the grocer.'

Adam slowly shook his head. 'Sir, I am sorry,' he said. 'We have turmeric in plenty if you will come tomorrow. But we may not trade today. 'Tis a holy-day, you know.'

'I had not forgot. But I need it urgently for an essence that I am brewing. Your brother said that you were an apothecary, and I had hoped for a fellow craftsman you might stretch a point.'

Adam coloured. Nan could see that he was pleased to be addressed as an apothecary.

'A fellow craftsman?' he repeated. "You are an apothecary yourself, good master?'

The man smiled, his thin lips parting over long yellow teeth. 'An apothecary, if you will. My name is Saloman Gross. I practise alchemy.'

Adam almost gasped. 'An alchemist! I never met an alchemist until now. I am honoured, sir.'

'An alchemist, like an apothecary, uses essences, but his object is to discover the secrets of nature,' Master Gross said rather pompously. 'Myself I seek a process that will change base metal into gold. I have at this moment an experiment hanging in the balance for lack of an ounce of turmeric. 'Tis so very small a quantity, yet so vital to my needs.'

'An ounce,' exclaimed Adam. 'I have more than that which is my own property. Though I may not sell it today I can give you some, if you will be pleased to accept it. Will you do me the honour to come inside while I measure it?'

He ushered the stranger through the little door that led into his own particular corner of the warehouse. Dickon remained on the wharf. Jenkyn and the boat had gone, so he climbed the wooden steps and sat down beside his sister.

'What time is dinner?' he inquired, pushing his fingers through his blown hair. 'Ye loaves and fishes, I'm so hungry I could eat an ox.'

Nan was shocked. '*What* did you say?' she cried. 'Was it an oath?'

'"Ye loaves and fishes"?' repeated Dickon unconcernedly. 'I don't think it's an oath, not a bad one anyway. Jenkyn often says it.'

'Jenkyn is a waterman and watermen always swear,' retorted Nan. 'You'd better not let Grandfather hear you. Don't you remember the beating you got when you said "By Cock and Pie"?' As he didn't respond she changed the subject. 'Who was that queer man you brought to Adam? Where did he come from?'

'Jenkyn knew him,' said Dickon. 'Jenkyn told him that he might get his stuff, whatever it is, from here. Listen! There go the noon bells.'

A single bell, not far away, began to ring the hour, but before it had reached its third note it was overtaken by a dozen others, high and low, from every quarter of the City; a regular cascade of bells. Nan first, and then Dickon, crossed themselves hastily as a token of their midday prayer, and began immediately to call out at one another above the clamour.

'St. Michael's,' cried Nan.

ST MICHAEL PATERNOSTER ST ANTHONY BUDGE ROW ST MARTIN VINTRY ST LAURENCE POULTNEY ALL HALLOWS THE GREAT ST MARY-LE-BOW

'St. Anthony's,' yelled Dickon.
'St. Swithun's.' 'Woolchurch.' 'St. James's.'
'St. Martin's.' 'St. Laurence.' 'All Hallows.'

Then they both shouted at once, counting how many of the bells they could name before the peal died down again: St. Paul's, St. Helen's, St. Andrew's, Trinity. It was an old game that they'd first played with Goody in the nursery, but they never tired of it.

'Bow,' cried Dickon triumphantly when Nan had given up for lack of breath. 'Bow Bells late again. Did you hear? It doesn't matter today because it's a holy-day, but the apprentices are all grumbling because they mayn't stop till Bow Bells ring and the clerk is always late. By the way did you hear that there was a great apprentice battle on Cheapside last night?'

'They are *always* fighting,' said Nan scornfully.

'Oh, but this was an extra big fight. The Fishmongers met the Mercers and broke a lot of heads, so the Mercers cried: "Clubs", and the Drapers rushed to help them. Then the Grocers came in to support the Fishmongers and there was a grand battle; the old story—Victuallers against Clothers, Food against Cloth. I wish I'd been there with the Grocers.'

'You're not an apprentice yet,' objected Nan.

'Oh, I shall be any day now,' said Dickon loftily. 'Grandfather said last week that it was high time that my indentures were signed. Then I shall work in the warehouse with Adam, and come out on to the wharf to see the ships arrive. I warrant I shan't stay inside all day with my nose over spices as Adam does. I hope I'm apprenticed before we fight the Mercers again.' He drummed his heels against the steps. 'Oh, I *am* hungry. Why is dinner so late?'

'Your head is so full of fighting that you forget all else. Master Whittington is coming. Aunt Isabel told you.'

'Dick Whittington? *He*'s a mercer too—a plague upon him.'

'Dickon!' exclaimed Nan in horror. 'You mustn't speak so of Master Whittington. He's your godfather.'

'Well, he *is* a mercer, isn't he? And everybody calls him that I heard some urchins on Cheapside yesterday crying out "Here comes Dick Whittington". How answer you that, mistress?'

'Grandfather will hear you say that one day and then he'll beat you.'

'Ah well,' sighed Dickon, 'one beating more or less makes little difference. Oh, I almost forgot. Jenkyn has promised to take me in his wherry to Ratcliffe-below-Tower to see the great ship built for the King. She's called the *Katharine-of-the-Tower* and she's due to set sail for Southampton soon, ready to carry him to France.'

'I wish I could come,' breathed Nan. 'But I'm certain that Aunt Isabel would never let me.'

'Then don't ask,' advised Dickon crisply. 'Do as I do; go first and ask afterwards. After all you won't be beaten with a stick; only with a slipper, and a slipper does not hurt nearly as much as a stick.'

Nan did not agree. A slipper could certainly hurt. She changed the subject.

'What shall we do after dinner?' she inquired. 'I'd like to cross the Bridge and go out in the country with Goody. There may be some bluebells out round Bermondsey.'

'Bermondsey is across the Bridge,' he reminded her. 'If you go there you'll have to go through the Drawbridge Gate, underneath all the traitors' heads stuck on poles. You don't like that.'

Nan shuddered. 'No, I don't. I wish they'd take them away. They've been there so long.'

'Some of them were put there after Oldcastle's Lollard rising last year,' said Dickon casually. 'But the crows have picked them clean by now anyway. As for me, I might have gone with Jenkyn to Ratcliffe-below-Tower; but if Grandfather and Dick Whittington sit over their wine, talking about when they were boys together, it will go on for ages and we shan't go anywhere at all.'

He swung his feet out from the ladder and Nan caught sight of them.

'Dickon, just look at your best shoes,' she cried out horrified.

Dickon pulled off one sodden shoe and examined it cheerfully. It was made of soft red leather elaborately looped and thonged, the finest he had ever possessed. But though it was sodden and coated with slime he was quite unabashed and wriggled his bare toes which projected beyond the strapping of his hose.

''Tis only mud,' he said lightly. 'It'll all brush off when it is dry.'

'There's some straw over there,' she pointed out; 'there, by the warehouse wall. You could wipe off the worst of it.'

Obediently Dickon vaulted to the ground. As he started to rub his feet, Adam and Master Gross emerged from the warehouse.

'It seems to me that you have a certain cure for the yellow jaundice in your formula,' the alchemist was saying. 'You are a young man of promise, and I shall be happy to give you any help that lies in my power. If you will visit my lodging in Southwark I can show you many things which may be of value to you. You will find me at the hostelry of Benedict Wolman, the sign of the *Green Falcon*, near the Marshalsea. You will not forget?'

Adam's eyes brightened. He said that most certainly he would not forget.

Master Gross lingered at the door. 'And on your part you will try to procure for me some of those rare earths we talked of?' He spoke earnestly laying hold of Adam by the doublet.

'I can get anything you want,' said Adam rather grandly. 'We deal much with the Hanse merchants—the merchants from Germany.'

'That is good,' said Master Gross with obvious satisfaction. 'It has been a fortunate meeting, and I am indebted to you for the gift of turmeric.' He looked round him as though uncertain of the direction.

'You want a boat?' asked Adam.

He shook his head. 'I will walk across the Bridge. I have plenty to think upon. Which way do I go?'

Adam led him to the corner of the warehouse and showed him the cobbled lane which led up the slope into Thames Street. He nodded his farewell, but after a few steps he returned.

'You will remember that all this is for your ear only,' he said.

'There are others who would be glad to know the elements I use, and how I procure them. It is vital that we should be secret.'

Adam reassured him, and after a searching glance in the direction of Dickon and of Nan, as though he were pledging them to secrecy too, he set off up the lane, walking with quick short steps, his black cloak streaming from his high shoulders.

'A plague upon him, I thought he would never go,' cried Dickon, vigorously rubbing his shoes with straw.

Nan peeped round the corner of the building to watch the retreating figure of Master Gross. 'I don't like him,' she announced. 'He pokes his nose like a ferret.'

'He is an alchemist of great esteem,' said Adam sharply. 'Many have sought the power of turning base metal into gold, but no one has come so near to finding it. His learning is wonderful and I shall be fortunate if he will impart some of it to me. Remember, Nan, and you too, Dickon, that you must not repeat anything of this. It must be kept entirely secret. In fact it will be best for you not to mention Master Gross at all.'

Nan stared at her elder brother, usually so silent. He must have been bewitched to make such a long speech. However, she promised that she would be careful. Dickon had already forgotten all about the alchemist, and was talking again, while he cleaned his shoes, about the great ship, the *Katherine* lying at Ratcliffe-below-Tower. So Adam, saying that he must put away his spices, went back into the warehouse.

He had hardly closed the door when there was a sound of shouting in the lane. Nan peeped round once more. The alchemist had already vanished and the noise came from some boys racing down the hill towards the wharf. There were four of them. A small boy, wearing a fishmonger's striped apron, was running for his life from three sturdy apprentices in the neat cloth tunics of the clothing guilds. As they drew near Nan could hear the child's terrified sobbing even above the howls and threats of his pursuers.

'Duck him!' they were yelling. 'Drown the stinking fishmonger. Throw him in the river. Drown him!'

Nan screamed and Dickson stopped cleaning his shoes to stare as the four swept onto the wharf.

Seeing himself cornered, with no way of escape except the water, the small boy turned and faced his enemies, his eyes screwed up and his arms raised to shield his head.

Though they were three to one, they did not spare him. In a second two of them had him on the ground and began to punch him mercilessly, while the third, a big red-haired fellow with a bright green hood across his shoulders, leaned over them and egged them on.

'Throw him in!' he commanded. 'Let him sink or swim. That'll teach him to push his way among decent mercers, the dirty little——'

He broke off abruptly, for suddenly from behind, Dickon rushed upon them. The red-haired boy was taken by surprise and went down with a crash. Dickon jumped over him to tackle the other two. They had dragged their victim to the edge of the wharf, and were holding him there. They were hampered by his hands clutching at them and could not defend themselves against Dickon's fists.

Nan, poised on the top step, shouted a warning, for the red-headed boy was on his feet again. Dickon had only just time to turn and meet the attack.

It was a hard struggle! Though Dickon was the smaller of the two, he was the quicker. But little by little the big mercer pressed him back towards the warehouse wall. Nan clapped her hands over her mouth, not daring to make another sound in case she should distract him. If the other two had joined in they would have decided it, but they stood gripping their wretched prisoner and gaping at the fight.

Nan saw Dickon glance quickly behind him. He had reached the heap of straw from which he had started, but he knew that it was there and took a quick side-step over it. His opponent following, put his heel on to a slimy clot of that rich Thames mud which Dickon had scraped from his shoe. He slithered, and Dickon, quick to seize the chance, landed him a blow full on the mouth and another on the point of the chin. Down he went, flat on his back, with Dickon standing triumphant over him.

At the same moment Adam opened the warehouse door. 'Whatever is going on?' he demanded. He looked quickly round and took in the situation. Obviously Dickon was in no need of help, so he went towards the two at the edge of the wharf.

But the smaller apprentices did not wait. They dropped the fishmonger boy, dodged Adam's long arms and ran off at top speed the way they had come, leaving their leader to his fate.

Nan scrambled down from her ladder and began explaining to

The fishmonger lad . . . stood snivelling

Adam what had happened, as he stood gazing down at the red-headed mercer, still on the ground beneath Dickon's threatening fist.

'You young knave,' Adam cried angrily. 'You might have done a murder if you had not been stopped. What's your craft? A mercer? You put shame upon a worshipful company.'

The apprentice sat up groaning and mopping his face with his green hood. His brow was cut, his nose bleeding, and two front teeth were broken. He mumbled some excuse about the whelp who had ventured in the mercers' quarter upon a feast day with his clothes stinking of fish. But Adam would not listen.

'Be gone,' he ordered, 'and think yourself lucky that I do not hand you over to the constable.'

Sulkily the boy scrambled to his feet and without another word limped away. Adam turned to the fishmonger lad who stood snivelling at the edge of the wharf. He did not seem badly hurt, but he was white-faced and puny, and the mercer had spoken no more than the truth when he said that he stank.

'You had best go home,' said Adam briefly. 'You can walk, can't you? No bones broken?'

The boy sobbed that he dare not. They would be waiting for him.

Adam frowned. 'Where do you live?'

'Southwark,' the boy sniffed.

'Southwark? Why, you'd better take boat. Can you row? Then borrow the one tied to the wharf. It belongs to us. Bring it back and don't fail, mark you, or you'll have the Grocers to deal with as well as the Mercers.'

Chapter Two

GRANTHAM'S INN

ADAM and Nan were silent as the three of them made their way single file up the narrow lane. Adam had already forgotten the fight and was thinking deeply of all that the alchemist had told him. Nan, having done her best to tidy Dickon up, was full of forebodings as to what would happen when Grandfather saw him. It was hopeless to try and conceal the fact that he had been fighting. He had a cut on his forehead; his hose and his doublet were torn and dirty, and one of his eyes was fast closing up.

But Dickon himself whistled cheerfully. Not even the swelling of his eyes and various aches and bruises could rob him of the satisfaction of having vanquished a mercer considerably bigger than himself. If only Grandfather would sign him on as apprentice now he would surely cut a fine figure among the other grocer apprentices.

Just before they reached home Adam briefly reminded them both not to talk about the alchemist in front of Grandfather.

'Can't we even say that we've seen him?' said Nan. It was odd for Adam to be so mysterious.

'No, you can't,' returned Adam quite sharply. 'You know what Grandfather is. He'd only make difficulties or take the

13

whole thing out of my hands. It's the chance of a lifetime for me to meet anyone like Master Gross and I'm going to make the most of it. You don't want me to spend all my days counting peppercorns and weighing rice, do you?'

Nan said, 'Of course not.' She *did* know what Grandfather was like, and yet in some odd way she felt uneasy.

At the top of the lane, before it joined Thames Street, they turned under a stone arch and entered a small paved courtyard. This was Grantham's Inn, where they lived with Grandfather, so called because it had been built by John Grantham, a Mayor in the days of Edward III. Nan was secretly very proud of living in a house called an Inn, for most of the Inns of London were the town houses of great lords who lived on their estates in the country and kept an Inn to stay at when they visited the city.

Grantham's Inn was built of stone and was very old-fashioned. It had a lofty hall, a kitchen and buttery, a room for the master, a solar for the ladies to sit in and sleep in, and very little else. To this stone house Grandfather had recently added a wing at each end, three storeys high, of oak beams filled in with mud. It really looked very odd beside the dignified hall, but it provided ample room for everybody. Aunt Isabel and Nan had a bed-chamber as well as the solar, the boys shared an attic, and even the journeymen and the apprentices and the servants had places to sleep instead of lying all night on the floor in the hall, as they used to do.

The main door stood open so that they could go straight in. Dickon now began to feel less sure of himself, and as they passed behind the carved screen which divided the passage from the hall, he dodged behind the others. Inside some sort of commotion was going on, more than the normal preparations for a feast-day dinner. All the servants seemed to be gathered in a chattering circle near the high table; the serving men, the cook, the house wenches, even the two scullion boys standing on tiptoes in their efforts to see over the shoulders of their elders.

Dickon seized his opportunity. Gently pushing Adam and Nan into the hall entry, he tiptoed quickly along behind the screen and vanished.

A little away from the crowd, his back to the screen, stood Grandfather, wearing a *houppelande* which hung in rich folds almost to the ground. It had wide fur sleeves and, with his great height and his forked white beard, it gave him an air of alarming dignity.

Adam and Nan hung back, but their grandsire heard them and turned round.

'Ah, here you are,' he announced in his booming voice.

Grandfather, wearing a 'houppelande'

'Here is Adam. Perchance he may be able to tell us what is wrong. Make way, all of you. Let Adam look at the fellow; he is our apothecary.'

The servants hastily drew back. On the floor in the midst sat Will the pantry steward, hugging his right arm and rocking himself to and fro, with loud groans and lamentations. Aunt Isabel hovered over him, her crisp white veil bobbing up and down like a sail in the breeze as she vainly tried to quiet him.

'Hold your peace, man,' Grandfather commanded. 'One would think that you had been dropped from a gibbet.' He pushed Adam forward. 'Find out what ails the groaning fool and let us get on with the dinner. Master Whittington will be here at any moment.'

'Tis his arm. He will not let me touch it. He vows that it is broken,' explained Aunt Isabel in a little pattering voice. 'He was bearing the roasted sucking-pig for your grandsire to carve when his foot slipped.' She poked about angrily with her toe. 'Those lazy wenches did not sweep before they spread new rushes. There are fish bones and gristly meat and Heaven knows what else, up here by the table. Someone will get a beating for this.'

There was an audible flutter among the maidservants, but Grandfather interrupted again.

'Beat if you will, but all in good time, daughter. First let us be quit of this bibble-babble.'

Nan stood staring with the rest as Adam bent over the steward. But she could not see much, so she looked round the room instead. The high table was spread for dinner with a vast linen cloth which almost completely enveloped it. In the shadow behind Aunt Isabel she suddenly saw a little head appear under the edge of the cloth. It was Button, Aunt Isabel's little dog. As Nan watched he edged his way to the forgotten sucking-pig which lay amongst the rushes and drew it firmly but unobtrusively under the table.

Nan caught her breath. Button was an adored family pet. He had belonged to Grandmother and his portrait actually appeared in the brass to Grandmother's memory in St. Anthony's

Button could not be allowed to steal a sucking-pig

Church. But however spoilt he might be, Button could not be allowed to steal a sucking-pig. Nan tiptoed round the table, lifted the cloth and pounced on him from behind.

It took a good deal of slapping and scolding to make him drop his prize, and she had only just succeeded when a chorus of 'Ohs' and 'Ahs', and a loud yell from the steward announced that something was going on. Clasping Button firmly she hurried back.

Will was on his feet again, though white and still groaning. Adam, undeterred by the groans, held the injured arm by a looped scarf and was gently bending it up and down.

'I 'faith it is not broken after all,' exclaimed Grandfather. 'That was a neat trick. Where did you learn it?'

Before Adam could answer there was a stir at the end of the hall. One of the scullions whispered loudly to the other—'Hist! Look! Here comes Dick Whittington——'

The cook smartly boxed the boys' ears, and they fled towards the kitchen, almost colliding at the screen with the slim quietly-dressed man who stood in the doorway.

Aunt Isabel rapped out orders to the serving men and wenches, who collected the dish, the sucking-pig and the grease-soaked rushes and took them away. Then she wiped her fingers on a napkin and hurried to her father's side to greet their guest.

Master Whittington smiled as he advanced into the hall. 'You look as if you had had the mummers here,' he said. 'Is it a feast-day frolic, or what's afoot?'

He kissed Aunt Isabel on both cheeks, and stood with his hand in friendly fashion on Grandfather's arm while he listened to the tale of woe.

Richard Whittington was a smallish man, approaching sixty, unassuming in manner and in dress. No one, seeing him for the first time, would have guessed that he had been already three times Mayor of London, the richest trading city in the world, and that he wielded immense influence, not only in the City but with the King. He was clean-shaven and he wore his hair short and brushed back from his forehead beneath his roundlet cap. His face was furrowed with many wrinkles. In repose it looked aged by a thousand cares. But when he smiled it lit up, his dark eyes shone, and he radiated merriment and perpetual youth.

He laughed heartily about the sucking-pig and wagged a solemn finger at Button who was still licking his chops in Nan's arms.

'Fie upon you for a thieving greasy little whelp,' he scolded. 'See what a mess you have made of Nan's fine gown.' He pulled the little dog's ear. 'You should take a lesson from my Madame Eglantine. She scorns to let grease stay for a minute on her dainty paws, and even her whiskers have to be washed after every meal.'

'By my troth, you have got the pig fat all over you, child,' cried Aunt Isabel, catching sight of Nan's dress. 'Put the dog down at once, and wipe it with this napkin.'

Before dropping Button Nan looked around to make sure

that Master Whittington had not brought his cat with him. His house was only a bowshot away and he often did so when he came to dine. Madame Eglantine followed him everywhere, even to church; and though she was a quiet little cat and sat peacefully on her master's shoulder or beneath his chair, Button hated all cats and there was bound to be trouble if they met.

However, on this occasion Madame Eglantine did not appear, so Nan gave her attention to rubbing her dress. Master Whittington stood with Grandfather watching Adam make a sling and settle the man's arm comfortably. Grandfather was greatly impressed.

A loop of linen cloth, a jerk with the foot

'That was very well done, my boy,' he declared. 'As neat a trick as ever I saw. I wish you had been here, Dick. A loop of linen cloth, a jerk with the foot, and lo! the arm was mended.'

'It was not broken, only out of joint,' said Adam modestly. 'I can show you on anybody's arm. Nan, lend me yours. I vow that I will not hurt.'

Nan hesitated, and Master Whittington drew her to his side with a protecting gesture.

'Nay,' he said firmly. 'You shall not plague Nan. And I have seen your trick—tho' it is no trick at all, friend John, but a matter of great skill. Adam must have learned it at the hospital of St. Bartholomew. I know he goes there, for the Master Hospitaller told me they rate him highly.'

Embarrassed by so much attention Adam began to set the stools for dinner. Aunt Isabel helped him.

'This is a pretty way to treat a guest,' she cried. 'Master Whittington must be well-nigh starved. Nan, go to the screen and clap your hands for them to bring in the meats.'

''Tis as well that I was late,' said Master Whittington, holding his fingers above the silver bowl while Adam poured water over them. 'I expected to get black looks from Mistress Isabel because

I was delayed so long. I could not help it. I have been with the King.'

'The King is at the Tower,' Nan broke in eagerly. 'I heard the trumpets.'

She was always happy when Master Whittington was there. They were fast friends. Long ago, when she was tiny, he used to set her on his knee and tell her stories. No one told such lovely stories as Master Whittington did. Even now she begged for one whenever she got the chance.

Master Whittington smiled at her. 'You are quite right, my poppet. His Grace is hard at work. He wastes not a minute. If it is not armour it is weapons; if not weapons then it is stores. We must talk, friend John, after we have dined. All that your warehouse can provide will be needed. Though the latest envoys have not come back from France, Harry of Monmouth is not idle. If there is to be war he will be ready.'

John Sherwood was thoughtful as he led the way to the table and took his place with Richard Whittington and Aunt Isabel on a high-backed settle facing down the hall. Adam waited at the sideboard to serve the meats, and Nan stood by Aunt Isabel's side until she was given permission to sit down on a stool at the end of the table.

She looked round, wondering what had happened to Dickon. He ought to have been here by now to help Adam and the serving men. The other servants had all filed in and taken their places for their own dinner round the trestle-board erected near the screen. Only Dickon was missing. Suppose he really had been hurt in the fight and was lying ill upstairs. But she dared not go and see. It would draw only attention to him. So she busied herself with the leg of chicken which Adam had put on her wooden trencher. She did her best to eat it as daintily as Aunt Isabel had taught her, nibbling the meat and not tearing it from the bone, dipping it carefully into the gravy and keeping her fingers dry, and not making a loud noise when she sucked them afterwards. She tried to forget about Dickon by fixing her mind on what her elders were saying.

'Will there be war, think you?' inquired Aunt Isabel as Master Whittington held out his trencher for a slice of sucking-pig, which, cleaned and regarnished, seemed none the worse for its adventure.

''Tis hard to say,' he answered cautiously. 'His Grace has

sent heralds to Paris to declare his wish for peace, but the Frenchmen must change their tune if war is to be avoided. Our Harry, as we all know, is partial to a jest, but the French Dauphin mixes his jests with insults. You have heard the story of the tennis balls?'

Nan leaned forward. A story! To her delight Aunt Isabel said that she had *not* heard about the tennis balls, and Master Whittington seemed quite pleased to tell it.

'It was more than a year ago, when his Grace was at Kenilworth; he had only been king a few months. Envoys came from the French Court bearing a gift from the Dauphin, as is customary from one prince to another. They brought a great tun, a vat, such as they send their wines in; we have all seen them down on the vintners' wharfs; each one holds 250 gallons. The King anticipated something rare in French wines. But when it was opened it contained nothing but tennis balls; tennis balls, mark you, in a 250-gallon tun.'

'It was an insult,' growled Grandfather angrily.

'Of course it was an insult and his Grace will not lightly forget it. I was told that the King was wonderfully master of himself. He would allow no hand to be laid upon the envoys, but in return he sent as answer a grim jest about matching his rackets to the Dauphin's balls and striking the French crown into the hazard. He has a very pretty wit, our Harry!'

He looked along the table as he finished and saw Nan's rapt expression.

'I know a little maid who loves a story,' he said. ''Tis finished now, Nan. You can go on eating your meat.'

'You were telling a story about the King; that is why Nan was all ears,' declared Grandfather. 'In the whole realm I do believe his Grace has not a more loving subject. She fairly dotes on him.'

'It began when he was Prince Hal and lived here at Coldharbour,' explained Aunt Isabel. ''Tis so near at hand that the children were always hovering about, and he was kind to them. He once gave Nan a ride across his saddlebow and she has never forgotten it. Dickon used to wait to hold his horse——'

She stopped abruptly with a little nervous laugh, and there was an awkward silence. All the family knew why. It was an old and sore story. Dickon had lined his pockets with ha'pence earned by holding the Prince's horse. He had made quite a profitable trade of it until Grandfather found out and beat him soundly. He might hold the Prince's horse as often as he wished. That was fit and honourable. But let him not forget that his grandsire was an Alderman, and Warden of the Grocers' Company. To take ha'pence for holding horses—that was an insult which must be wiped out——

Richard Whittington saw that some painful memory had been stirred. He tried to change the subject.

'I have not seen Dickon today,' he remarked. 'What has become of him?'

Nan caught her breath. What ill luck could have prompted Aunt Isabel to mention Dickon's name? And where on earth could he be? Then to her astonishment Dickon himself answered, from the back of the high oak settle where the grown-ups were sitting. He must have come into the hall so quietly that she had not noticed him, and now he was keeping himself carefully out of sight. And small wonder, for in the interval his black eye had almost closed up, and his face was swollen and blotched. To try to cover the cut on his forehead he had wetted his curly hair and combed it down in Adam's fashion so that it lay in watery rats'-tails. The jagged tear in his hose could not be concealed and in trying to brush the mud from his doublet he had only succeeded in making it a great deal worse.

Nan stared in dismay, her half-eaten chicken leg in mid-air. Adam, pouring wine, saw him too, and spilt the wine on to the cloth. Grandfather looked from Adam to Nan and back again.

'What's afoot?' he demanded. 'What ails you both? Is Dickon there? What are you doing, boy? Come out at once.'

Slowly and reluctantly Dickon appeared from behind the settle, carrying a dish of chicken. There was a moment of shocked silence. Aunt Isabel crossed herself and invoked St. Thomas of Canterbury. Master Whittington was very obviously trying not to laugh. Grandfather looked Dickon slowly up and down.

'You have been fighting,' he boomed.

Dickon answered simply, 'Yes, sir.' He could not make up his mind whether to add that he had been defending a fishmonger apprentice against quarrelsome mercers. In the ordinary way Grandfather would have been quite pleased, but today Dick Whittington was there and he was a mercer. To tell the truth

Dickon appeared . . . carrying a dish of chicken

might be rude to a guest, and make Grandfather angrier than ever. It was best to be discreet. So he began to mumble a garbled account of what had happened on the wharf.

That was more than Nan could bear. Dickon had fought three big boys to rescue one small one. Unless Grandfather understood that, Dickon would get a most terrible beating. She jumped to her feet.

'Sir!' she cried aloud. 'I was there. I saw it. The mercers would have drowned the little boy but Dickon saved him. Please *please* hear me.'

Quite regardless of Dickon's signs to her, she poured out the story in a high clear voice, even forgetting to be frightened of Grandfather. She had no thought about Master Whittington.

She left them in no doubt that the mercers were the villains and Dickon the hero of a most valiant fight.

The effect was not in the least what she had expected; nor what Dickon feared. Grandfather did not frown. He began to chuckle. Master Whittington, sitting beside him, began to laugh too. There seemed to be some joke between them, for Master Whittington laid his hand on Grandfather's arm, his face screwed up with laughter.

'Did you mark that, my friend? The boy begins boldly,' he cried, as soon as he could speak. 'He downed three mercers, the young fighting cock. *Mercers*, did you hear?'

The two of them went on laughing till the tears came. It was Dickon's turn to stare. He could not understand it. He had hoped Grandfather might not be *too* angry, but he had never dreamed that it could be regarded as a *joke*. For himself he could not see that it was funny, but all the same he began to laugh too. Then Nan joined in with little shrill peals of laughter; so did Aunt Isabel; and Adam; till everyone was laughing and nobody but Grandfather and Master Whittington quite knew why.

Suddenly Grandfather pulled himself together. He glared at Dickon.

'What are *you* laughing at, you young fool?' he roared. "Tis no laughing matter for *you*.'

Everybody was immediately sobered, except Master Whittington, who went on shaking and wiping his eyes. Grandfather did not attempt to explain what he meant. Dickon began to feel anxious again. There was some mystery here he felt sure.

'The boy does not understand. How could he?' said Master Whittington. 'Shall we tell him, friend John?'

Grandfather mumbled something like 'As you will' into his beard and Master Whittington began to fumble in the folds of his *houppelande*. From within he produced a small roll of parchment which he held out to Dickon.

'Look at it,' he said with a smile. 'It concerns you.'

Dickon carefully unrolled the parchment. It was covered with neat writing. He noticed his own name, Grandfather's name and the name of Richard Whittington, but he was too nervous to take in the sense of it.

'Don't you know what it is?' asked Grandfather gruffly. "Tis your indenture, boy.'

'Possibly he has not seen an indenture before,' said Master Whittington. 'An indenture, Dickon, is a deed of agreement which, when it is completed, is cut in half so that each party to it may keep one half. This is the indenture of your apprenticeship, drawn up between your grandsire and myself. It is all ready to be signed. Give it back to me now. We will talk about it after dinner.'

Arms of the Grocers' Company

Sitting on the edge of the wharf

Chapter *Three*

THE NEW APPRENTICE

ALL this talk about indentures was rather above Nan's head.
Nor did she know what the laughter was about. But anyway
there seemed to be no danger of a beating, so she returned happily
to her dinner.

Dickon also was puzzled. He considered that he had got
off pretty lightly. As for being apprenticed it was exactly what
he wanted. Ever since the fight he'd been thinking that if only
Grandfather would sign him on now, he would start off with a
pretty good reputation among the other grocer apprentices.

But there was something odd about the whole business. He
knew that he looked funny, for he had crept into Aunt Isabel's
bed-chamber and peeped in her mirror of polished steel. But
Grandfather seldom laughed at anything. The sight of Grandfather and Dick Whittington sharing some tremendous joke at his
expense worried him.

And why should Dick Whittington have been the one to show
him his indenture? Surely it ought to have come from
Grandfather. He brooded over that while he helped Adam to

He peeped in the mirror of polished steel

serve at the table, but presently a solution occurred to him. Every new apprentice had to be sponsored by some respectable grown-up. As Grandfather was becoming his *master* he could not very well be his sponsor too. In that case it would be quite natural for Dick Whittington to take his place, for he was Dickon's godfather. Of course that must be it! Satisfied with this explanation Dickon sat down to his own dinner and began to listen to the conversation at the table. Grandfather and Dick Whittington were still discussing the King's preparations for war.

'We shall all be in it,' Master Whittington was saying. 'There is not a craft among us which will not be called upon to work for his Grace's needs. If I were you, John my friend, I should order some shiploads of corn from the Baltic. In a good harvest we grow enough at home for the whole of England, but this year we shall have to feed an army in France, and if the harvest is poor we might go hungry ourselves. If it is not needed you can always re-ship it to Gascony in exchange for wine. Speak with the Hanse merchants about it, and do it betimes. There will be many things for them to bring from Germany and the North.'

John Sherwood nodded. 'You are right,' he growled. 'There is a Hanse ship due to sail within a few days—her master is Hans Stein; she is bound for Hamburg. There should be large orders for the Hanseatic League, iron and copper for the armourers, sulphur and saltpetre for gunpowder, bowstaves for the archers, drugs for the apothecaries.'

Nan glanced quickly at Adam. There had been talk with the alchemist about some rare earths from the Hanse merchants. She found that Adam's eye was already upon her. He made no sign, but his look warned her again not to say a word.

When dinner was finished Grandfather said grace; then he and Master Whittington sat down again while the servants cleared away the dishes, dismantled the trestle-board on which they had eaten their own meal and went back to the kitchen. Adam and

Dickon placed flagons of wine before Grandfather and two fine silver dishes, one piled with nuts and raisins, the other with doucettes and comfits and every sort of sugar plum. Then they made ready to leave the hall with Aunt Isabel and Nan. But Grandfather nodded to them.

'You may stay,' he said, looking up at them from under his bushy brows. 'There are matters to be discussed which are meet for you to hear.'

'And Nan?' Master Whittington broke in with his little wry smile. 'You are not going to take my poppet away, good mistress? Leave her here with me and we will share a sugar plum.'

He pulled Nan down on to the settle beside him and picked out a sweetmeat for her—one made of almond paste and topped with pink sugar. John Sherwood filled his guest's cup with wine and bade his grandsons fetch cups for themselves. There was something so unusual about all this that, in spite of the reassuring glow from the wine, Dickon began to feel anxious again. To make it more impressive Master Whittington after a 'By your leave' to Grandfather dispatched Nan to look behind the screen at the end of the hall to make sure that all the servants had really gone. When she reported that there was no one there Grandfather told her to close the heavy iron-studded door that shut off the kitchen quarters. She returned, ill at ease, to Master Whittington's side and for a few moments there was silence. Dickon sat watching his Grandsire's face, certain that there was going to be some portentous announcement.

But in the end it was Master Whittington who broke the spell. He spoke lightly in quite an ordinary tone.

'What think you of Lollardy, friend John?' he inquired.

John Sherwood frowned. 'Lollardy,' he repeated. 'Why, it is a heresy and a sedition. What else?'

'It could be a great deal else,' returned Master Whittington decisively. 'It could mean rebellion and bloodshed. Let me remind you that it is only just over a year since Sir John Oldcastle led an armed attack on London in the name of Lollardy. You and I both remember what it is like for the City to be in the hands of a rebel mob. We had not long finished our apprenticeship at the time of Wat Tyler's rising, but we are neither of us likely to forget it.'

Nan, startled, ceased nibbling at her sweetmeat. She had

heard terrible stories about Wat Tyler's rebellion. Even Goody talked about it. Was that going to happen again?

Grandfather took it quite calmly. 'Oldcastle's attempt failed,' he said sipping his wine. 'They never even reached Newgate, and things have been quiet enough since then. Methinks the heads displayed on the Bridge are a sound warning.'

'But Oldcastle himself is in hiding somewhere, and probably planning more mischief. He is a desperate man. If you remember, he was in the Tower condemned for heresy when he escaped to lead his rebellion. What makes it worse is that he and the King are old friends. Why, they fought side by side in the Welsh wars. They were Hal and John together. When he was first sent to prison for heresy his Grace went himself to reason with him. He did all in his power to save him from being condemned. And now, in return, the man plots against his kingdom and his life.'

'When I was a young man,' Grandfather began, thrusting out his feet under the table and twisting his cup of wine by the stem, 'Lollards were poor priests who went from place to place preaching against the riches of the Church and the worldliness of the clergy. Many thought that they had right on their side.'

'It did not remain like that for long,' said Whittington. 'They would not be content with simple matters. Soon they were floundering in heresy, and from heresy it is but a short step to treason.'

'Yea, yea,' boomed Grandfather solemnly. Then he lifted his head. 'But why are we discussing this? I thought that we were speaking of war. Surely Lollardy will fade into the background now.'

'That is just why his Grace is uneasy. Evil in the open is less dangerous than evil that lurks in the shadows. On the surface all is well. But where is Oldcastle? Do not forget that he escaped. You may be sure that he is not quietly tilling his Herefordshire acres. Remember that Parliament itself declared that the intention of Oldcastle and his Lollards was to "destroy the Christian faith, the King, the spiritual and temporal estate, and all manner of policy and law". I quote their words. The realm was to be a commonwealth with Oldcastle as its ruler. Treason of that sort is not to be cured by a few heads stuck on London Bridge, you know. If the King goes to war, traitors may well seize their opportunity.'

'You speak strongly,' said Grandfather. 'Have you news, then, of some fresh plot?'

'News is too great a word. When rats burrow you can perchance trace which way they go by pressing your ear to the ground.' He glanced at Adam and then half-smiling, at Dickon. 'We must seek news among humble citizens—among apprentices for instance. It is very possible that we may learn something among the apprentices.'

Dickon's interest which had faded was at once rekindled. He was an apprentice now.

'I will be open with you,' said Whittington. 'We are all trustworthy people here. What we say between these four walls must never be talked about outside. Do we all understand that?'

He glanced round the table, beginning with Adam and ending with Nan, who nodded her head like a wooden manikin on a stick.

'Well then, I will tell you that the King has laid a charge upon me. I am to watch what goes on underground within this City. We are not without our rats; I am sure of that; and it is *my* task to discover them, *my* ear which must be pressed to the ground. Now in this family I have *two* pairs of ears, young quick ears that I can depend upon. Adam and Dickon will hear more among the apprentices than I could ever hear. I want you to be ever watchful, and if you come across anything that seems to you to hint at treason, say no word to any man but let me know immediately. Will you do this, both of you?'

Adam said 'Yes' with proper gravity. Dickon's answer was a ringing 'Yea, sir'. Master Whittington nodded, satisfied.

'That is good. Between the two of you we shall cover a good deal of ground. Adam will be on the look-out in the grocer's craft, and Dickon among the mercers.'

Dickon looked at him, startled. He could not have heard aright.

'Among the *mercers*?' he repeated, too taken aback to remember to say 'Sir'. 'Why among the mercers?'

Dick Whittington smiled at him. 'Because you *are* a mercer now, or will be when your indenture is complete. Did you not understand?'

Dickon stood up. The blood in his swollen face throbbed and burned. The hall began to swim round him.

'I'm *not* a mercer,' he protested hotly. 'How can I be? I've just been apprenticed *grocer*. You told me so. I *hate mercers*.'

Grandfather's voice boomed suddenly. 'Dickon! Have you taken leave of your senses? How dare you speak so to Master Whittington? By my faith, boy, I'll beat the life out of you.'

Dick Whittington laid his hand on Grandfather's arm.

'Calm yourself, John. He has not understood. He is crippled by his fight. I beg you, deal gently with him.'

Grandfather made a visible effort to control his wrath. After a moment of mumbling into his beard he began again in a long-suffering tone.

'It seems, you young fool, that you have not taken in your good fortune. There is no lord in England who would not gladly see his son in your place. You are apprenticed to Master Whittington. Because you are his godson, and also, I flatter me, for the love he bears to me, he has consented to receive you as a mercer apprentice under his own charge. You are the luckiest young whelp in London. You should be going on your knees in thanksgiving.'

Still bewildered Dickon stared first at Grandfather and then at Dick Whittington, but he scarcely saw them. The truth was slowly sinking in. His head throbbed till he thought that it would burst. Suddenly to his own dismay he began to cry. With a sob that would not be suppressed he turned and ran from the hall.

The main door stood open. He crossed the forecourt and turned down towards the river. There was no one about. The wharf was deserted. He leaned against the warehouse, all among the straw and the clots of slippery mud where so short a a time ago he had stood in triumph over the red-headed apprentice. He did not want to cry. It hurt too much. So he pulled himself together and tried to think.

He was to be a mercer! At that moment he felt that nothing more dreadful could happen to him. He had grown up in a grocer's household, and gone to school at St. Anthony's Hospice in Broad Street where most of the scholars were grocers' sons, because St. Anthony was the patron saint of the Grocers' Company. There was always bad blood in the City between the Guilds of the Victuallers, the Grocers and Fishmongers who dealt with food supplies, and the Guilds of the Clothiers, Mercers and Drapers and Haberdashers who handled cloth, silk, and other luxuries. The great men of the respective Companies might be civil enough to one another, and even do business together when it suited them; but the apprentices broke one another's heads regularly, and schoolboys on both sides made it a matter of honour to keep up the feud.

And now he, Dickon, grandson of John Sherwood, Warden of the Grocers' Company, was to be turned into a mercer. The triumph of the morning faded completely away. Far from starting a new life with a feather in his cap, he looked like being in a pretty tight corner. What would happen when he met the red-haired boy again? He did not care to dwell on that point.

Then he would be leaving the river. Most of the mercers' shops were in the centre of the City, along Cheapside, close to the church of St. Mary-le-Bow. For the future his life would be ruled by those wretched Bow Bells. They would ring him to work in the morning, ring the time for dinner, ring for him to stop work at night. Their noisy peel would take the place of the river sounds that he loved; the ships' bells, the clatter of ropes and pulleys as sails went up or down, the gentle slap of water when the wind blew with the tide, and incessant creaking of oars in row-locks.

He moved from the warehouse and sat down on the edge of the wharf, dangling his legs. Ferry boats at the bottom of Dowgate were doing a brisk trade this holy-day afternoon. He could not see his friend Jenkyn. Perhaps he had taken passengers down the river to view the *Katharine* at Ratcliffe-below-Tower. Dickon sighed. *He* could never see the *Katharine* now.

Beyond Dowgate stood a group of buildings enclosed by a high stone wall. It was the Steelyard, the stronghold of the Hanseatic League, where merchants from Germany and the Baltic lived together and carried on their trade. A sea-going ship was moored at their quay. Dickon guessed that it was the ship from Hamburg which Grandfather had mentioned at dinner. He eyed it critically. From the way that it lay low in the water he judged that it must be almost fully loaded and ready to sail.

He was always interested in the Hanse merchants because they came from distant ports with strange and exciting cargoes. He'd seen bear skins unloaded there, and such wonders as rowing-boats from Danzig, packed like walnut shells one inside the other, and ready to be launched straight away on the waters of the Thames.

It was all these things that he had to give up in order to be a mercer, to work in a shop or a counting-house in the middle of the City, toiling over cloths and silks and women's fal-lals.

As he sat hugging his misery he heard a quick footstep behind him. He knew without looking round that it was Adam.

'So here you are,' said his brother briskly. 'Grandfather was enraged when you bounced out of the hall like that. Are you fretting because you are to be a mercer? If I were in your shoes I should be thankful. Dick Whittington will be a master in a thousand.'

'Were you sent to find me?' asked Dickon. It was plain that he would not get much sympathy from Adam.

'Nay, they were still talking of the King's matters. When I had filled their wine-cups again they gave me leave to withdraw. I am going across to Southwark to seek out Master Gross. He invited me. As it is a holy-day Grandfather will not be calling for me endlessly as he does on other days.'

'The boat is not there,' Dickon reminded him. 'The fish boy took it. You'll have to go by ferry or else walk across the Bridge.'

'I forgot. A plague upon the fish boy. No matter, though. If I go by ferry I can call at the Steelyard on the way, and then I'll be able to tell Master Gross that I have seen the Hanse merchant for him.'

Dickon began to scramble to his feet. 'Wait a moment,' he cried. 'I'll come with you.'

Adam turned back. 'I'd rather you didn't,' he said. 'You see, if anyone looks for you it would draw attention to me, and then Grandfather will start asking questions.'

Dickon nodded. He understood, but nevertheless it was the last straw. As Adam set off again he called after him.

'If you see Jenkyn tell him that I shan't be able to come and see the *Katharine—ever*.'

His voice cracked on the last word. He picked up a stone and flung it savagely into the water. Then he sat down again feeling completely alone.

But he had scarcely settled when once more he heard somebody moving behind him. Again he did not look round. He wanted first to know who it was. Not Grandfather, that was certain; nor Nan; one was too heavy, the other too light. Perhaps it was Aunt Isabel come to fuss about his bruises. He was genuinely surprised when he heard the voice of Dick Whittington.

'I guessed that I might find you here. It is pleasant by the river. Nay—do not get up. I will sit beside you. I used to come here myself when I was an apprentice.' He lowered himself somewhat stiffly. 'But my old bones do not take to it as easily as they used to do.'

They sat in silence for a minute. Dickon felt that he ought to say something, but he could not think of anything that seemed right. Then Master Whittington spoke again.

'I think I should crave your pardon, godson,' he said gravely. 'It was ill-mannered of me to laugh so heartily at your mischance. But at the time it seemed uncommonly funny that you should have chosen this day to triumph over the mercers.'

'If I had known I would not have done it,' began Dickon shyly.

'Oh, yes, you would, at least I trust you would. You would always interfere if you saw a small boy bullied and outnumbered. Even among the boys you fought, I think it will do you little harm. You will begin your new life marked as a fellow who can take care of himself and that is no bad thing.'

Dickon was not so sure, but he said nothing, and after another minute his godfather began again.

'To be a new apprentice is a cheerless business, but you are better off than I was when I was in your shoes. You are a London boy. I was country bred. My home was in Gloucestershire, at Pauntley, beyond the river Severn. I was the youngest son. My brothers inherited the manor and I was sent to London to earn my living. The City is a fearsome place for a lad reared among trees and meadows, I promise you.'

'Were you apprenticed mercer then?' inquired Dickon shyly.

'Yes, I was sworn prentice, just as you will be tomorrow. My master was also a west country man, Sir John Fitzwarren, a good friend of my family. He was the best of masters, and the best of fathers too, for later he gave me his daughter to wife. But however good the master, 'tis no light matter to be a new apprentice. The best cheer I can offer is that it soon passes.'

Again there was silence. Then Dickon ventured another question.

'Sir, where shall I live?'

He held his breath as he waited for the answer. It was too

much to hope that he would remain at home. But there was just a chance that he might be in Master Whittington's own house, only a short way away, in a street called The Royal, just across Thames Street. Most apprentices lived on their master's premises, sleeping often enough under the counter in the shop, or in the vaults or warehouses among the goods. If only he were at the house in The Royal it would not be so bad. It was near enough for him to run down to the river whenever he had a moment to spare.

Master Whittington's first words raised his hopes only to dash them again.

'You will live in mine own house; not where I am living now, in The Royal, but a house outside Cripplegate, facing the open country. I have a master mercer in charge there, Will Appleyard. He is a grand trainer of prentices. There are other lads in the house. You will be happy enough.'

Dickon's heart sank. Outside the Wall. No hope of running down to the river from there. The City gates were shut from curfew to dawn.

'"Tis a fine place for apprentices for it is close to Moorfields,' Master Whittington went on cheerfully. 'They play games on Moorfields. When first I came to London the smells turned my stomach and as soon as I made enough money I built a house where I could breathe fresh air. You will enjoy the country.'

'It is a long way from the river,' said Dickon gloomily.

'The river, eh? Tell me, boy, if you could follow your own will what craft would you choose?'

'I would be a shipman,' replied Dickon promptly. 'I'd like to set sail and see other lands. The spices in Grandfather's warehouse come in wonderful ships. The mariners often have rings in their ears and once they had a monkey on board. It sat at the masthead and wouldn't come down.'

Master Whittington laughed. 'You speak as though grocers were the only people who dealt in foreign merchandise. You, a London boy, have you never heard of the Merchant Adventurers? *That* is the company that brings more wonders from abroad than any other, and it is ruled, I would have you know, by the *Mercers'* Company. I'll warrant that you have clothes on you now which you owe to the Merchant Venturers. Your shirt, for instance, is made of Cambrai linen; the buttonholes on your doublet are sewn with Paris silk; your red shoes are made of leather from Cordova in Spain—very fine shoes they are, too, though they, like their owner, seem to have been in the wars.'

Dickon actually laughed as he looked down at his feet. They were still coated with mud as they had been before the fight.

Shoes made of leather from Cordova

Master Whittington began to raise himself.

'Come, boy, help me up. We have sat here long enough. I'm going to walk up to Cripplegate now, before Vespers, and you had better come with me. You will see where you are going to live, and I will present you to Master Appleyard. Then you will not feel so strange when you begin your new life.'

To go *now* was a good idea. Dickon pulled at his godfather with a will. Master Whittington, back on his feet, began to brush the dust from his gown.

'We are both a little disarranged,' he smiled, glancing at Dickon's torn hose. 'As we pass Grantham's Inn you might run and tidy yourself a little. I will stroll slowly up the hill and you can catch me up.'

Arms of the Mercers' Company

Cheap . . . with St. Paul's against the western sky

Chapter Four

PROGRESS TO CRIPPLEGATE

MASTER WHITTINGTON had, as he promised, started to stroll up the hill. Dickon hastened after him, across Thames Street and up the next turning, The Royal. No sooner had he rounded the corner than he saw his godfather ahead, standing outside his own house. To Dickon's surprise Nan was there too. The pair of them were busy petting Dick Whittingon's little black and white cat, Madame Eglantine. As Dickon approached Master Whittington delivered her into Nan's arms.

Madame Eglantine

'Take her indoors, my poppet,' he said. 'Doubtless she would like to come with us, but it is too far for her to walk and I have no mind to carry her. Beg a dish of milk from the cook maid for her; set her down with it in my parlour and shut the door.'

36

Nan vanished into the house, which opened straight on to the cobbled street. It was a modest house of oak beams filled in with yellow plaster. True there was glass in the little leaded windows, but it was plain glass, not painted. As he looked up at it Dickon thought it strange that a great man like Master Whittington should not have a grander house.

'This is what I call my little house,' said Whittington suddenly, almost as if Dickon had spoken his thoughts aloud. 'I

Buckets of Thames water

have two other houses but this one is big enough for me now that I am alone. Alice, my dear wife, lies buried next door, in the church which you know well—at least you have been in it often enough. I rebuilt it to provide a fit resting-place for her. That work is only partly done. There is to be a college as well, and a hospital of almshouses for a master and a dozen poor old men. They will be given money for their needs and their task will be to pray for her soul, and for mine when I go to join her. One day I will show it to you, but we have no time now.'

Dickon stared up at the new stone tower of St. Michael Paternoster. He had watched the church being built, but he had never realized that it was all paid for by Dick Whittington. It must be rather fine to be rich enough to build churches and colleges.

At last Nan reappeared and they all continued their way up the hill The roadway of The Royal was wide enough for them to walk three abreast. It was also clean, for at Master Whittington's own cost, water-carriers brought buckets of Thames water each morning to swill it down, so the cobbles were free from slime and only the merest trickle of dirty dish water drained down the kennel, or gutter, in the middle of the road.

It seemed to be taken for granted that Nan was coming with them to Cripplegate. Dickon was quite pleased. Though Nan was a girl she was never in the way. She began to chatter to Master Whittington at once, telling him all over again about Button and the sucking-pig, and Dickon was free to look about him and think his own thoughts.

At the top of the hill they reached the Tower Royal, a massive stronghold from which the street, The Royal, took its name. Dickon never failed to stop and peer under the archway whenever he passed, for it was a place where exciting things had happened in the past. King Richard II had put his mother there for safety during Wat Tyler's rebellion, when the Tower of London was captured by the mob. Nowadays it was used by knights donning their armour before they went out to practise tilting at the lists on Smithfield, outside the City walls. There was always a chance of seeing one of them come prancing forth on a splendid charger.

Only a week ago he had been lucky. He had been just passing

Dickon ran alongside

on his way home from school when Sir Thomas le Strange clattered out in a suit of glittering plate armour. Dickon had been able to run alongside all the way down Knightrider Street (so called after the knights who used it) and had kept up until he reached Ludgate. Once outside the walls the knight had spurred his horse and ridden away, along by the Old Bailey, leaving Dickon hopelessly behind. Still, that had been exciting enough, and he had enjoyed afterwards the satisfaction of finding without any possible doubt who the knight had been from the two silver lions on his red shield.

But today the Tower Royal seemed deserted, and after linger-

ing a minute or two to gaze into an empty courtyard, he had to
run to catch the others.

Nan was trotting along by Master Whittington's side, taking
two little steps to each of his long ones, and even then giving a
skip now and again to keep up. But she was happy at last after a
thoroughly wretched afternoon.

When Dickon had rushed out of the hall, she had wanted to
run after him, but Grandfather bade her keep still. Dickon
seldom cried; he was much too old; but she was quite sure
that he was crying then. Aunt Isabel, to whom she went for
comfort, told her to leave him alone. He would get over it
more quickly by himself. So she had hung about miserable and
forlorn, waiting for something to happen. Adam did not want
her, he had gone off somewhere alone, and she had nothing to do.
Presently she had seen Dickon come in and hurry upstairs. Then
Master Whittington had noticed her in the forecourt and invited
her to come to Cripplegate with them to see Dickon's new home.
Aunt Isabel had said yes and here she was, feeling very important.

She was so glad that Dickon looked quite cheerful when he
arrived dressed in his best clothes, and she talked without ceasing
all the way up The Royal, and all along Budge Row and Soper's
Lane. Wasn't it funny, she cried, that you could always tell by
the smell just where you were? Budge Row was full of furriers'
shops, so it smelt of rabbit skins; Cordwainer Street was all
shoemakers, and had a nice smell of leather; Soper's Lane was the
grocer's part, and the spices and the pepper almost made you
sneeze.

Master Whittington smiled at her. 'So I suppose you smell
garlic in Garlick Hithe, and candles in Candlewick Street, and
and cats in Catte Street?'

They all laughed at that and Nan gave an extra big skip. It
was such a lovely day. The sun was shining and everything was
going to be all right.

'Oh, I'm so glad we came,' she cried. 'I wanted to go with
Goody across the Bridge to Southwark to look for bluebells, but
I'm glad I didn't. This is much better.'

'I'm glad you didn't too,' said Master Whittington gravely.
'Southwark is no place for a well-brought-up little maid to
wander, and you wouldn't have found many bluebells there.'

'I didn't mean Southwark; I meant Bermondsey,' Nan

corrected herself. 'But why shouldn't I go to Southwark? Is it a bad place?'

'I suppose one cannot call any place bad in itself, and the Bishop of Winchester has his Inn there. But nobody respectable lives in Southwark. It is the haunt of rogues and vagabonds.'

Nan grew a little sober. How very strange; she had never thought about Southwark before, and today it kept cropping up all the time. Master Gross, the alchemist, lived there, and so did the fishmonger boy.

'It's funny,' she said aloud. 'Everything has to do with Southwark today.'

'Has it?' Master Whittington questioned quickly. 'Why? What have you been hearing about Southwark?'

Dickon made a wry face at her. She knew what that meant. She was not to mention Master Gross. She gave her head a little toss. Did he really think that she would have forgotten Adam's secret?

'The fishmonger boy lives there,' she said calmly, 'the boy Dickon rescued from the mercers.'

She met Dickon's eye triumphantly. He turned red. She thought that it must be because she had mentioned the mercers; but Dickon knew, as she did not, that Adam was at that moment visiting Master Gross in Southwark. He knew also that what Dick Whittington said about Southwark was quite true.

'Oh, *that* boy,' said Master Whittington satisfied. 'But I think that we will not talk too much about Dickon's fight. It is best forgotten.'

At the top of Soper's Lane they came out into Cheap. Cheap was the City's principal market-place, very long and very wide, with Cheap Cross and the Water Standard as landmarks in the middle. Cheapside, the main road through London from east to west, ran along the edge.

Cheap was always an exciting place. Nan came there on such great occasions as the Eve of St. John at midsummer to see the torchlight march, or Mayor's day to watch the new Mayor's procession. It was a treat on any day to come shopping with Aunt Isabel, buying a hood from one of the mercers' stalls or a pair of shoes at a cordwainer's shop. Almost anything could be bought in Cheap or in one of the streets leading out of it—Bread Street, Milk Street, Honey Lane, Ironmongers' Lane and The Poultry.

But today Cheap seemed different from ever before. That struck her as soon as she looked at it, though she could not tell why. Of course as a rule there was so much to see, with the crowds and the bustle and the market stalls with their bright-coloured awnings, but now the stalls were bare, like skeletons, and the shops were all shuttered. There was nobody about except a few people filling pitchers at the Water Standard.

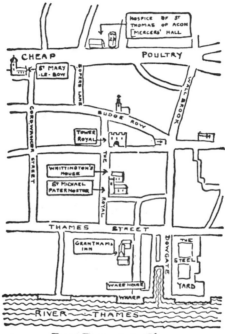

From Dowgate to Cheap

The first thing she noticed today was St. Paul's, rising like a great cliff against the western sky, its lofty spire shooting right up to Heaven. St. Paul's was always there, of course, but when she was busy shopping she had barely noticed it. Nan gave a big sigh. It was beautiful. She had never realized that before.

Master Whittington heard the sigh and looked down at her inquiringly. She smiled up at him.

'I've never noticed St. Paul's from here before,' she said. It sounded silly because of course she must have looked at it dozens of times. But Master Whittington understood.

'It's big enough to be seen,' he teased gently, 'the longest cathedral in the whole of Christendom; did you know that? That's something for London to be proud of, I think; don't you?'

He stopped and pointed to a church on their left. 'Since you have overlooked St. Paul's, perhaps you have not noticed St. Mary-le-Bow. Dickon is going to know Bow Bells well after this—and hate them too. Every apprentice hates them. I know I did. That big stone balcony at the side of the church was built by the King, King Edward the third, so that he and his Court could watch the processions and the tournaments in Cheap. We've not had a tournament for quite a long time, not since the one that took place on London Bridge about twenty years ago.'

'A tournament on London Bridge?' echoed Nan, scenting a story. 'Oh, do tell me about it.'

But before he could begin, the quiet of the empty streets was broken by the sound of horses approaching behind them. He looked round, then quickly pulled Nan and Dickon out of the way on to the steps of Cheap Cross.

A group of horsemen were approaching from the direction of Cornhill. The leader wore full armour and his companion a rich velvet cloak. Behind them were men-at-arms in steel caps and breastplates, with pennons showing the King's badge on their lances.

As they neared Cheap Cross the leader recognized Master Whittington and reined in his horse. The whole company pulled up short behind him, with hoofs stamping, harness jangling, and armour plate rattling and clattering.

Dickon was breathless with excitement. His eyes devoured every detail of the men-at-arms; their helmets, the steel gorgets to protect their throats, the plate armour that showed glimpses of chain mail beneath it.

But Nan was watching Master Whittington, who stood talking beside the leader's stirrup. She could not hear what they said, but presently the leader turned to his companion who threw back his cloak and produced a roll of parchment. Nan pulled Dickon's sleeve.

'Look!' she whispered, 'a herald!' Beneath the cloak the second man wore a herald's tabard, emblazoned with the arms of England.

Master Whittington unrolled the parchment and read it. Then smiling broadly he allowed it to roll up again and passed it

Master Whittington stood beside the leader's stirrup

back to the herald. There were hand wavings and cries of
farewell. The leader touched his horse and with more jangle and
clatter they all moved on westward towards Newgate.

Master Whittington stared after them. 'I wish I were going
with them,' he said. 'They are actually going to Gloucestershire,
my own country. That was one of the King's Commissioners of

Array. He is going to recruit an army for the French war. He will bear the King's summons to the Sheriffs, and the Sheriffs will visit every village and every manor to decide how many men each landowner must provide. I wonder how many they will require of my brother at Pauntley, my old home; perhaps three horsemen or half a dozen archers. Maybe my nephew Guy will lead them.'

'Will they come to London?' Nan asked.

'Nay, I hope not. We do not want to have to feed an army here. They are to muster at Southampton by the beginning of July. But come, both of you. At this rate it will be curfew time before we reach Cripplegate.'

He swung on his heel, and leaving Cheap behind turned northwards into Wood Street. For Nan this was new ground. Even Dickon did not know it well. St. Anthony's Hospice, where he went to school, was in the other direction, over towards Bishopsgate. Wood Street was very long and very narrow, closed in by tall timber houses which jutted out so far at the top that they almost shut out the sky. It smelled sour and stuffy, like all the streets that didn't get enough fresh air. Nan thought it dull.

Master Whittington now began to talk to Dickon, explaining what it would mean to become an apprentice. At first Nan listened. She had never heard it put as clearly as that before. She did know that an apprentice was bound to his master for seven years, and that during that time he lived and ate and slept under his master's roof. But she had no idea that the master also had obligations to the apprentice. He must give him a good bed and feed him properly, and not use him like a servant or a slave. When he beat him it must be with a stick small enough to pass through a finger ring. Nan gave a quick glance at the heavy gold signet on the first finger of Master Whittington's left hand, and hoped that Dickon would not be beaten very often.

But after a while she lost interest and began to look about her. The smell was really dreadful. The kennel in the middle of the road was nothing but a stagnant ditch, the scum on its surface only broken when a woman came out from one of the houses and emptied a bucket of slops into it. Still talking Master Whittington drew Nan to one side and made her walk in the best place next to the wall, as if she were a grown-up lady. Dickon on the outside had to pick his way among the puddles.

Suddenly Nan noticed two boys walking ahead of them.

They were quite a long way off but even at that distance she could see that one of them had red hair and wore a bright green hood hanging down his back. She glanced quickly at Dickon. He had seen them too. There was no doubt about it. The red-headed boy was the mercer whom he had fought.

Nan held her breath. What was to be done? Then Dickon caught her eye and frowned at her. She understood. She was to say noth-

Master Whittington's Signet

ing. That meant that he was not going to tell Master Whittington. It also meant that he did not want to overtake them. She walked a little more slowly and, without noticing, Master Whittington slowed down too. He was still talking about apprentices and about the Mercers' Company. Dickon began to ask intelligent questions, a device, Nan realized, to keep his godfather's attention in case the boys happened to look round.

'You will have to appear before the Mayor tomorrow,' Master Whittington was saying. 'As it happens he is a mercer too. I shall come with you and we will both sign the indenture. Then you'll pay over some money which your grandsire will give you. There'll be two shillings towards the city funds, and two shillings to the Mercers' poor box for charity, and forty shillings for the privilege of being received as apprentice of the Mercers' Company.'

'*Forty shillings*,' cried Dickon with a brave show of eagerness. 'Forty shillings is a great sum.'

''Tis a costly entrance, I admit,' said Master Whittington. 'Forty shillings is more than a skilled labourer earns in a year. But it is done with a purpose. Mercers often handle merchandise of fabulous worth and deal with noble customers. We want only apprentices of good birth.'

To her dismay Nan saw that the two boys had stopped, and were scratching about with sticks in a lay stall, or refuse dump, piled at the corner of a side street. Something must be done. Suddenly inspired she began to limp, and then clung to Master Whittington's arm while she took off her shoe and shook out an imaginary stone. By the time she had got the shoe on again the boys were once more well ahead.

But the conversation had flagged. Master Whittington was silent. At all costs she must keep him talking.

'What happens next?' she inquired. 'I mean, when Dickon has finished his seven years as apprentice?'

'Then he will be admitted as a freeman of the Mercers' Company and have the right to serve any master he wishes as a journeyman; that is a man who works by the day, a *journée* man; the French call him *homme de journée*. Later on if he wants to start business on his own, he must show himself worthy and pay a fee to wear the Company's livery. Then he could be elected Warden of the Company, or Mayor of London for that matter. How would you like to see your brother Mayor? It is a position of some small honour, I believe.'

Nan and Dickon both laughed at that, for Master Whittington himself had already been Mayor *three* times. Nan believed that the danger was past. The boys had gone. She had lost sight of them round the last curve of Wood Street, and now ahead stood the Wall, the high stone rampart that ran right round London except on the river side. Wood Street ended at Cripplegate, one of the six gates of the city, a narrow archway through a square stone tower in the Wall.

The boys might have gone out through Cripplegate, but somehow it seemed much more likely that they had turned off along one of the many small alleys to right or to left. Nan peeped down each one as they passed it, hoping that they had vanished for good.

The gatekeeper of Cripplegate recognized Master Whittington, and seizing a broom swept the cobbles under the arch as a mark of respect. Master Whittington gave him a warm 'God be with you', and they all passed through.

Chapter Five

THE HOUSE IN GRUB STREET

OUTSIDE Cripplegate they crossed the City moat, where a family of white ducks swam, and immediately found themselves in what seemed to be a different world.

They stepped out of London into a country village. The village green was ringed round with ancient cottages; the parish church of St. Giles stood back a little way with a pond beside it and a row of almshouses beyond; there was a farmyard where cows lowed and hens cackled, and all the roofs were thatched, which in one stroke gave the place a countrified air, for thatch was no longer permitted within the City.

Behind the cottages lay a number of prosperous modern houses, built among trees and gardens, with an occasional glimpse of a line of distant wooded hills.

Master Whittington paused for a moment to fill his lungs with fresh air, while Nan gave a little cry of delight and darted to pick some buttercups growing on a grassy bank.

From this vantage-point she could see a side road leading away towards the east. Over the farther hedge two heads were visible going along the road. So they *had* come out of Cripplegate after all.

Master Whittington's back was turned for the moment. She beckoned to Dickon and pointed excitedly. He guessed at once what she meant, but before he could come and look for himself, church bells inside the City walls began one after another to ring for Vespers, and Master Whittington faced round.

'We *are* late,' he exclaimed. 'I had meant to be there and back by Vespers' time, but——' The end of his sentence was lost in a sudden peal from the belfry of St. Giles' close beside them; but they gathered from the signs he made that he was bidding them come to Vespers there and then.

They followed him obediently across the green. Under cover of the bell-ringing Nan managed to whisper to Dickon that to delay was the best thing. The boys would have gone by the time they came out of church. But Dickon looked very glum.

'*Pray hard*,' he muttered into Nan's ear as they waited to let Master Whittington go first through the porch. 'It would be awful if *he* were living in the same house.'

Nan gasped. There was no doubt whom Dickon meant by 'he'. The idea had never occurred to her, but now it put everything else out of her head. She looked round the church, which was old and dark, without seeing it. Dickon beside her joined in the Latin psalms and prayers mechanically—he knew them all by heart—and in her turn she sang the evening hymn at the top of her voice. But she was paying very little attention. All her real praying was done when she buried her face in her hands and begged over and over again that the red-haired boy might live *miles* away.

Dickon came out of the church so tired of suspense that he wished they could hurry up and reach the house. He would rather know the worst. What would happen if his enemy *was* there? Would there be another fight straight away? If so surely Dick Whittington would move one or other of them elsewhere. But by that time of course all the other boys would know and they would all take sides against him.

He was tempted to ask Master Whittington right out if there was a red-haired apprentice there, but he decided that it was better to wait and see.

But now that they had been to Vespers Master Whittington showed no sign of haste. He was enjoying his leisurely stroll. He even paused to watch some cows being driven knee-deep into the pond to drink.

'That pond is fed by a pure spring,' he remarked frowning. 'Yet every day it is so fouled that it is good for nothing. Methinks that I will have a pipe set to carry the water to a boss in the wall, so that people may drink without harm. Remind me, Dickon, if I forget.'

He turned away at last and led them along the very road that the boys had taken, which ran close to the edge of the moat. But by now it was quite deserted except for a family of ducks which waddled away across the grass verge and plunged quacking into the water.

'We go to the left here,' observed Master Whittington, indicating a tree-hung lane. 'This is called Grub Street; why I

A large house, three storeys high

know not. It is an ugly name for a fair spot. Here we are. We have arrived.'

They stood in front of a large house, three storeys high. Its framework of stout timbers was filled in with whitewashed plaster, like the new part of Grantham's Inn. The only unusual thing about it was an odd-shaped tower in the middle, with a wide roof that suggested a broad-brimmed hat. There was nobody about, and, above all, no sign of any boys. Master Whittington rapped on the door.

It was opened by a tall bony man dressed in a gown of dark brown fustian.

'Will, I have brought you the new apprentice,' said Master Whittington as he stepped inside. He led the way into a long low-ceiling room with a broad wooden counter board, and great rolls of cloth stacked round the walls. Will Appleyard drew out a joint stool and Master Whittington sat down thankfully.

'I've been on my feet since the first mass this morning,' he declared. 'I'm getting old for so much exercise. Will, I have already told you of this lad, my godson. He is bound apprentice to me, but I purpose to put him in your care. You are to be in all things as his master.'

The mercer looked Dickon up and down. 'He is well grown,' he remarked. 'And you say, sir, that he is lettered?'

'He has been to school at St. Anthony's Hospice, though it would be as well not to mention it, for our lads love not grocers. He can read and write and I'm told that he casts up a reckoning correctly as often as not. Also'—he looked from one to the other of them with a little smile—'he can use his fists, as you may notice.'

Will Appleyard did not respond to the smile. 'There is a good deal too much fighting nowadays,' he said. 'There was a cry of "Clubs" on Cheap last night, so I am told, and plenty of heads broken. By good fortune none from this house was there. There is virtue in being beyond the City gates. After curfew they cannot get in or out.'

Dickon's spirits sank still lower. Will Appleyard seemed a gloomy fellow. He listened while the two men discussed a few business matters, about tidings from agents in the wool-growing district and what cloth could be expected to arrive from Reading and Newbury. He wished to goodness that they would say something about the other boys. He was still in suspense. But he did not have to wait much longer.

'The lads are all out on Moorfields making the most of the holy-day.' Will Appleyard volunteered. 'Would you wish me to call them in to take charge of the boy?'

Dickon's heart pounded. Now at last he would know. But Master Whittington shook his head.

'There is no hurry,' he said. 'By your leave I would like to show Dickon round. But first let me commend him to your good wife. Is she at home?'

It was clear that Mistress Appleyard was not only at home but hovering outside the door. At the first mention of her name she

He presented Dickon with great ceremony

appeared as if by magic, bobbing and smiling at everybody.   She
was a dame as stout and merry as her husband was thin and sad.

Master Whittington stood up and greeted her as an old friend.
Then he presented Dickon with great ceremony, as if she were a
fine lady, and Dickon, taking the hint, swept her a low bow.

She beamed at him, called Nan her chick-a-biddy, and then, in spite of Nan's anxious glances at Dickon, swept her off to the kitchen to help in making gingerbread.

When they had gone Master Whittington led Dickon upstairs to the room on the first floor which he described as his parlour. The strange tower that Dickon had noticed from outside proved to be a broad circular stairway, twice the width of any normal winding stair. It was, Master Whittington explained, specially built for bales of cloth to be trundled up to the top of the house or simply rolled down.

'I will warrant that finer English cloth comes to this house than to any other in London,' he claimed proudly. 'There are advantages in being outside the walls besides the blessing of fresh air. We avoid the toll we should have to pay did the cloth pass in by the gates, and it is far easier to unload packhorses here than to pilot them through the narrow streets.'

Dickon looked eagerly round the upstairs parlour. He caught Master Whittington's eye upon him.

'I suppose,' said his godfather with a twinkle, 'that you are looking for marvels from across the seas? You are thinking that all this business about English cloth is dull, eh?'

Dickon reddened. It was just what he had been thinking.

'Remember, then, that your marvels have to be paid for. There would be scarcely enough coin in the whole City to buy one shipload, they are so costly. How then do you think that we pay for them?'

Light broke upon Dickon. 'With English cloth,' he cried. 'I had never thought of that.'

'Then I trust that you will think of it for the rest of your days. We do not sell English cloth in London. The Drapers' Company does that. But we send it over the seas to markets and fairs in France and Flanders and Germany, and anywhere else where there is a sale for it and we bring in its place things that are rare and precious. See you here.'

He opened a tall press standing against the wall and laid upon the table various objects, naming the land from which each had come. There was a purse of deep blue velvet, the pile cut and picked out with silver thread. That had been bought in Venice for a piece of English broadcloth. A tiny altar piece of carved ivory with little figures of the Crucifixion, made in France to stand upon somebody's prayer desk, had cost a roll of ordinary

Kersey. A sword belt and scabbard of Spanish leather that made Dickon's eyes sparkle were the price of a mere woollen gown.

'Some day you will come to my house in Hart Street,' Master Whittington said. 'It is the receiving place for treasures from the big merchant ships which anchor below Bridge. There I will show you the cloth of gold which the Lady Blanche, the King's sister, wore at her wedding to the Prince of Bavaria, and the silk broidered with pearls from Sicily for the Lady Phillipa's bridal gown.'

But another idea had crossed Dickon's mind. Perhaps, if his enemy was here, in Grub Street, Master Whittington would let him go to this other house.

'You have a lot of houses, sir,' he ventured,

'Why, yes. I have three. Does that seem strange to you? I have told you how I came here for the fresh air. But later my affairs called for a finer place so I built a great house in Hart Street, near Aldgate. The apprentices call it Whittington's Palace, I believe, but it is far too grand for my simple needs; so when my wife died and I was alone, I moved back to The Royal, where we had lived when we were young. You will go to the Hart Street house presently, but you must first learn the trade here. Now we must put these things away. Judging by the clatter downstairs I think the prentices are back from Moorfields.'

Dickon's heart was pounding as they entered a large cheerful kitchen. The place seemed to be full of boys clustered round Goodwife Appleyard who was baking little cakes over the fire, with Nan beside her holding the bowl of batter. Everyone seemed to be laughing and exchanging noisy jokes, so that at first nobody noticed Master Whittington. Dickon looked quickly from one face to another. Then he breathed a sigh of relief. The red-haired boy was not there.

Suddenly one of the apprentices looked round, and hissed a word of warning. The group broke up and melted away, till only three remained.

Master Whittington nodded genially to everyone. 'Don't stop your cooking,' he said to Goodwife Appleyard. 'I only want to make these lads known to each other and then I will sample your cakes.' He pulled Dickon forward. 'This is your new fellow,' he said to the boys. 'His name is Dickon. One of you had better take charge of him. Robert, you are the eldest; nay, perhaps you are too old, and Toby scarcely old enough.

Owen, it had best be you. Will you show him his sleeping place?'

The three boys were widely different in appearance. Robert was almost a man. Toby looked like a fat schoolboy. Owen, who led Dickon upstairs, was a tall dark boy with shaggy black hair and deep-set eyes.

Up and up they went until at last they emerged through the floor boards of a long garret in the roof. It was lit by two small dormer windows filled with panes of transparent horn, and it seemed to run the entire length of the house. Bales of cloth were stacked closely on both sides but Dickon could see no sign of beds. Owen tipped a bale over. It was a roll of bedding tied with a cord.

'Here is your bed,' he said. 'There was another prentice here till Easter, but he finished his time and has gone as journeyman. You are Dick Whittington's kinsman? Do you come from Gloucester too?'

'Nay, I live in London,' said Dickon cautiously, 'and I'm not his kinsman, only his godson. You are not from London, are you? You do not speak like a Londoner.'

'I'm from Monmouth. My aunt married the steward of the Whittington manor in Gloucester.' He looked curiously at Dickon who had crossed to the window. 'You've been in a fight. Was it a prentice battle?'

Dickon said yes. He had dreaded this question, but anyhow *that* was true. It was a battle between apprentices.

'The big one, in Cheap, clothiers against victuallers?'

'Not the big one,' said Dickon carefully. 'Just a small one.'

'Who won?'

'I did.' It was a boast, but he could not avoid it.

'Did you draw blood?' As Dickon nodded he said 'Good!' apparently satisfied at last. 'Then you are already one of us. A new mercer must always punch a victualler till he draws blood before we will admit him to our prentices' club.'

Dickon's face was crimson. He felt a craven and a liar because obviously Owen thought that he had fought on the mercers' side. He tried to screw up his courage to say that he was of a grocers' family but the words just wouldn't come. To hide his confusion he went to one of the windows, from which the horn shutter had been taken down, and stuck his head out.

The view was so astonishing that for a moment he even forgot his worries. Beyond the garden fence lay the Moor-fields, a green expanse of marshy land. On the drier parts there were playing fields, with archers' targets and football grounds, while cows and sheep grazed on the lush grass of the swamp. Farther away stretched un-broken country, dotted with farms and villages, to the wooded hills of Hampstead and Highgate.

Wrestling

He had only once been out on Moorfields and that was in winter, when it was flooded and frozen and everybody put on skates made from mutton bones. Now the place swarmed with holy-day crowds, some playing games, some practising at the butts, or with the quarter-staff, or wrestling, while parties of sedate citizens with their wives strolled across footpaths and enjoyed the air.

But it was what he saw in the other direction that took his breath away. Not much more than a bowshot distant lay Lon-don Wall, with the moat in front of it reflecting its grey stone battlements. Inside the Wall the roofs and gables and soaring church towers of the City stood packed together as close as her-rings in a barrel. He tried to pick out build-ings that he knew; the tall spire of Austin Friars and the smaller one of St. Helen's Priory in Bishopsgate, both quite near his school; farther to the right the scaffold-ing round the new Guildhall, still unfin-ished, and beyond it, in the distance, the familiar arched belfry of St. Mary-le-Bow.

Quarter-staff

He'd never seen

London like that before. 'Ye loaves and fishes!' he exclaimed half under his breath.

Behind him he heard Owen give a little gasp. Then there came a whisper almost in his ear.

'The net is full!'

Dickon turned round, puzzled. 'What did you say?'

Owen repeated, 'The net is full.' Then seeing Dickon's face, he continued: 'You *did* say "Loaves and fishes", didn't you?'

'Of course I did. Why shouldn't I? Lots of people say it.'

Owen seemed confused. 'Yea, of course lots of people say it. I thought you meant it.' He changed the subject quickly. 'Look, the football is over. I wonder who won.'

'Who was playing?' asked Dickon, anxious to avoid a silence.

'Oh, just a friendly game between clothiers—mercers against haberdashers. Everyone's going back to the City. I suppose there'll be dancing in the streets tonight. We miss all the fun out here.'

But Dickon's attention was riveted on a small group of apprentices passing the end of the garden. Among them was a boy with red hair and a green hood. It was his enemy! So it was to Moorfields that he was going when they saw him in Wood Street.

He drew a little way back into the shadow.

'Who are those passing now?' he inquired. 'Are they mercers or haberdashers?'

'Mercers of course,' returned Owen promptly, as though everybody ought to know that. 'That big fellow with the red hair is Kurt Bladebone. He's one of the best wrestlers we've got; and he can wield the quarter-staff too, I can tell you. But d'you know he was set on this morning by a fishmonger and half a dozen grocers, somewhere down by the river. They knocked him down and broke two of his teeth. His hood was all covered with blood. We shall take it out of the dirty knaves when we find them!'

Dickon was divided between rage and dismay. Half a dozen grocers; the liar! He almost threw discretion to the winds and cried out that it was he, all alone, who had vanquished Kurt Bladebone. But he pulled himself up in time.

'Where does he work?' he inquired cautiously.

'Oh, a long way off; just within Aldgate. He is apprenticed to Master Falconer, the Mayor. But you'll see him at the prentices' club next time it meets. That'll be—let me see—on Corpus Christi day I suppose.'

Dickon breathed more freely. Corpus Christi was three weeks ahead. By that time, he told himself, he would have found his feet in this new life, and he could meet Kurt Bladebone boldly and show up his cowardly lies. Six grocers indeed! But for the present it was best to keep quiet.

As he turned from the window the boy Toby came clattering up the stairs to say that Dick Whittington was ready to go.

Back in the kitchen Master Appleyard looked Dickon up and down once more. 'And when will the boy start work?' he inquired.

Master Whittington smiled. 'There's no point in delay,' he said. 'He had better begin tomorrow.'

The Bridge chapel

Chapter Six

NAN ALL FORLORN

EARLY the next morning Dickon left home, his possessions in a
sack slung over his shoulder.   There was very little excitement
about his going.   Grandfather had given him a talking to and his
solemn blessing the night before, while Aunt Isabel, with Nan to
help, collected and packed his clothes.   He needed little except
shirts and hose and shoes, with a warm gown for cold weather and
of course some kerchiefs and his ivory comb.   She also slipped in
a little Primer, a book of simple prayers, written so small yet so
clearly that it seemed as if the scrivener who copied it must have
worn spectacles.   His best doublet could remain at home, for he
would be donning the plain cloth tunic and cap worn by apprentices of the clothiers' crafts.

Dickon himself was extremely calm.   The only sign of anything unusual was that instead of scrambling ill-dressed to mass
long after Aunt Isabel and Nan were already in church, he got up
and went by himself to the morrow mass, the very earliest of all,
at dawn.   They met him coming back as they were going out.

He ate a good breakfast of bread and cheese and ale with a
slice of eel pie as a treat for a special occasion.   Then he said
his grace and picked up his sack as casually as though it were his

school satchel. He suffered himself to be kissed by Aunt Isabel and by Nan, knelt before his Grandsire, and then walked alone across the forecourt and up the hill.

'I would have given him some salve for that black eye but he would not have it,' fussed Aunt Isabel as she and Nan stood at the gateway watching him go. 'Perchance Goodwife Appleyard will look after it. A mess of goosefat pounded with St. John's wort is better than anything.'

Nan, who until now had been busy and excited, all of a sudden felt utterly miserable. Last night everything had been so lovely. Dickon had whispered to her that it was all right—Red-head lived *miles* away—and she had been perfectly certain that her prayers had done it. Then, as they walked back through the City, people were already dancing in the streets, as they always did on fine holy-day evenings. At every open space little parties were gathered with a piper or two, and her toes had itched to join in. But now Dickon had gone and nothing would ever be the same again.

Aunt Isabel, hearing a stifled sob, gave one look at Nan's face and began to bustle. They must be quick, she cried. All this business about Dickon had put everything behindhand. This morning, come what may, those lazy wenches were going to scrub the hall floor and lay fresh rushes. The grease from the sucking-pig had soaked right through.

As a rule Nan found Aunt Isabel's household tasks dull and wearisome, but this time she welcomed them. For one thing the work was different from the usual routine of spinning and mending, or a long hour at Aunt Isabel's loom with Aunt Isabel beside her to rap her knuckles when she passed the shuttle clumsily and made a fault in the weave.

The first thing was to make the big bed where she slept with Aunt Isabel, usually the job of the house wenches who were cleaning the hall. Nan enjoyed bed-making. Years ago, in the days of Goody Doubleday, there had been a special game in which little Nan was tossed with the feather bed. Though she was much too big to be tossed now, the happy memory remained, and she went for the heavy bag of feathers with a will, pummelling it with all her might. Aunt Isabel checked her quite crossly.

'Stop, child. We do not toss the bed today; it is Friday. For shame! Would you sleep soft on a Friday, the day our Blessed Lord died for you?'

The rebuke almost brought Nan to tears again, and she did not cheer up until, bed-making finished, they visited the kitchen to inspect the dishes in the larder. Aunt Isabel's sharp eye was turned upon the cook. The remains of sucking-pig and chicken and meat pasties all piled on wooden platters raised a storm. Why were these things still here? she demanded. They should have been put out on the alms dish yesterday. Had not the needy poor come to the back door for a meal as they always did? And what were they given, pray? Dry bread? Now it was Friday and it was all wasted. She would let nobody defile the Friday with *her* broken meats. The chicken and the pork could be put into the cauldron for a hotchpotch, but the pasty would have to be given to the pigs.

That left nothing for dinner. Aunt Isabel lifted the lid off the last barrel of the winter's salted herrings and did not like what she found. She turned to Nan.

'Fetch my cloak and the baskets, child,' she commanded. 'And you had better put on your pattens. The streets are muddy. We will go to market.'

Nan wasted no time. To go to market was a treat. Better still Aunt Isabel decided that they would go all the way to Billingsgate instead of to the old Fish Market towards St. Paul's. The fish was fresher. Boats with fish from the open sea put in at Billingsgate. They did not often come up through the Bridge. Nan ran to fetch the pattens and the other things. The way to Billingsgate was all along Thames Street, past the gate of Cold-harbour where she had once sat on the King's horse, and past the end of the Bridge. Perhaps, if there was time, they might even go *on* the Bridge and see Goody.

It was a lovely morning. There was a fresh breeze across the river to temper the hot sun. Stepping out into Grantham's Lane, Nan felt the sadness lift just as though she had suddenly taken off her winter cloak. Her heart became wonderfully light. If Aunt Isabel had not been walking just behind her, she would have skipped along Thames Street. They walked single file, close to the wall, and Nan peeped surreptitiously into each house as they passed. All the shutters were down and the rooms open to the spring sunshine, and it was fun seeing how other people lived.

The marketing was quickly done, for Aunt Isabel caught sight of a shop on Fish Street Hill where the fish was all glittering from the sea, so they did not even have to go as far as Billingsgate.

Aunt Isabel bought a fine young codling

Fish Street Hill was the main road leading up from the Bridge, and Nan gazed longingly in the direction of Goody's house. Aunt Isabel saw the look and actually bought a fine young codling over and above their own needs.

'I thought that perhaps we might take it to Goody,' she said innocently. 'There will be just time if we do no more than leave it at the door; but, mark you, we must not stay to gossip or dinner will never be cooked by noon.'

This time Nan really did give a little skip. Quite apart from the joy of seeing Goody, it was always exciting to go along the Bridge. Although it was a street with houses and shops, it was quite different from any othe. street because every now and then there was a peep of the river on one side or the other, and always there was the noise of the water rushing underneath. Everyone shouted on the Bridge, for, as well as the roaring and swishing of the river, cart-wheels clattering along the narrow way between the overhanging houses made a din like a constant thunderstorm.

From Fish Street Hill which caught all the sun, they plunged suddenly into deep shadow. One of the thrilling things about the Bridge was the way that some of the houses stretched right across the road, like little bridges over a Bridge. This gave a startling pattern of bright light and heavy shade. Nan had invented a game for it. The open parts, where the sun shone, were dry land, and the tunnels of shadow counted as water, which she had to hop through without getting wet! It seemed a very real game because the tunnels were so cold in contrast to the sunny parts that it was just like plunging into water.

When they were nearly half-way across they came out suddenly into the open, where, for a few yards, there were no houses at all, but just a parapet along the edge. Nan darted to the side to gaze downstream at all the fine ships anchored between Billingsgate and the Tower. But Aunt Isabel called her back.

'Come along, child. There is no time to dawdle. We must spare a moment to pop into the chapel and say a prayer for Dickon, starting his new life. Here is a silver farthing. I dare say you'd like to light a candle for him.'

The chapel of St. Thomas of Canterbury, the wonder of the Bridge, opened from one corner of the little square. It was a fairy-like building with slender fluted pillars and delicate tracery, tapering up to the little belfry. The stone looked very white and crisp for it was but newly built.

Clutching her farthing, Nan followed Aunt Isabel through the door. The chapel was deceptive, for inside it seemed quite a big church. It was, she knew, really two chapels, one over the other, and it jutted right out into the river, built upon the largest pier of the Bridge. She knelt down on the stone floor to say her prayer, but she could not resist looking round her. The sun poured through the stained glass in the tall windows and it was like kneeling in a rainbow.

To light a candle was a great affair. She took her time about it, chose one with a good wick, and kindled it with a taper from a tiny lamp burning in a niche. Then she spiked it carefully on a long pricket candle stand, and knelt again to offer up her prayer for Dickon.

She was just getting up to go when she hesitated, looked at Aunt Isabel and then deliberately went back to the candles again. A farthing was a lot of money; it would certainly pay for more than one; so she took a second, lit it and stuck it up beside the first. She felt that Adam was being left out, and, she did not know why, she had an idea that he could do with an extra prayer too.

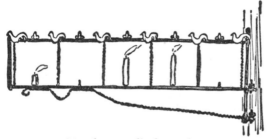

Nan lit a candle for Dickon

Aunt Isabel smiled at her as they went back to the open air. She asked no questions about the second candle but only said once more that they must be quick.

Goody lived with her son-in-law, Simon the glover, in a house on the right-hand side only a few doors short of the Drawbridge Gate. To Nan's satisfaction the next house farther on stretched across the road so she could not see the horrid heads stuck up on poles, but she kept her back carefully turned so as to be quite sure.

Goody came to the door at once. Her son-in-law was out and she was keeping her eye on her two little grandchildren in a play pen in the workshop, so that she could attend to customers at the same time.

She was overjoyed to see them and delighted with the fish. Aunt Isabel shouted into her best ear that Dickon was apprenticed to Master Whittington and that they would come and see her again soon, and Nan just had time for one hug in the comforting scrubbiness of Goody's woollen gown, and then it was all over and they were hurrying back to Grantham's Inn as fast as they could go.

It was very hot, and by the time they got home Nan was tired; so Aunt Isabel told her to take her spindle and sit on the window-seat in the hall. But spinning alone was dull work and Grand-father, coming in from the warehouse, found her asleep. She looked so forlorn that when she woke he asked her, less gruffly than usual, if she would like to go and see Adam. He would probably find her something to do in the spice closet.

Goody's grandchildren in their playpen

Nan jumped up at once and bobbed her thanks. The ware-house as a rule was out of bounds. She was making for the door when Grandfather told her to see Aunt Isabel on the way and ask her how many bundles of rushes she wanted. A barge load had just arrived.

Pleased to be useful Nan hurried to the kitchen. She found Aunt Isabel standing by the back door talking to a woman and a boy. They were obviously poor people. The boy's thin white face seemed familiar, and so did the way that his shoulder-blades stuck out under his tunic.

'My nephew is not here,' Aunt Isabel was saying. 'He has gone to be a mercer. He is apprenticed to Master Whittington.'

Nan heard the boy give a gasp of astonishment.

'A mercer,' he cried. 'But it was only yesterday that he fought the mercers.'

Instantly Nan remembered. He was the fishmonger boy, the cause of all the trouble. She had not recognized him now that he was clean and tidy. His mother had brought him to thank Dickon for having saved him and she was now busily pouring out her tale to Aunt Isabel. She was a poor widow with nothing belonging to her except her boy.

Aunt Isabel, well accustomed to dispensing charity at the back door, plied her with questions. Where did she live? What work did she do? And how was it, if she was so poor, that she could apprentice her boy to the Fishmongers, which was one of the noblest and richest of the crafts.

The woman managed to account for herself. Her husband, she explained, had been a journeyman fishmonger, and his master, out of charity, took Lob without fees. She in the meanwhile worked at the sign of the *Green Falcon*, a tavern in Southwark, scrubbing, and cleaning the ale pots.

Aunt Isabel was plainly shocked about the Southwark tavern. Surely, she said, a respectable woman could find something better than that. But she sent Nan upstairs to fetch an old shirt that Dickon had outgrown, while she loaded the woman with the remains of the chicken and the sucking-pig, though with strict instructions that they must be cooked up for the morrow and not used to break the Friday abstinence.

On her way to the warehouse with a message about the rushes Nan cudgelled her brain. The woman had said 'the sign of the *Green Falcon*'. She was sure she had heard the name before but she could not recall where.

In the warehouse she found Wat, the journeyman, among rolls of canvas and rope and twine, busily counting bow staves that had arrived yesterday. The warehouse was an exciting place, for it was stocked with chests of rice and raisins and figs and dates, and jars of honey and soft soap and varnish and lamp oil, among dozens of other things. When she had delivered her message Wat sent two apprentices down to the wharf to fetch the rushes, while he opened a crate of raisins and gave her a handful of them.

Clutching these she tapped on the small door that led into the spice closet, Adam's own particular corner.

Here everything was neat and trim. A window, from which

the shutter was down, looked out on to the wharf. On the opposite wall there were shelves arranged neatly with jars and canisters, each labelled in Adam's neat script: Cinnamon, Ginger, Borax, Mace—row after row of them. There was a desk beneath the shelves with some big books on it, a jar of quill pens, a pestle and mortar, and a delicate pair of balancing scales with tiny weights. Nan's eyes brightened. Once before Adam had trusted her to weigh out herbs and spices for him. Perhaps he would let her do some today.

But Adam was not alone. Nan recognized the back of the man who stood with him by the window. It was the alchemist, Master Saloman Gross. They did not notice her come in and she wondered if she ought to creep out again. But the opening and shutting of the door a second time might disturb them, so she decided to stay. Their talk sounded very dull, all about drugs and spices with funny names, Sal ammoniac, Hartshorn, and something that was mentioned over and over again called Silver Steel. Nan did not listen. She leaned on the desk and drew patterns in the film of spice dust on its surface. She remembered now where she had heard of the sign of the *Green Falcon*. It was where the alchemist lived. Lob's mother must be a servant there. But how odd that they should both come from the same place. She added some sand from the blotting sifter to the spice dust and began to build tiny castles with it.

Then a remark by Master Gross caught her attention.

'We must have it ready before the King sets sail for France,' he said. 'I shall need some Hartshorn from Germany, as well as the Silver Steel. Can you hasten the Hanse merchant to bring them with all speed?'

''Tis but early May,' said Adam calmly. 'If the muster at Southampton is in July, it should give us time enough.'

This did not seem to satisfy Master Gross.

'But recall that I have to compound the mixture. We can prepare the other elements, it is true, but until you bring me the Silver Steel all is useless. I would have you remember, young sir, that this is for your honour and fame as well as for mine. For years beyond count learned men have sought the Panacea which will cure all ills, and you, a mere stripling, have I believe discovered it. With my help, and this potent earth, Silver Steel, to complete your formula, you can place the Panacea itself before the King. Think what it would mean in his wars if none of his wounded should die. Think of the number of men who will live to fight another day. Think of the suffering saved. Think of the honour that will be yours. All this you can do if you will but see the merchant who is to bring the Silver Steel and bid him make haste!'

Nan, at the desk, listened spellbound. She did not understand what it was all about, but clearly it was something for the King which was very wonderful and would make Adam famous. At the end of the alchemist's harangue she let out a deep sigh of excitement. The alchemist looked quickly round.

'I thought we were alone,' he said sharply. 'When did the child come in?'

Adam almost scowled at Nan. 'Who told you to come here?' he demanded.

Nan's eyes grew big. It was something unheard of for Adam to speak so to her.

'Grandfather said I might come,' she returned timidly. 'I have been here but a moment.'

Adam relented. 'She is a good child,' he said to Master Gross. 'She will not prattle.'

The alchemist still looked doubtful. 'You must be certain,' he said. 'I have warned you that all depends on secrecy. If any should hear of the Silver—of the earth you are to get from the Hanse, you might find that another has succeeded with the Panacea before you.'

'I will be careful,' Adam promised.

'Be careful indeed, and by all you value be speedy.' Master Gross gathered his gown around him. 'Come to me soon at the *Green Falcon* and let me know your fortune.'

Adam opened the door and escorted Master Gross across the wharf to a waiting boat. Then he returned to Nan. All his gravity was gone. Bubbling with excitement he seized her by her hands and whirled her round.

'Did you hear?' he cried. 'I've found the Panacea. I can scarce believe it, but it is true. I shall be rich. I shall be famous. I can be apothecary or chirurgeon or physician, whatever I please. Any of them will welcome me because I have found the Panacea.'

Nan came to a standstill panting.

'What *is* a panacea?' she inquired mystified.

The plain question sobered Adam. 'The Panacea is the elixir of health.' Then seeing that she was still puzzled he went on.

'It is the magic remedy which will cure every disease. Nay, I speak wrong. It is not magic. It is a particular mixture of simples and earths and essences distilled together. Alchemists have sought it for years and years, and Master Gross says that I have found it. It needs but the addition of one special element which comes from Germany, from the silver mines near Freiburg. I must go at once to the Hanse. There is a merchantman sailing this evening.'

He ran his fingers through his hair excitedly, then stepped to a mirror of polished steel which hung on the wall and smoothed it down again. As he stood looking into the mirror, he caught sight of Nan reflected in it. He swung round and came back to her.

'Was I sharp with you, Poppet?' he said gently. 'It is because I am in a ferment. I want above all things to be a physician and cure diseases and I know not how to achieve it. Pray for me, Nan, that I may get my way.'

Nan nodded, her eyes very bright. When Adam spoke to her like that there was nothing that she would not do for him. She was just going to tell him about that candle when the door opened and Grandfather came in.

'Who was that who was here?' he asked gruffly. 'He went away by boat.'

Adam became very quiet. Nan noticed that he spoke carefully.

''Twas a Master Gross from Southwark. He wanted some essences. He has been here before.'

'Essences? Is he an apothecary?'

'Yes,' replied Adam. 'That is to say he is an alchemist.'

'An *alchemist*,' repeated Grandfather with surprise. ''Tis not often we have an alchemist here. What did he need?'

'He wanted some Hartshorn of a particular sort, and asked that we would obtain some specially for him from one of the Hanse merchants. It is ground from the horns of deer in the Harz Mountains. I thought me that Master Hans Stein, the German, sails today.'

'That is true,' said Grandfather approvingly. 'Go to the Steelyard and talk to him at once. Bespeak the order. You had best hasten. He will go out on the tide.'

'May I come with you?' begged Nan eagerly. She wanted to be *in* this with Adam.

Grandfather rounded on her suddenly. 'By my troth, 'tis well that you spoke, child. I had almost forgot. Master Whittington is at home. He brings news of Dickon. And he has a treat in store for you. This afternoon he goes to Westminster by river. If you have your dinner quickly he will take you with him.'

Nan needed no second telling. Adam and the Steelyard were forgotten. She darted out of the warehouse and up the hill. She had almost reached home before she remembered that although Adam had told his grandsire about the Hartshorn he had not mentioned the Silver Steel.

St. Paul's from the river

Chapter Seven

BY BARGE TO WESTMINSTER

WHEN she reached the house, Master Whittington had already gone, but Aunt Isabel reassured her that everything was arranged; she was to go to Westminster with him. She must be at Dowgate, where the boat would be waiting, in an hour from now. There was no reason to get flustered. She had plenty of time to eat her dinner and change her dress too. The fish that they had bought together was cooked in milk with lots of herbs, and Aunt Isabel gave her some in a bowl with a horn spoon, and some crusty bread to eat with it. While she was swallowing it, too excited really to taste it, Aunt Isabel gave her the tidings about Dickon. He had already been before the Mayor, his indenture was signed, and he was now a full-fledged mercer apprentice. Master Whittington would tell her more about it on the way.

Dinner finished she was bustled upstairs to dress. She must wear her very best, Aunt Isabel decreed, because Master Whittington was going to Westminster on special business for the King.

Awestruck by such an important errand, Nan stood very

still while Aunt Isabel fastened her dress, a rosy pink surcoat, sleeveless and cut away at the sides, worn over a smock of fine linen embroidered by Aunt Isabel with little flowers in pink Paris silk. It would be nice and cool for her, Aunt Isabel said chattily, as she arranged one of her own fine lawn veils on Nan's head, pulling the edge forward to shade the eyes, and securing it with a circlet of twisted silver. The afternoon bid fair to be a warm one.

But when, escorted by Joanna, Aunt Isabel's tiring woman, she reached the dock at Dowgate, Nan was more awestruck still, for the boat was not an ordinary wherry, as she had expected, but a richly painted barge with six rowing men and an awning brilliantly striped in the colours of the Mercers' Company.

Master Whittington was already there directing the arrangement of cushions. He greeted Nan with his merry smile and

Soon they were swinging upstream

handed her down the steps and into the barge as though she were a great lady. When Joanna was also safely seated he signed to the watermen to push off.

Sitting like a queen under the awning with Master Whittington Nan felt very small and shy. It was a comfort to recognize among the oarsmen the familiar face and cheerful grin of Dickon's friend Jenkyn. In a few powerful strokes the barge shot out beyond the little bit of London River that was known to her. Soon they were swinging upstream past crowded wharfs and warehouses, behind which a jumble of roofs and church towers clustered round the towering mass of St. Paul's.

Master Whittington did not let her feel shy for long. He began to talk to her at once, pointing out everything as they passed; first Baynard's Castle, its massive stone walls rising straight out of the water; then the church and cloister of the Dominican friars, the 'Blackfriars'; then London Wall, which ran down to the Thames by the mouth of the Fleet river—the same wall, he reminded her, that she had passed through at Cripplegate. Beyond the Fleet river they came to a line of fine houses with gardens running down to the water's edge. Some of them were the Inns of great lords or of bishops from different parts of England who used them when they came to attend Parliament, and some were religious houses, like Whitefriars, the priory of the Carmelites, or the Temple, with its round church, built by the Knights Templars.

The afternoon was very hot and Nan felt sorry for the watermen who had to sit in the sun and row the heavy barge against the stream. Between London and Westminster the river swung round in a big curve, but, it seemed, they could not make a short cut because the water near the south bank was shallow and full of rushes.

Even under the awning it was stifling. Master Whittington glanced enviously at Nan's cool smock. 'You are dressed wisely,' he said ruefully. 'Men are fools about clothes. You can wear a piece of gossamer, but if I were to come to Westminster in my shirt, what think you that my Lord Abbot would say?'

Nan smiled back at him. She was enjoying herself, but she did wish that he would tell her about Dickon.

'I wonder if Dickon is as hot as we are,' she ventured.

Master Whittington laughed right out. 'Dickon? I'll wager that he is a great deal hotter, though I doubt not that Will Appleyard will be merciful with him on his first day. I suppose you are on tenterhooks to hear about this morning's doings, eh? Well, help me loosen my gown and I will tell you. Lord Abbot or no Lord Abbot, I must get cool while I may.'

Feeling very grown up she helped him to drag his *houppelande* half off his shoulders. Underneath he wore a fine lawn shirt, exquisitely gathered and tucked with silk thread. She wished Aunt Isabel could have seen it. Even the best ones she did for Grandfather were not so finely stitched as this. As for the gown, Nan did not wonder that he was hot. The cloth was heavily embroidered and actually edged with fur.

When he was comfortable Master Whittington was as good as his word and began to describe vividly how Dickon had become a mercer apprentice. To start with he had turned up punctually at the Mercers' Hall escorted by Will Appleyard. He was already dressed in his working tunic and his round cap, and he looked, said Master Whittington, as though butter would not melt in his mouth.

'He went down on his knees in front of the Mayor and took the prentice's vows without stumbling over a single word. Doubtless Will had made him go over them half a hundred times between Cripplegate and Cheap.'

'What are the prentice's vows?' inquired Nan. She had never taken much interest in apprentices before.

'The prentice's vows? Oh, he lays his hand on the Gospels and vows solemnly that he will pray faithfully to God, and be zealous in industry, in obedience, and in duty towards his master. Poor lad, he had an air as if he had thrown away a noble and picked up a groat, but he did his part valiantly.'

'What happened next?' pressed Nan as he stopped for breath.

'When he had finished his vowing it was my turn. I only hope I did it with as good a grace as he did. Then we both signed the indenture, and then it was chopped up the middle and divided between us.'

'Why is it chopped up?' demanded Nan. It seemed such a funny thing to do with a parchment.

'Bless you, my poppet, it is hot for so many questions,' he protested. 'An indenture is an agreement between two people. After it has been signed it is cut with a jagged line, _indented_ do you see? Each person keeps one half and if any dispute arises it's easy to prove that they are both part of the original because they fit together. It's very simple, isn't it? But look! We are almost at Westminster.'

They had just passed Charing, the village where there was a cross like the one in Cheap, and Nan looked eagerly ahead. She was the only one of the family who had never been to Westminster, and she had heard so much about the King's Palace and the Abbey where the King was crowned that she expected some sort of fairy city of towers and pinnacles.

But at first sight Westminster was disappointing. There was no great spire like St. Paul's, but only a jumble of buildings with scarcely a tower between them.

'That high roof is Westminster Hall,' said Master Whittington, struggling back into his gown as the barge glided up the last reach. 'And the one behind it with the little turrets is St. Stephen's, the royal chapel. The Abbey lies beyond. . . . You can only just see the top of it. It has no tower yet.'

'Is the King at the Palace?' she inquired eagerly.

His eyes twinkled. 'Alas! no,' he is at Eltham. I forgot your devotion to his Grace or I might have begged him to be here to receive you. But I will show you his Hall if we have the time. It is very ancient, but King Richard had it all renewed a few years ago, with a wonderful new roof. He gave a splendid feast there during his last Christmas. I was invited to it. It took twenty-six oxen and three hundred sheep a day to feed everybody

Hand in hand they passed under the arch

that Christmas-tide. I tell you, Richard the Second was a very lavish prince.'

The watermen shipped their oars and the barge slid alongside a landing-stage jutting out from the Palace wall. At the top of some steps there was a small stone watergate. Master Whittington disembarked and waited to help Nan. Then hand in hand they passed under the arch.

They emerged into a huge square courtyard, with buildings all the way round it.

'This is New Palace Yard,' he told her, 'and that is the main entrance to Westminster Hall on your left. All that you see on that side is part of the Palace.'

Nan stopped to gaze at the archers guarding the door. The King might be away, but all the same there was a constant stream of people in fine clothes coming and going between the Palace and the big stone gateway at the far end of the courtyard.

'Did you go in by that door when you went to the feast?' she questioned.

'Yes,' he said smiling. 'And I came in a barge, just as we came today, except that it was the Mayor's barge and very splendid. I was not Mayor myself that year, but I had been Mayor the year before, and so I shared in the honours. If you had been there with me then, we would have walked through that watergate, hand in hand, just as we did today; and we would have been conducted through those doors by the King's chamberlain, and shown into the Great Hall, where King Richard was waiting dressed in a gown of cloth of gold trimmed with pearls and precious stones.'

'Go on,' she begged as he paused for breath.

'Well, remember then that it was Christmas and very cold. There were flurries of snow driving into the barge, and we were all huddled up in cloaks over our fur-lined gowns. But there was a great fire burning in the Hall. The children of the King's chapel sang carols while we feasted.'

Nan stood staring up at the Hall as if the scene was actually there before her eyes. He had to call her back to earth.

'Come along, my poppet. Look at the clock behind you. My business is at the Abbey, you know.'

She turned quickly. A clock was an exciting thing to see in any case, and this one stood in a tower all by itself. There was a story connected with it, Master Whittington told her, as he led her away from the Palace. More than a hundred years ago a judge in the Law Courts at Westminster had taken a bribe of eight hundred marks. He was found out and ordered to spend the money on building this tower with a clock which would strike the hours and remind other judges in the courts of his disgrace.

'The houses all round the clock tower are used by the merchants of the Wool Staple,' he said chuckling to himself. 'It was very clever of the King who established them there—King Edward III I think. You see, most of the royal money comes from taxes on wool, so having the wool merchants just opposite the Palace must be rather like keeping a cow in the garden.'

Nan laughed too, though really she wasn't paying very much attention. There were so many things to look at in New Palace Yard. A bishop was arriving in a horse litter, his mitre carried in front of him; two lords with hawks on their wrists came riding in from a day's sport in the marshes; tonsured clerks carrying rolls of parchment hurried about everywhere, and ordinary men and women drew water from the conduit in the middle. Certainly Westminster was a very exciting place.

As they were passing out of the stone gate it occurred to her to wonder why they were going to the Abbey. Aunt Isabel had said that Master Whittington was on the King's business.

'Sir, what are we to do at the Abbey?' she ventured.

New Palace Yard

'They are building a new nave to the Abbey church, and I have to see how they are getting on. The King has made me watch-dog over the money to be spent on it. I am a good watch-dog, you know. So far I have not bitten anybody, but I often come and rattle my chain just to let the builders know that there *is* a watch-dog. Master masons are all the same. They have no idea of money.'

Outside the stone gate they crossed a muddy street and turned to the left under another gateway. There were high stone walls round them now and she knew at once that they must be inside the Abbey enclosure because the gatekeeper was a monk in a black habit.

It was not at all what she had expected. She could scarcely

see the Abbey church, for they were passing through narrow alleys of gloomy tumbledown houses, deep in shadow. Strange-looking people hung about in doorways and peered out at them suspiciously, as they went by.

Nan kept close to Master Whittington's side. This was the Little Sanctuary of the Abbey, he explained. Surely she must know about the Church's laws of Sanctuary, how anyone who was pursued or in danger could claim the protection of Holy Mother Church. But what it meant in practice was that all sorts of evil-doers ran for shelter to the Abbey and lived there, on and off, safe from the law.

At last they came out of the dark shadows into the graveyard, where it was all sunshine, and the Abbey church itself towered up before them, misty and blue against the light, the near end of it partly hidden by scaffolding.

Nan gave a sigh of relief. Here life was going on busily again. There were men working everywhere, chipping stone blocks, pushing them about on barrows, carrying them up ladders, or sending them up with ropes and pulleys to other men so high up on the scaffolding that they looked like flies against the sky.

All the workmen seemed to know her companion and greeted him respectfully with friendly grins. A monk with his cowl over his head stood with his back to them talking to a man in a leather apron. The man said a word and the monk looked round.

'Ah, Master Whittington,' he exclaimed, and murmured a Latin blessing. 'We were expecting you. The master mason has plans ready for you to see.'

Master Whittington crossed himself in acknowledgement of the blessing. 'I thank you, Father Prior,' he said. 'I should have been before, but yesterday his Grace required me to wait on him at the Tower. Where shall I find the plans? In the Lord Abbot's lodging?'

The prior nodded. 'They are laid out ready for you. Master Colchester is there.' Then he looked at Nan. 'This little maid? Is she your grandchild?'

'Alas, no. I am childless. But Nan has been good enough to adopt me. I suppose, though, as our Lord God has seen fit to make her a girl and not a boy, I had best not take her into the monastery. We will leave her here with Peter. This is Peter the plumber, Nan. He has charge of all the lead for the roof. If

Father Prior gives leave, he will take care of you. There is plenty for you to see, and I shall not be long.'

Nan, on her best behaviour before so important a person as Father Prior, whispered 'Yes, sir'. She felt like Button, when Button was tied up outside a church where they were strict about dogs, and as she looked up at Master Whittington she was sure that her eyes must be as beseeching as Button's. But in the distance she could see black-robed monks everywhere, and she decided that anyway she would be too shy to go any further.

The man with the leather apron had a kind face. As soon as the prior and Master Whittington had gone, he asked her if she would like to see the church. When she said yes he took her inside the new nave and helped her to clamber over the piles of squared stones. It was so strange to be in a church that had only

In the distance she could see black-robed monks

part of a roof. The walls seemed to be almost complete, and the pillars and arches were growing up like trees in a wood. But it was so high that it made her quite dizzy to crane her neck and look up at men like midgets balanced on the top.

Peter the plumber was very nice. When they were outside again he told her that he lived at Lambeth, across the river, and came to work by the ferry every morning.

'Lambeth?' said Nan, to be friendly. 'I've never been to Lambeth. It is by Southwark, isn't it?'

'Nay, it is not by Southwark,' retorted the plumber quite indignantly. 'I grant that it is not far away across the marsh; I sometimes walk over the cut to get to London Bridge. But

Lambeth is a village on its own, and Lambeth folk have no dealings with those of Southwark.'

An idea came into Nan's head. This was a chance to find out something.

'I heard of someone who lives in Southwark,' she said, 'at the sign of the *Green Falcon*. Do you know it?'

He stared at her. 'The *Green Falcon* is a tavern, a Southwark tavern. Who would a young maiden like you be knowing at a Southwark tavern?'

Nan took fright. Suppose he told Master Whittington!

'Oh, no one,' she replied airily. 'Only a poor apprentice I heard of.' Then she changed the subject quickly. 'Can I go and watch them carving those stones?'

But before they reached the stonemason's shed, she saw Master Whittington coming towards her. He was accompanied by a man in a flat cap whom Peter said was Master Colchester, the master mason. Behind them walked a lay brother carrying a basket.

'See what we have been given,' Master Whittington called gaily. He took the basket from the lay brother and showed it to her. On a bed of green leaves lay half a dozen shining trout. 'What do you think of that? The Father Cellarer told me that they were caught this morning in the Tyburn brook, and have been only a few hours in the Abbot's fishpond. You shall eat them with me. We will send a message to your grandsire that you will be supping at my house.'

They went back to the river a different way. Master Colchester led them through the churchyard by a small postern gate and a network of passages, out into New Palace Yard again. The two men were deep in conversation, and they did not pause, as Nan had hoped, at Westminster Hall. At the landing-stage they stood at the top of the stairs, still talking, so Nan jumped into the barge. She was amusing herself by looking for the ferry by which Peter the plumber crossed the river, when someone behind her said quietly, 'Ye loaves and fishes!'

She glanced round. That was what Dickon said. It was one of the watermen who spoke, but she could not be sure which. While she was looking a voice from among a group of men loitering on the quay added softly, 'The net is full.' But just then, before anything more could happen, Master Whittington stepped into the barge and they started on their way down-stream.

Master Whittington was lost in thought, and Nan was thinking too. 'Ye loaves and fishes!' She would love to know if it was a very bad oath. Softly she tried it out, to see its effect on Master Whittington.

'Ye loaves and fishes!' she murmured under her breath.

She had thought that he might be shocked, but she was not prepared for the amazement in his face.

'*What* did you say?' he demanded, raising his voice a little, because the slap of the water made it difficult to hear. 'Say that again. Nay, do not be frightened. I am not angry, but I want to be sure what you said.'

'"Ye loaves and fishes",' she repeated timidly, sorry that she had ever begun. 'Oh sir, your pardon. Is it a very bad oath?'

He smiled at her. 'It is not a mortal sin. You need not confess it. But I would like to know where you heard it. Can you remember?'

Nan nodded cheerfully, relieved that she did not have to mention Dickon.

'One of the watermen said it just now, and someone on the wharf answered "The net is full". What does it mean?'

'I do not know myself,' he said. 'Did you notice which waterman it was? If you speak quietly they cannot hear you in this wind.'

Nan shook her head. It *might* have been Jenkyn but she was not going to say so, in case it meant trouble for him.

'A pity,' said Master Whittington, as though to himself, and relapsed again into silence.

But the combination of Dickon and Jenkyn and the memory of yesterday on the wharf when Dickon had used this strange oath, put another idea into Nan's head. Her heart began to beat quickly. If only she *dare* ask Master Whittington, she might do something really big for Dickon. Drawing a deep breath she laid a hand on his knee and started before she had time to get frightened again.

'Worshipful sir,' she ventured. 'Jenkyn has promised to take Dickon to Ratcliffe-below-Tower to see the *Katharine*, the King's ship, before she sails away. May he go?'

'What's that?' he demanded in astonishment. 'To see the King's ship? And who is Jenkyn? Oh, of course, that fellow pulling in the bow there. I forgot he was a friend of yours. But, my child, how can Dickon go? Remember that he is newly apprenticed. An apprentice cannot leave his task to go a-voyaging.'

'There are holy-days,' said Nan, surprised at herself. She wished that Dickon could have heard her. He wouldn't call her a frightened rabbit any more.

'True, there are holy-days,' he repeated, a twinkle in his eye. 'There is, for instance, Corpus Christi, not so very far ahead. 'Twas that you had in mind maybe?'

Nan shook her head. Really she had nothing in mind except to win this treat for Dickon.

'Well, we will see,' said Master Whittington tolerantly. 'But, mark you, I do not offer much hope. I have passed Dickon to Will Appleyard who is a strict master. He does not smile upon giddy apprentices. Look, the Bridge is in sight. And yea, in truth, the drawbridge is open. Can you see it? 'Tis that German merchantman which is going down river. Her master is Hans Stein, from Hamburg. I heard that he was to sail today.'

Nan nodded. She had heard it too, though she did not say so. But silently she wondered if Master Hans Stein carried Adam's order for that strange earth, Silver Steel.

Turn again, Whittington

Chapter Eight

'SUPPER FOR TWO'

INSTEAD of sending a message to Grandfather, Master Whittington himself returned to Grantham's Inn with Nan, and begged permission to take her home with him. They had been fishing in the Tyburn brook, he said with a twinkle, and had brought back some trout for their supper. Grandfather entered into the joke at once and Aunt Isabel hurried Nan upstairs to tidy her veil and her hair. Her hands too must be washed; and Joanna was sent scurrying down to fetch some water from the cauldron in the kitchen. Nan lingered over the luxury of warm water and Castile soap in the pewter basin. Cold water in a tub was her usual lot, but now Aunt Isabel inspected her hands carefully. It would be a shocking thing if she were to dip them in the finger-bowl at the table and leave black marks on the napkin.

So, fresh and tidy, Nan walked up the hill with Master Whittington. As they neared the house they were met by Madame Eglantine who came hurrying towards her master, her black tail very erect, mewing and purring and throwing herself against his legs in a transport of delight.

'Thou bold little wench,' he cried as he stooped to pick up the cat. 'Didst thou smell the fish all that way off? Take hold on the basket, Nan, or we shall have no supper. Ah, my pretty sweeting, my Madame Eglantine, I fear that thou art but a false lover; 'tis the trout that thou lovest, more than thine old master.'

It seemed that he misjudged her. Madame Eglantine was intent upon nothing but upon being stroked and petted. Only

82

when they were actually in the house and Master Whittington had delivered the trout to the steward to be grilled would she consent to take any notice of the fish. Then, when she was put down, she sniffed the air delicately and followed the basket towards the kitchen.

'She wanted to come with me this afternoon,' laughed her master. 'I allow her to come sometimes when I am about the City, but I thought that my Lord Abbot might deem it strange if the King's agent should arrive accompanied by his cat.'

There was a question which, secretly, Nan had wanted to ask for many a day. Her chance came when supper was almost finished and the two of them were sucking the last delicious taste of buttery trout from their fingers.

Supper with Master Whittington

'Sir, why do you call her Madame Eglantine?' she ventured.

'Because she is just like Madame Eglantine,' he smiled, dropping a piece of fish to his pet. 'Madame Eglantine is the name of the nun in *The Canterbury Tales*. You have heard of *The Canterbury Tales*?'

Nan nodded. Of course she had heard of *The Canterbury Tales*. Grandfather was always quoting them. But still she could not see the connexion between a nun and a cat.

'She was prioress of a nunnery,' he went on, 'a very dainty lady clad all in black, with a white wimple, as most nuns are. I wish I could remember the lines by heart. Master Chaucer describes her exactly, especially her table manners. She was so well brought up that never a morsel of food fell from her lips or a drop of gravy spilled on her breast. She took care not to dip too far into the sauce, and when she had finished her meal she wiped

Chaucer's Madame Eglantine

every little trace of grease from her mouth. It's a perfect likeness of *my* Madame Eglantine.' He glanced down at the cat and began to laugh. 'Come and look at her now and you will see what I mean.'

Nan slipped down from her stool and came round to Master Whittington's side. Madame Eglantine, having enjoyed her fish, was sitting up primly, cleaning her face and her whiskers. Certainly with her smooth black coat and white throat, she did look rather like a little nun.

'I *do* see,' she agreed. 'She *is* a dainty lady, isn't she?'

'Simple and coy", that's how Geoffrey Chaucer described her,' he persisted. 'They both sing through their noses, mark you, and they both have a soft spot for a mouse. There's a slight difference between them when it comes to little dogs, but we can forget that part. Come along, my poppet, we had best follow her example and clean ourselves after our meal.'

He dipped his fingers into the bowl, wiped them on the napkin and passed it to Nan. When she was ready he stood to say a grace and led the way into the garden.

It was quite a small garden, for the church of St. Michael Paternoster cut it off on one side, and the half-finished buildings of the new hospice on the other. But it was large enough to hold a little fishpond and some neat beds of pot herbs and scented flowers. A dovecote for his pigeons stood in one corner, and there was a stone seat so placed that anyone resting there could enjoy a glimpse of the river and the Bridge.

Master Whittington made the seat comfortable with cushions from the hall, and picked two nosegays of rosemary and gilliflower to banish the smell of the Wallbrook which ran near-by. As soon as they were settled the doves flew down looking for food and he threw them some pieces of manchet bread saved from supper. Madame Eglantine jumped on to his lap and watched them placidly; she knew better than to interfere with them.

''Tis pleasant here after a hot day,' he said, burying his nose among the flowers. 'If you are not longing for your bed we might sit still till curfew, and then I will take you home. In so short a distance we are not likely to be seized by the watch and cast into prison for being in the streets without a light.'

'Surely they would not seize *you*,' said Nan, missing the joke.

'Perhaps not,' he agreed gravely. 'Hark, there go Bow Bells. Apprentices stop work. And there is the angelus-bell too. Say your Ave where you are. You've had a long day. Our blessed Mother will forgive you for not standing up.'

As she said her prayer she thought of Dickon. It had indeed been a long day for him. How weary he must be. It seemed like a week since he left home.

The doves flew down

Master Whittington heard a little sigh and looked down at her.

'You *are* tired, my poppet,' he said softly. 'Shall I take you home now?' Then, as Nan shook her head, he smiled. 'Well, would you like a story? What sort of a story shall it be?'

'About Madame Eglantine, please.'

She curled herself up among the cushions. The cat on his knee purred softly. As he began she sighed again, but this time it was with sheer contentment.

She thought that the story would be the one from *The Canterbury Tales* about the nun. But it wasn't. It was about a poor boy who came to London with a bundle on his back to make his fortune, because he had heard that the streets were paved with gold.

'What was his name?' she inquired sleepily.

'His name was Dick,' said Master Whittington.

'This poor boy soon found that there was no gold in the streets and very little bread either. A rich merchant took him in and made him scullion in the kitchen, but the cook was cruel to him and knocked him about, and the other servants all jeered at him. His only friend was his cat, a little black cat with a white wimple, which caught the rats and mice in the garret where he slept. After a time he could bear it no longer. He decided to run away. So he took his bundle and his cat, and he crept out of the house and left the City by Cripplegate. They walked and they walked till they came to a high hill, and there they stopped to rest. From where they sat he could see London with all its towers and spires. And then Bow Bells began to ring for all good apprentices to go to work. He could hear them quite clearly. They seemed to be playing a little tune, and the tune they played was

> Turn again Whittington
> Thrice mayor of London.'

Nan, who was almost asleep, sat up with a start:

'It's about *you*,' she cried.

'Hush!' said Master Whittington. 'You'll wake Madame Eglantine. Now rest, if you want me to finish the story.'

Obediently Nan curled up once more. She wished that she did not feel so sleepy for it was a lovely story.

'Where had I got to?' he asked. 'Oh, I know. It was where Dick was sitting on Highgate Hill listening to Bow Bells. *Bow Bells*, do you understand? He was a runaway apprentice and Bow Bells were calling him back to work. They were reminding him that if he went back and was faithful to his duty he might become Mayor of London.'

He paused and Nan began to fear that the story was over. 'Go on!' she said. She was so comfortable that she did not want him to stop.

But the story wasn't finished. It became quite exciting—all about a merchant ship setting out upon a venture. The ship was called the good ship *Unicorn*, and lots of people lent their money, hoping to become rich. Poor Dick had nothing to lend except his cat, so the cat went with the ship and caught rats and mice for the King of Barbary. There was something about the merchant's

'Softly, friend Thomas. Do not wake the little maid'

beautiful daughter, too, but by the time they came to that part, Nan was fast asleep.

She was woken by Master Whittington dumping a warm sleepy Madame Eglantine on to her lap. Someone had come into the garden. She recognized the voice of the steward an-nouncing Master Falconer.

She peeped round doubtfully. Master Falconer was the Mayor. She ought to make her curtsy, but she couldn't without disturbing Madame Eglantine, so she closed her eyes again. If they thought she was asleep they would not expect her to get up.

She heard Master Whittington speak in a whisper.

'Softly, friend Thomas. Do not wake the little maid. She is the sister of the new apprentice you saw this morning. We have been supping.'

The two men began to pace up and down together, talking in low tones. Nan could only catch part of what they said; it was all about business and very dull. After a while she heard some-thing about Lollards which reminded her of the discussion at dinner yesterday, when Master Whittington spoke of his charge from the King, but she was too drowsy to pay much attention. But suddenly Master Whittington said something that caught her ear.

'Tell me, Thomas, have you heard of an oath about loaves and fishes? "Ye loaves and fishes"; that is the form of it.'

'Why, yes,' said Master Falconer. 'I have heard it often enough, though I could not tell you where. It does not sound to me too grave a blasphemy.'

'It is not the blasphemy that I was thinking of, but the meaning.'

'Surely it is just a reference to the feeding of the five thousand in the Gospels. I cannot see any other meaning.'

'I would not be too sure.' Master Whittington's voice sounded grave. 'I have several times heard it receive an answer, and always the same one. "The net is full." *That* has no mean-ing on the surface, but we should watch it, and learn more of it.'

Master Falconer halted quite near the bench. 'What is your idea? That it may be some sort of password?'

'It is possible. At any rate it supposes an understanding between the people who use it.'

'We must find out,' said the Mayor decisively. 'If you are right their number must be immense. We had best apprehend one or two for question.'

'Nay, I beg you, don't do that,' exclaimed Master Whitting-ton earnestly. 'Let it go without comment. It will be the greatest help in discovering their circle. Just note the names of those who say it, and let me have them. It is in shallow streams that the current is near the surface, you know, and I believe that it is by watching the apprentices that we shall learn which way the stream is bound.'

'Have you any young Lollards among your lads?'

'I think not. Will Appleyard has a sharp eye and he has no ill report to make. How about yours?'

'Now that I come to think of it,' said the Mayor slowly, 'there *is* one of my lads who uses the oath about loaves and fishes. He is a great hulking red-headed fellow called Kurt Bladebone; a truculent oaf, in the thick of every fight. Only yesterday he came in with a bloody nose and lacking two front teeth.'

Nan was wideawake now, and so alert that she had all that she could do to keep still.

'Yesterday? And you say he is a red-head?' Dick Whittington began to laugh. 'I think I could tell you how those front teeth went. Do you recall that Dickon, my new apprentice, had been fighting too? You remarked at it this morning.'

'God save us,' cried Master Falconer. 'I thought that Kurt had been in battle with half a dozen victuallers. In fact he told me so.'

'Then he is a liar, at least about the half-dozen. So far as I can learn 'twas only half a grocer that he fought. It all happened just before Dickon was told that he was to become a mercer. He thought himself certain for the grocer's livery. It was an odd chance that set that pair at each other. Methinks their guardian angels must have been enjoying a jest.'

'You always see a jest in everything, my good Dick,' retorted the Mayor. 'But for my part I think it would be as well if those two should not meet yet-a-while. We do not want bloodshed within the craft.'

'We can arrange that,' said Whittington. 'I will keep Dickon to Cripplegate for a bit. I will not let him go to the Hart Street house, if you on your part will keep your lads to Aldgate. Their blood will cool in time.'

'Yea, but how about holy-days?' objected Master Falconer. 'The prentices' club gathers on holy-days. That is when the mischief brews. They meet to choose their leaders and elect their officers, for all the world like their betters at the Guildhall. At Corpus Christi, for instance; they are bound to meet then.'

'Humph!' muttered Master Whittington thoughtfully.

'Corpus? Well, by chance I have a plan even for Corpus.' Once more he began to chuckle. 'You chide me for too many jests; but does it not strike you as funny that you and I should be solemnly conspiring together, not on the City's business, but to save our apprentices from murdering each other?' He laid his hand on the Mayor's arm. 'Before you go I have a letter that I would like to show you. It concerns an order for sails painted with the King's device. Come you inside a moment.'

Nan heard the rattle of the door latch. It was growing dark in the garden, and soon after the two men vanished indoors the curfew rang. The white doves, as though at a signal, fluttered one by one to their dovecot. But she did not move. She was very comfortable and the cat on her lap kept her warm. She had heard so much that her mind was quite confused with it. Tomorrow, she told herself, she must remember it all carefully so as to tell Dickon. But in the meanwhile she was getting drowsy again. When Master Whittington returned a few minutes later he found her fast asleep.

'You must wake, my poppet,' he urged, feeling her hands to make sure that she was not cold. 'You will catch your death in the night air. I am mightily to blame in leaving you so long.' Nevertheless as she roused herself, he picked up Madame Eglantine and sat down on the bench beside her.

'I have been thinking,' he said. 'I am going to grant the favour that you ask. Dickon may go to see the King's ship on the feast of Corpus Christi.'

Chapter Nine

SHADOWS OF THE NIGHT

THE lanes were dark and deserted when Master Whittington took Nan home. With the summer curfew as late as nine o'clock most people were in bed before it rang. They had to be up at dawn, and to use precious candles, which were needed for the winter, was sheer extravagance.

In one window, however, a light was burning. Through the small glass panes of his parlour, they could see Grandfather, spectacles on nose, bending over his ledgers, the yellow candle glow reflected on his white beard.

Master Whittington did no more than hand Nan over and say a brief good-night. She was left standing by her grandsire's side, waiting for him to give her his blessing and send her up to bed. Apparently Aunt Isabel had already gone. But Nan was now wideawake again and quite excited. In her whole life she had never been out so late before.

John Sherwood had returned to his accounts. His quill pen squeaked upon the parchment. Only when Nan shuffled her feet did he remember her. Then he laid down his pen and his spectacles and looked at her kindly.

'How now!' he said. 'We are coming to a pretty pass when our little maids are running abroad at curfew time. Did you enjoy your supper? I could have fancied one of those trout myself. And what did you afterwards? Play backgammon?'

Nan shook her head. 'We sat in the garden, and Master Whittington told me a story. It was a lovely story, all about how he came to London as a boy. Do you know it? Shall I tell you?'

Grandfather smiled at her. He poured himself some wine from a silver flagon and gave her a sip. So, as he sat swilling it round the goblet and sniffing the aroma, she began. Somehow Grandfather by candlelight, with walls of shadow shutting in the two of them, was quite a different person from Grandfather who boomed at them during the day. She told him the story as fully

Grandfather by candlelight

as she could remember it. It seemed that he must be enjoying it because there was a smile on his face.

'That is a pretty tale,' he said, 'but of course it is not about Master Whittington. *He* was never a poor scullion. He is the son of a knight of the West Country, a gentleman of coat armour with estates in two counties. His brother is High Sheriff of Gloucestershire. You have confused it, child. 'Tis the story of some other boy.'

Nan shook her head. 'It *must* be about Master Whittington,' she insisted. 'He told me himself. He heard Bow Bells ringing, and they said "*Turn again Whittington, thrice Mayor of London*". It was about Madame Eglantine too.'

Grandfather chuckled to himself as he pinched her cheek.

'"Tis just one of his humours. Without doubt he made it all up as he went along, to amuse you. You see *I've* known him since we were both apprentices, and I can vouch for it that he was no scullion. Still, three times Mayor of London is true enough. 'Tis a mixed confection, half-true, half-fancy. He loves such trifling.'

Suddenly the hour-glass on the table caught his eye. All the sand had run through to the bottom.

'It must be very late,' he cried. 'I forgot to turn the glass. You must go quickly to bed or we shall have Aunt Isabel after us.'

He held the candle to light her up the winding stairs. As she climbed them her own shadow twisted ahead of her in fantastic shapes.

Aunt Isabel's room was lighted too, and Aunt Isabel herself, her night shift wrapped round her, was kneeling at the prayer desk holding her Book of Hours close to a flickering rush taper. As Nan came in she crossed herself devoutly and put the book away. Nan hoped that this was a signal that she might talk, for she was bursting to tell all her news. But Aunt Isabel would not allow it. It was past ten o'clock, she said quite crossly—more than an hour since curfew. What was Master Whittington thinking of to keep a child up so late? Nan must just kneel down and say one PATER and one AVE and then hurry into bed.

Nan sighed. It was sad not to be able to tell Master Whittington's story again before the morning. As she lay by Aunt Isabel's side in the feather bed, between lavender-scented sheets, she went through it for herself all over again, fitting together the parts that she had missed by being so sleepy until it seemed more than ever a lovely story. It was silly of Grandfather to say that it was not true. Had not Master Whittington told her himself? He must know better than anyone else.

She was not at all sleepy. It had been such an exciting day, and so much had happened since Dickon went away. First of all she'd been to market with Aunt Isabel; then she'd actually been on the Bridge and seen Goody. That poor boy and his mother had come, and Grandfather had allowed her to go to the warehouse. She'd found Adam with the alchemist and heard about the pana—, pana—, — she tried to think of the word and couldn't— about the wonderful cure that Adam had invented. And when that horrible man had gone, Adam had told her about his secret and asked her to pray for him. Though she was lying in the dark she screwed up her eyes tight and said one more Our Father . . . there and then, just for good measure.

Then there had been the trip to Westminster and the Great Hall, and the Abbey, and Peter the plumber who lived in Lambeth, and the tiny little men up against the sky, and the silver trout in a basket. The list was so long that she really could not remember it all. She was feeling very uncomfortable; not sleepy but *hot*. Aunt Isabel liked such a lot of bedclothes and try as she would Nan could not find a cool place in the feather bed. She pulled herself up a little on the pillow and tried to get some air. That was the trouble—air. The room was like an oven. If only she could get a breath of fresh air.

She was suddenly tempted to get up and open one of the windows. Of course they were both closely shuttered. The night airs were dangerous. But she felt that she would suffocate, and one might as well die of a fever from breathing night air as die of suffocation.

Quiet as a mouse she slipped out of bed and tiptoed across the room. Even the rushes on the floor felt deliciously cool to her toes. It was pitch dark but there was no furniture on that side of the room that she could trip over. With her outstretched hand she felt the wall and moved along till she reached the shutter. The bolt was quite easy; she knew it well for it was her task to open it in the morning.

With the utmost caution she drew it back. There was no glass in the lower part of the window, only in the upper which did not open, so when the shutter swung out, the cool air struck her like a blow, and she gave a delicious shudder at the sudden chill. She glanced back, but Aunt Isabel had actually begun to snore. Of course the bed curtains would shield her; she would not be likely to notice the draught.

Nan unhooked her cloak which, conveniently, was hanging on a peg close to the window. She wrapped it round her shoulders and ventured to lean a little way out. The night was dark and still. The window faced south, towards the river, and the air that floated towards her carried the smell of tar and river mud.

An owl hooted not far away, and it was so still that she could hear the fluting bubbling call of water-birds in the dim distance. Another faint sound caught her ear, the sound of oars in rowlocks. Someone was rowing on the river.

As she listened it became more distinct. It must be somebody crossing from Southwark. The very thought of Southwark made her hold her breath. The sound came nearer and nearer. It seemed to be coming straight at her, as if a boat were rowing up the lane. Then the oars ceased. There was a muffled bump. She was certain that the boat was mooring at Grantham's Wharf.

Her heart was thumping but her brain was alert. What was anybody doing out so late? There were guard boats on the river at night to protect merchant ships and their cargoes, but it could not be one of those, for they went up and down the river, not across it, and they made much more noise. She wondered what the time was, but there was no means of telling. From this side of the house she could not hear the night watchman's call.

Then, because she was listening intently, she heard footsteps in Grantham's Lane. They were so soft that, even though she had been expecting them, she could hardly be certain of them. After a moment they passed under her window. She had known that they would, for she had been certain for some time that it was Adam. He had been to Southwark.

When he had gone she closed the shutter and crept back to bed, her ears strained to catch a sound of him on the stairs or in the attic overhead. Once she thought that she heard a creaking board, but she was not sure.

The warmth of the bed was very welcome. She slid down stealthily and lay rigid, as, for a moment, Aunt Isabel stirred. She felt more wideawake than ever now, for she was worried. Of course anything that Adam did must be all right, but everybody said such dreadful things about Southwark, and what was he doing there in the middle of the night? She tried to think it out, but bed, after all, was very cosy, and quite suddenly she went to sleep.

At the other side of London Dickon also was lying awake, but there was no feather bed nor lavender-scented sheets for him. His portion was a straw mattress on the floor of the apprentices' garret in Grub Street. It was stuffy between the bales of cloth and one of the other boys was snoring. There were the three in the garret beside himself: Owen, who had showed him round; Robert, the quiet, broad-shouldered young man whose seven-year apprenticeship was nearly finished; and Toby, the fat boy, son of a wealthy miller of Henley-on-Thames, sent to better himself by becoming a London mercer.

Bales of cloth had to be lugged upstairs

It had seemed an endless day, and Dickon could hardly believe that it was less than twenty-four hours since he left home. After being sworn apprentice he had returned to dinner at Grub Street, a large and noisy meal with a dozen or more journeymen and apprentices gathered round the trestle-board, all of whom looked at him curiously. As he took his share of the sturdy chops which Will Appleyard carved from a side of mutton at one end of the table, and of the sticky mess of frumenty, boiled wheat sweetened with honey, which Goodwife Appleyard ladled into bowls at the other, he glanced quickly up and down the line of faces, wondering how much they knew about him. He was uneasy because he did not know how he stood.

After dinner he joined in what was apparently a normal afternoon's work. Packhorses arrived from country weavers bringing bales of local cloth which had to be lugged upstairs by the apprentices. He had not got the knack of carrying them as the other boys had, and after he had laboured up and down a dozen times Will Appleyard caught sight of his crimson sweating face and called him over to help with the tally sticks. Except by name tallies were strange to Dickon as they were not much used in Grandfather's business. They were a very old-fashioned way of keeping accounts, Will Appleyard told him, but they were still very useful for people who could not read or write. The system was to cut notches across a length of wood, one notch for each bale delivered; or if it were money that had to be calculated, then the notches would represent pounds, shillings and pence. The stick was split lengthways into two halves; one-half was given to the packhorse drover to take back to the weaver, as a receipt, while the merchant kept the second half. All the weaver had to do, when he claimed payment, was to present his tally to the merchant, and if the notches on the two halves matched, he was given the money.

When he had mastered the lesson about tallies he was shown the great leather-bound ledgers in which business was written down. Master Whittington, it seemed, had given particular instructions that he was to be taught all about the accounts. This was flattering and Dickon felt rather pleased with himself as he perched on a high stool and began to copy a long list of figures with a newly-made quill pen. But after an hour or two he began to find it rather dull. Try as he would his script did not look neat and beautiful like the pages written by Robert. He was quite glad when he was given a broom instead of a pen and told to sweep out the houseplace at the end of the day's work.

Now as he turned and twisted in his bed, trying to find a comfortable spot, it was not of the work that he was thinking, but of his position with the other boys. He wished to goodness that he had never concealed the fact that his family were grocers. He could see now that it would have been easier if they had known from the beginning. It was not too late; he could mention it casually to Owen or Robert, and leave them to tell the other boys. But the difficulty was that he had allowed them to believe that his black eye, which was still all the colours of the rainbow, had been received when he was fighting on the side of the mercers. Of course he had not *said* so; that would have been a downright lie, and a grave sin; but when they jumped to that conclusion and received him warmly because of it, he lacked the courage to contradict them and tell them the truth.

In the long dark hours all these matters went round and round in his head till they took the nightmare shape of a great snowball which rolled slowly and relentlessly towards him to crush him. He struggled and panted to free himself from it and woke to find that Toby was shaking him. The pale light of dawn showed through the horn panes and the bells of St. Giles were ringing for the morrow mass.

He felt better when they were all gathered in the kitchen for a

breakfast of bread and cheese and small ale before starting the day's duties. It was Saturday. Work would stop at the noon bell and then there would be games on Moorfields.

'We usually play trapball in the summer,' said tall Robert, who seemed to take the lead; 'or can you wield a quarter-staff? You're scarcely heavy enough for the wrestling ring; you look more like a runner. We could do with a sprinter in the mercers' team.'

Dickon admitted that he was not much good with a quarter-staff. He preferred shooting with a long-bow. He was cautious about what he said. He had been the fastest runner among the boys at St.

Every appren- Anthony's, but he did not want to provoke inquiries.
tice has a club At the archery butts he would be more out of the way if Kurt Bladebone turned up again.

But there was no sign of Bladebone on Moorfields that after-noon, and Dickon quite enjoyed himself. At the butts only two of his six arrows failed altogether to hit the target, though he was shooting at the grown man's range of 440 yards; and in a game of trapball he did so well that he was invited to play with the bigger boys. He walked back to the house between Robert and Owen feeling that life was not so bad after all.

They were sluicing their faces in the trough by the well when Robert said suddenly, 'By the way, have you got your club yet?'

Dickon shook the water out of his hair. 'No. Do I have to have one? Who gives it to me?'

'You'll get it from Appleyard,' said Robert. 'Every appren-tice has one. Officially he gets it so that he can guard his master in the London streets at night, but of course it's useful for prentice battles. You must always carry it, you know; then if you hear a cry of "Clubs" you can go and see what the trouble is. If it's just an affair between two other crafts you need not join in; but of course you always use your club to support another mercer.'

'Or any other clothier,' cried Owen fiercely.

They both looked at Dickon. He said 'Of course' as calmly as possible. He felt he was getting on to dangerous ground.

'I'll take you to the mercers' meeting myself,' said Robert with the air of conferring a great favour. 'I expect you know all about the prentices' fellowships. Every craft has one, and if needs be they are ready to draw clubs to defend their rights. Some people actually call the fellowships "clubs".'

Dickon murmured into the towel as he dried his face. He was glad to be hidden.

Robert rolled down his sleeves, ready to go indoors. 'The next meeting is on Corpus Christi,' he said pleasantly. 'You'll meet all the mercer prentices there.'

With this happy prospect in front of him, Dickon went in to supper.

The next day was Sunday. The boys at Grub Street took it in turns to get up betimes and draw water from the well and tend the kitchen fire for Goodwife Appleyard. Dickon was told that he was to do the early shift with Owen, while Robert and Toby lay late in bed if they wanted to. After High Mass there was dinner, a gigantic meal of good roasted lamb, which was turning and spluttering merrily on the spit when they came in from church, filling the kitchen with blue haze and a most appetizing smell.

After dinner everyone went their own ways. Robert's home was at Kensington, and as he had leave he started off to walk the four miles through country lanes. Owen went into the City with some other boys from neighbouring houses. Dickon was not told that he could go home and he did not want to ask. Neither did he want to hang about the City streets looking for trouble. He decided to explore the wooded hills to the north, and he set off with Toby for company. But they lost their way and ended up by wandering about rich water meadows in the neighbourhood of the little village of Islington. Dickon had not been out in that direction before, and he was delighted by the wonderful view of St. Paul's with his beloved river behind it.

He found that he and Toby had one thing in common, the river. Though Toby's Thames at Henley was narrow compared with London River, nevertheless it was the same Thames. Barges went up and down the sixty-odd miles between, and much of the flour ground at the mill owned by Toby's father came to London to be made into bread by London housewives.

When they reached Grub Street on their way home, they were met by Owen who had been sent to look for them. Dickon was bidden by Goodwife Appleyard to make haste because his sister was waiting to see him.

Dickon was not too well pleased. Nan? Here? What was she thinking of? He wished that she would keep away. It might lead to questions about his home and his family which he would rather answer at his own time.

Nan was in the kitchen beating up eggs for Goodwife Appleyard, while Joanna, looking superior in her Sunday clothes, sat with her hands folded in her lap by the kitchen table.

At any rate Nan had the sense not to rush up and kiss him, but she did set down the bowl and greet him with a little cry of joy.

'Master Whittington bade me come,' she declared, 'and Aunt Isabel sent you another shirt.'

Dick Whittington? What was afoot? He glanced round. Toby had just come into the kitchen and was peeling off his muddy shoes. Whatever it was that Nan had to say he did not want Toby to hear it.

'Come outside,' he said. ''Tis over hot in here.'

She came with obvious gladness, leaving Joanna behind. He led her through the garden and on to the edge of Moorfields. There were quite a lot of people gathered round the archery butts, but nobody within earshot. She chattered as they went, just like a sparrow on the eaves—all about going by boat to Westminster. Did every maiden talk as much as this, he wondered?

'What is the message?' he inquired as soon as he could get in a word edgeways.

She took a deep breath and looked at him with very bright eyes.

'I begged Master Whittington for you,' she said, 'and you may go with Jenkyn to see the King's ship on Corpus Christi.'

He stared at her, scarcely able to take it in.

'On *Corpus Christi*?' he repeated.

'Yes, to see the King's ship.' To her mind that was the part that mattered. '*I* asked him.'

For a moment he forgot their surroundings enough to give her a quick hug. It seemed too good to be true. 'Are you sure he said Corpus Christi?' he persisted.

'Quite sure. He said no at first, because you were newly apprenticed. Then I asked about a holy-day, and in the end he promised that you should go on Corpus Christi. And this morning he said that I could come myself and tell you.'

She watched him, hoping that he would say how brave she had been to ask, but after that first excited hug he forgot her. If she had only known it, it seemed to him so great a miracle that his guardian angel was getting the credit for it. Nan tried something else.

'I've heard about that red-headed apprentice,' she volunteered; 'the one you fought.'

'What about him?' he asked quickly.

'His name is Kurt Bladebone. He's prentice to the Mayor, and he lives somewhere near Aldgate.'

'Oh, I knew all that.' He did not mean to be unkind, but the news about Corpus Christi had dwarfed everything else.

Nan at last was silent. She decided that she would not tell him any more. Anyhow she had been so sleepy that night in Master Whittington's garden that she had forgotten most of it.

Her quietness stirred his conscience and he grinned at her.

'You are a good little wench,' he said. 'What's it like at home now? Have you seen Jenkyn?'

'It's very quiet.' She looked carefully behind them. It was her turn now to make sure that there was no one there. 'Dickon,' she said. 'It is true about Southwark. It *is* a wicked place.'

'Well, what of it? Everybody knows that.'

'Adam goes there, late at night.'

He was really startled this time. 'How do you know?'

She told him about opening the bedroom shutter. She was sure he had been to see the alchemist at the *Green Falcon*.

Dickon frowned. Secretly he was shocked at the news, but he was not going to say so to Nan. He and Adam always stuck together.

'Adam knows what he is about,' he told her. 'Why shouldn't he go there? Don't be a little busybody.'

Then as he saw her stricken face he relented. 'Listen,' he said, 'you've done me a good service and I'll not forget it. If you are going home now, I'll walk with you as far as Cripplegate.'

He stood under the archway and waved her good-bye till she and Joanna vanished round the curve of Wood Street. On his return walk he was very thoughtful.

What was Adam up to? If his Master Gross was really such a wonderful person why did he live in a Southwark tavern?

He was disturbed about it, but not for very long. His sense of relief about the prentices' meeting was strong enough to banish every other thought.

Goodwife Appleyard told her husband that night that the new lad was settling down.   She'd actually heard him singing as he filled the pitcher at the well.

Chapter Ten

THE *KATHARINE-OF-THE-TOWER*

WHEN the first week at Grub Street was over, the time passed quickly. Now that Dickon no longer dreaded Corpus Christi day the rest of his worries seemed to fade away. Nobody asked him questions about his family; he was Dick Whittington's god-son; that was good enough. And for some mysterious reason Kurt Bladebone was seen no more on Moorfields.

For some days Dickon never ventured out without giving a quick glance round in search of that ominous red-head. But he was not the only person to notice its absence.

'What has happened to Bladebone?' inquired Robert one night, as they were all going to bed. 'I haven't seen him lately.'

'He has given up coming to Moorfields,' returned Owen. 'They go to Mile End to play now, I know not why.'

Dickon, hearing it, marvelled. This was another miracle. He must indeed remember to offer a thanksgiving. He had to remind himself that he'd be bound to meet Bladebone *some* day. There would be other prentices meetings and he would not be able to dodge them all. But, with any luck, by that time the fight on the wharf might be completely forgotten. The danger had passed for the moment, and the future must look after itself.

He began to enjoy his new life. It did not take him long to learn the different grades of cloth, and the names of the agents who travelled the country buying it from the weavers. He got quite used to the ledgers and soon was trusted to make entries alone. In fact, being a mercer, which he had expected to be so dull, turned out to be quite interesting.

On certain days he was sent to a mercer's shop in Cheap, where he learned to sell coifs and kerchiefs and ribands and sewing silk to London housewives who thronged the market with baskets on their arms. This was entirely to his liking, for it meant standing outside the open shop among the jostling crowds and bawling at the top of his voice: '*What will you have? What do you lack? Buy! Buy! Buy!*' He found that he could yell

One of the new horned head-dresses

as loud as any other apprentice, and louder than most; and also that he could sell things where others couldn't. He began to take a pride in his salesmanship. It was fun to send a trim young mistress away satisfied with a red hood when she had come determined to have no other than a blue one, or to persuade a stout goodwife that one of the new horned head-dresses would become her better than her present sober wimple.

He watched the apprentices of other crafts and felt sorry for them; butchers and fishmongers with their striped aprons, grocers with canvas ones, armourers and cordwainers aproned in leather. Mercers needed no aprons. He pushed his cap to one side and began to walk with a slight swagger.

By the time that Corpus Christi day arrived he was as sure of himself as if he had been a mercer all his life. He walked under the Mercers' banner in the parish procession at St. Giles', and attended the High Mass with other members of the craft who lived near-by. Then, having received Master Appleyard's permission, he ran home as fast as he could go.

He and Adam embarked in Jenkyn's boat directly after dinner. Everything had been planned beforehand, the tides studied, the wind and the moon calculated. Jenkyn had brought two other watermen and there were extra oars in case Adam and Dickon should be required to lend a hand. Nan, who had begged unsuccessfully to be allowed to join the party, had hurried off, escorted by Joanna, to Goody's on the Bridge, so as to hang out of the window and wave to them as they passed underneath.

Jenkyn greeted Dickon with a grin of friendly understanding. 'You're lucky, young master. You could hardly have timed it better. Did you know that the *Katharine* sails this afternoon?'

'Sails?' gasped Dickon. 'For sure I did not know. Shall we be in time to see her?'

'In the nick of time,' declared the waterman. 'She won't get away till the tide is right for her, though when she does come out she'll have wind and tide both with her. It's a valiant sight, I can tell you, to see a great ship set sail for the first time.'

'Where is she bound for?' Adam inquired, as he settled himself in the stern of the wherry.

'Southampton,' said Jenkyn briefly. 'She's to wait there for the King's pleasure.'

Dickon crouched in the bow. It was even better than he had expected. The tide was flowing gently downstream. They would need to balance the boat neatly at the Bridge, Jenkyn warned them, for the current would be running pretty strongly through the arches. It would be daring but not dangerous. The dangerous time was just before flood-tide, and, still more, immediately afterwards, when the water rushed through like a mill race.

It was very still on the upper river. The sun was shining, and the wharfs and half-timbered houses along the bank were reflected dazzling black and white. As they paddled downstream the Bridge grew larger and larger, like a great wall in front of them. They felt the current when they were still many yards away. Jenkyn issued a sharp order to his fellow watermen. Each took a couple of strong strokes, then with a drilled precision shipped his oars.

Dickon gripped the sides, tense with excitement. The

starlings, the great boat-shaped piers on which the Bridge was built, suddenly loomed very large. They were made of stout elm piles filled in with rubble and baulks of oak. From the bank they appeared to be little more than a line of paving stones at the base of the Bridge. But now, as the wherry swept on towards them, they looked like a mighty barricade through which the little craft must force its way. Above them towered the stone arches and buttresses of the Bridge itself, and higher still the houses, which seemed to grow taller and taller as the boat shot underneath.

Dickon glanced upwards to please Nan, who must be hanging out of Goody's window. He had a swift impression of tiny faces and of kerchiefs waving. Then they were in darkness. The moment had come. The roar of the water deafened him. He drew a deep breath. It was like being lashed to an arrow. The little boat darted swift and straight on the foaming current, and before his breath was finished they were out on the other side.

'That was well done,' shouted Jenkyn as soon as his voice could be heard. 'The tide was just a shade too near the full to be pleasant, but we had to risk it or we should have missed the *Katharine*.'

The roar of the water died away behind them, as they swept down into the wide reach by Billingsgate.

Dickon relaxed and gazed eagerly about. Everything was different here. The houses were tall and closely packed. The ships lying at anchor were mostly sea-going vessels and every wharf was furnished with cranes and pulleys for handling heavy cargoes. He glanced back at the Bridge. Even that seemed different from this side, for the chapel, built out on a pier, looked as if it rose sheer from the water. He had never realized before that there was a door into the lower chapel at river level, so that people could come to church by boat.

'I believe the King's standard is flying at the Tower,' announced Adam.

Dickon looked quickly round. The Tower was still some way ahead. Adam must have wonderful sight if he could distinguish one device from another at that distance. Flags fluttered from every turret. But as they swung down the middle of the stream he saw that Adam was right. From the White Tower, the keep itself, floated three standards; the red cross of St. George, the banner of England; a chained antelope, which was the King's personal badge; and the Royal Standard, the lions of England quartered with the lilies of France.

The Tower from the river looked far more imposing than it did from the land. Dickon shaded his eyes and stared at it, as though he would see through those great stone walls.

'I did not know that the King was there today,' he said with bated breath.

'He's here today and gone tomorrow, like a jumping Jack,' returned Jenkyn shortly. 'Eltham, or Sheen, or Westminster, you never know where he is.'

Dickon glanced at him quickly. It seemed an odd way to speak of the King, but just at that moment they locked oars with another wherry and were nearly jerked into the water.

The Tower from the river

The river now swarmed with small boats, all heading in the same direction. Apparently everybody knew that the *Katharine* was about to sail. It was impossible to keep up the pace, at which Dickon was rather pleased; it gave him more chance to see everything. Adam called to him to notice Bermondsey Abbey among trees on the south bank, but he was more interested in the marshes on the Essex side. The river swept in a big curve round an area of mud flats, covered with coarse windswept grass and devoid of human habitation. Why did great birds of prey, kites and blackbacked gulls, sail and circle overhead? Searching for the answer he noticed a row of gibbets standing near the river's edge, some of them bare, but others carrying the grisly remains of corpses.

'Wapping flats,' said Jenkyn resting on his oars. ''Tis where they hang pirates. The raiding of ships would be without limit if the law did not make an example.'

Dickon gazed with horror at the bones swaying gently on creaking chains. Suddenly Adam broke the spell.

'Look!' he cried, 'that great sail! Is it the *Katharine*?'

A low spit of land jutted into the river ahead of them, over the top of which they could see a cluster of roofs and a forest of masts. From this small haven a great ship moved slowly out into the river, one huge painted sail unfurling as she came.

'God save us, it *is* the *Katharine*,' cried Jenkyn. 'Either she is early or I have miscounted the tide. Here, you fellows, pull clear of the crowd and we will stay here, near the bank. We shall see better from here than if we tried to round the promontory. She would be gone before we could get there.'

It was perfectly true. The *Katharine* was already gaining speed as the wind filled out her sail. But the neck of land was no more than a belt of marshy hillocks, scarcely high enough to hide even her waterline. Groups of cheering people ran along its length, and the sound of answering cheers from the mariners on the ship came floating across the water. Dozens of little figures moved about on the forecastle and the sterncastle, swarmed up the rigging to the fighting tops, and waved from the cross masts. Flags and pennons ran up and down in salute and the sun glittered on the steel of halberds on the upper deck.

'Don't you wish you were going with her?' gasped Dickon, swept by the thrill of the moment. 'What is the picture on her sail? I can't make it out from here. It is something round, isn't it?'

'St. Katharine's wheel of course,' declared Adam. 'There's a golden emblem on her masthead too.'

'The cresset and the antelope, two of the King's badges,' said Jenkyn. 'The new great ships all carry something of the sort. The *Cog John* has a crowned lion, and the *Holy Ghost* has a swan.'

The *Katharine* was proceeding slowly down the river. They watched her as she tacked across the wide curves of the waterway. Many of the small boats followed her, and Dickon wanted to go too. But Jenkyn shook his head.

'This is too heavy a craft,' he said. 'Remember that we'd have an ebbing tide against us all the way back. You can stay and watch her from here, if you like. She will be in sight for an

A great ship moved slowly out into the river

hour or more.' To show that he was in no hurry, he produced some hooks and some bait and proceeded to set a line. Then he stretched himself in the bottom of the boat and went to sleep.

Adam and Dickon stood watching the retreating ship. As she turned and twisted round the curves of the river the sunlight caught first one bit of her and then another. It shone on the vivid line of shields hung round the stern; then it picked up the colour of her carved and painted rudder. Her sail gradually merged into the tone of the sky and almost the last they saw of her was a brilliant glint of gold on the antelope at the masthead.

When at last she had melted into the distance, Dickon gave a great sigh of contentment and began to look up river instead of down. They might have been far away in the wilds instead of little more than a mile from the Tower. All there was to remind them of the nearness of London was a faint drift of blue wood smoke across the marshes, and a skyline of church towers, with the spire of St. Paul's tapering high above them all.

The little boats had all gone and they had the river to themselves. Jenkyn got up yawning, pulled in his line and took a fine large eel from it. He knocked it on the head and left it to finish its lifeless wriggling in the stern of the wherry.

It did not seem far back to the Bridge again. The water round the starlings was calmer now and the only problem was one of physical strength, to pull the boat from the lower river to the upper. Jenkyn roared orders to his crew, ONE—TWO—THREE—timing their strokes for one great effort.

They made the passage easily at no more cost than a good deal of water shipped. Above Bridge they were in a calm lake once more. Adam leaned over and said something to Jenkyn in a low voice. To his surprise Dickon saw that they were heading not for Dowgate or for Grantham's Wharf, but for the Southwark bank.

'Where are we going?' he asked as the boat grounded.

Adam stood up. 'I have some tidings for Master Gross,' he said. 'I shall not be long. Or would you like to come too? 'Tis not far to the *Green Falcon*.'

'I'll come,' replied Dickon cheerfully. He was always ready for anything new, and this deep secret of Adam's might prove exciting. Besides, the longer he stayed away from London the less chance there was of getting mixed up with the prentices' meeting.

The 'Green Falcon'

Chapter Eleven

AT THE SIGN OF THE GREEN FALCON

FROM across the river Bankside looked pleasant enough. It straggled along the margin of the Thames on the only strip of ground high enough to be built upon. Seen close up it was very different. Round the Bridge-foot there were fine churches and palaces, but gradually the scattered houses became meaner, till they were little better than shabby hovels giving on to lanes deep in mud and filth.

Adam led the way over the river strand, where the tide washed up its refuse without wharf or wall or quay to stop it. Dickon had stood often with Jenkyn waiting for passengers at the one point where a paved way led down to the water's edge—the ferry to Dowgate, the most ancient route across the river, older than the Bridge itself. But never before had he ventured inland. Now he followed Adam along the narrow alleys, picking his way and sometimes holding his nose. Everyone in London was accustomed to smells, but this was beyond anything permitted in the City. Had they no scavengers in Southwark?

At last under a signboard showing a green bird, they turned into the yard of a tavern. It was a poor enough place, but at least it was cobbled and there was a trough of water in the middle which looked reasonably clean.

An outside stairway led up to a wooden gallery. Two men

leaned over the rails talking together. One was red-faced and over-fat, and wore a taverner's apron. The other was Master Saloman Gross, the alchemist. They both greeted Adam as though they expected him. The taverner made some joke which Dickon could not catch, and rumbled with wheezy laughter, while Adam sprang up the steps and began an earnest conversation with the alchemist.

Left by himself at the bottom, Dickon felt stupid and adrift, but almost at once the taverner came down, the stairs creaking and groaning under his weight.

'What can I do for you, young master?' he cried jovially. 'How about a pot of ale? Or I can give you a fine heady mead. You look as though you could carry your liquor bravely. You're the young Jack who laid low the giants on Grantham's wharf, if I mistake not.'

Dickon stared. How on earth did this fat old tavern-keeper know about the fight?

'We heard of it from Lob, the poor little rat whose life you spared,' returned the taverner, as though he read the question. 'His mother cleans the pots here. He's a miserable little wisp of a lad and they would surely have killed him if you had not rescued him.'

Dickon squared his shoulders and grinned. He'd got used to looking upon that fight as something to be concealed. It was good to find himself praised for it. When Adam leaned over the gallery and called to him to wait just for a few minutes, he followed the taverner into a house-place which smelled strongly of stale ale. He accepted a horn full of frothy liquid and took a sip. It was mild enough, and pleasant at the end of a long afternoon.

'You're a prentice now, I see,' remarked his host. 'I'll warrant you'll make a good use of your club. You've the makings of a fighting man. Have you ever thought of following the armies to France?'

Dickon was startled. The idea, he said, had never entered his mind.

'There's room for such as you,' said the taverner, wagging his head till his fat dewlaps quivered. 'The City trained bands would gladly have you.'

'They would not let me go to France. I'm sworn apprentice.'

'Well, there are other ways. The best advancement comes to the free lances, who attach themselves to the train of any great leader. We've one such here now, Thomas Bason, a soldier from the West Country. He's my Lord Scrope's man, and as my Lord Scrope is King Harry's dearest coz, you may be sure our Thomas is on his way to the top of the tree. He's sleeping now; he was journeying all night; but he'll be down at any moment.'

An ale horn

Dickon stared into the remains of his ale. The taverner filled up his horn and poured some for himself from a different jug.

'I'm an old soldier too,' he volunteered. 'I was a hobler—that's a light horseman, in case you don't know—I was a hobler in King Richard's day. My name is Benedict Wolman. I've been most things in my time, including a marshal at the Marshalsea prison here. That's why I set up my sign by its gates when I retired. A prison near-by makes for good trade.'

Dickon glanced round, as though the shadow of the Marshalsea were overhanging the room.

'It lies just beyond the yard; behind that stone wall,' volunteered Wolman. 'One can hear the groans of the prisoners some nights, when the customers are not too lively. Southwark abounds in prisons, the Marshalsea, the King's Bench, the Clink; prisons, and bishops and monks to leaven the rogues and vagabonds. They are cleaning up the borough to make it meat for milksops. Aye, but the world was a merrier place in King Richard's day.'

'So I've heard my grandsire tell,' returned Dickon, unable to think of a better answer.

Benedict Wolman leaned forward. 'Have you heard it said that King Richard is alive?' he asked in a confidential tone.

'Alive?' said Dickon startled. 'How can he be alive? King Harry brought his body back in state to Westminster. He has masses said for his soul.'

'Nevertheless 'tis said that he is alive and in safe keeping at the Scottish Court. There are some who have seen him. But maybe 'tis only a cock-and-bull story. Don't quote me. Ah, here comes Thomas Bason; him that I spoke of, in my Lord Scrope's service.'

From a low doorway at the back another man entered the

house-place. He was short and stocky, with a pock-marked face and a sword-cut that ran in a long red weal across one cheek, distorting both nose and mouth. His hair and beard were bristly as a badger, the one too short and the other too long. He stared at Dickon and then glanced at the landlord.

'Ye loaves and fishes,' he exclaimed gruffly, 'I have almost slept the day through.'

'The net is full,' replied Benedict Wolman cheerfully. 'Here is your ale. Drink it down and it will restore you. The young master here is thinking of going for a soldier. I was telling him that you might get him preferment in my Lord Scrope's train.' He ignored Dickon's interruption and went rattling on. 'I promised that he could not do better. My Lord Scrope is very close to the King.'

'To the King he is as a brother,' declared the pock-faced man, wiping the ale from his beard with the back of his hand and shaking it into the rushes. 'The King's Grace will do naught without him. When we are on the march he shares the King's bed.'

Dickon managed to get a word in. 'I do not want to be a soldier,' he said firmly. 'I would like to go to sea. If all is well Master Whittington may let me sail with the Merchant Adventurers.'

'Whittington,' exclaimed Wolman sharply. 'What has Whittington to do with it?'

'He is my master. I am prentice to him.'

'Prentice to Whittington?' repeated the taverner, obviously taken aback. 'I did not know. No one had told me.'

It crossed Dickon's mind to wonder why anyone *should* have told him. The taverner went rattling on.

'Dick Whittington is a great man. I heard recently that he has a new office—to hunt out traitors in the City. Is that true, think you?'

Dickon stared. How on earth did the man know that? Dick Whittington had said that it was a close secret. He decided to bluff.

'That's a pretty story,' he laughed, and emptied an imaginary last drop from the bottom of his ale horn. 'Where did you hear that one?'

'I can't remember,' said Wolman calmly. 'There is always gossip in a tavern, you know.'

At that moment footsteps on the outside stairs heralded the arrival of the alchemist, followed by Adam. Master Gross glanced quickly round the company to see who was there. He greeted Dickon with a poke of the head and invited Adam to have a pot

Pestle and mortar

of ale. But Adam said they must go. The waterman would be tired of waiting.

The taverner and the soldier both raised their drinking-pots to Dickon and he gave them a grin as he went out, but he was glad to be quit of the place all the same.

He followed his brother and the alchemist across the yard. Near the forbidding stone wall of the Marshalsea prison a boy was pouring pig swill into a trough. He set down his pail to stare at them as they passed. The pale wizened little face was familiar to Dickon but he could not place where he had seen it. Then the boy smiled shyly, and at once he remembered and smiled back. Of course, it was Lob, the fishmonger's apprentice.

Jenkyn was waiting for them all alone, patiently whittling a stick with his sheath knife. Master Gross nodded to him and slipped a coin into his hand. Dickon wondered immediately why the alchemist should have paid their waterman. He must have found the visit valuable if it was worth his while to reward Jenkyn for waiting. But he gave Master Gross a respectful salute in return for a watery smile and joined Adam in the boat.

Both he and Adam were completely silent during the river crossing. At Grantham's Wharf he remembered his manners enough to copy Adam's example and tell Jenkyn what a splendid afternoon it had been. When Jenkyn had rowed away he followed Adam into his little spice room in the warehouse.

As it was a holy-day the place was deserted. Adam went straight to his bench, took a little silver phial from his pouch and, emptying some crystals from it into his little mortar, proceeded to grind them with the pestle.

Dickon watched him. He was profoundly disturbed. The *Green Falcon* was an ill-favoured spot. It had a furtive air. If all Southwark was like that, he did not wonder that it had a bad name. But it was the taverner's talk that worried him most. First of all there was that strange saying about the loaves and fishes. He had noticed before that when one person said 'loaves and fishes', another answered 'the net is full'. What did it mean? Until today he had thought that it was some sort of popular catchword, but now he began to have misgivings.

Above all how did Wolman know about the task given to Master Whittington by the King? That was the really startling question. He recalled how careful Master Whittington had been that day after dinner when he had told them the news; how he had even sent Nan to discover if there was anyone within earshot. And yet it was already known in Southwark. Dickon watched Adam's careful measurements with a knitted brow. Though he tried to put the idea aside, he could not help remembering that Adam had gone straight from that dinner table to the *Green Falcon*. He felt that, come what may, he must ask Adam. And yet he could not bring himself to make a beginning. Adam was his elder brother, his senior by several years. It had never entered his mind, until now, to question anything that Adam did.

He drew a deep breath and took the plunge.

'What are you doing?' he asked.

Adam glanced round, his eyes bright with interest. 'This is some antimony,' he said. 'Master Gross gave it to me. It is of a very precious sort. He thinks that if it were blended with dregs of white wine, it might replace the mercury in my Panacea. You know about my Panacea, don't you? By the Rood, I forgot that you had left home before it all happened.'

'Before what happened?' asked Dickon. Definitely there was some mystery here. He listened intently to Adam's long explanations of his experiments and the future that the alchemist promised. Certainly the idea of inventing a remedy which would cure every disease was exciting. He did not wonder that Adam was beside himself at the thought of it. And yet Dickon was not satisfied. He dared not say so, but it seemed to him a little too good to be true.

'And so,' said Adam at the end of his recital, 'all we are really waiting for now is the Silver Steel, and that cannot come for another month at least; it may be two months.'

Dickon, still troubled, asked a direct question.

'What do you *do* at the *Green Falcon*?' he inquired. 'Where did you go to just now, while I was in the tavern?'

'To Master Gross's workshop,' said Adam promptly. 'He has taught me a lot already. He has a furnace for reducing metals, and the finest crucibles and retorts that I have ever seen. I'll ask him to show them to you if you like.'

Adam sounded so completely frank that it was impossible to imagine anything wrong. All the same Dickon shook his head.

'I don't think I like the *Green Falcon*,' he said. 'The taverner knows all about Dick Whittington's mission to look out for traitors.'

'Does he?' replied Adam unmoved. He was tipping the crystals back into the phial again.

'Did *you* tell him?'

'Of course I didn't.' He spoke quite casually. He was not even cross.

'*I* believe they are Lollards,' said Dickon bravely. 'I wish you wouldn't go there.'

Adam set down his phial and faced his brother.

'Don't be so silly,' he said, as if he were speaking to a child. 'You don't realize that it is the chance of a lifetime for me. Master Gross is a man of great learning. He has no time for Lollardy and such churchmen's matters.'

'It is not churchmen's matters; it is treason,' retorted Dickon hotly. 'I think we should tell Dick Whittington.'

Adam at last was frowning too. 'Now, look you here,' he said, 'I will not have you interfering in my business with your schoolboy notions. I have shared my secrets with you and you are bound to hold your tongue. Consider, boy, it ill becomes you to take this tone with me. You are younger than I am, yet *you* were chosen for Dick Whittington's favour because you are his godson. *You* have the chance to make your way in the world, while *I* am left to serve Grandfather and humour his whims. To cap it, you start disapproving of where I go and what I do. I tell you, I care not a jot what Master Gross's views are on church matters. I do not ask him. He opens for me the road that I would travel, and I must be free to better myself if I can.'

Dickon was silent. When Adam put it that way there was very little he could say.

'Well?' urged his brother at last. 'Are you still pledged to keep my counsel?'

Dickon looked at him and grinned. After all, Adam came first.

'Of course I am,' he said.

     .   .   .   .   .

But in spite of this pledge he was still far from easy as, after a pleasant family supper, he walked back to Cripplegate.

The idea that in taking *him* as an apprentice Master Whittington had passed over Adam had never entered his head until now. He had looked upon Adam as the lucky one, remaining at home to work quietly under Grandfather in the family business and living among the scenes and sounds of the river. But now he began to see it rather differently. For him the world was beginning to open up, while Adam was still like a child under Grandfather's thumb.

St. Anthony's pigs

But Adam or no Adam, he had his suspicions about the *Green Falcon*. He was now perfectly satisfied that it was not Adam who had revealed Master Whittington's secret, but the fact remained that it was known there. And there was that strange story about King Richard too. He went through the whole business again as he trudged along the London streets, still thronged with holiday-makers on their way home. What ought he to do? He could not tell Master Whittington without giving Adam away. He could not even pass on his suspicions about loaves and fishes. Master Whittington would worm the whole story out of him and then Adam would not be allowed to go there again, and perhaps his invention would be ruined.

What it all came down to was a choice between his duty to Dick Whittington and his loyalty to Adam, and his mind was already made up. He would stand by Adam.

He reached this decision as he crossed Cheap. It was beginning to get dark and he suddenly felt very weary. It had been a long and exciting day. He was plodding along Wood Street when suddenly he heard a familiar sound, a series of grunts accompanied by tinkling bells. He knew at once what it was— St. Anthony's pigs, rootling in that garbage dump at the corner of a side lane. The brothers of St. Anthony's Hospice, his old school, enjoyed the privilege of keeping pigs to roam the streets and pick up a living under market stalls or anywhere else. They were the only pigs in London allowed to go free; all others had to be kept in sties. Often and often he had been sent out with a stick to round them up, and the very sound of the bells which they had to wear round their necks took him back to his childhood and made him feel better. He turned aside to look at them, a fat old sow and a couple of young pigs. He gave them each a friendly kick on the rump for the sake of old times, noting that the youngsters were nearly as big as their mother. He remembered when they were born. It showed how quickly time flew.

To his dismay the curfew sounded while he was still dawdling with the pigs. He had to run for it. The gatekeeper at Cripplegate saw him coming and waited for him under the archway with a lighted lantern, holding open one half of the heavy doors.

When he had passed through and the bar clattered down behind him, he took to his heels and did not stop until he reached Goodwife Appleyard's cheerful kitchen.

The Marching Watch

Chapter Twelve

THE EVE OF ST. JOHN

ONCE back at work, Dickon's concern about the *Green Falcon* faded away. There were other things to think about.

Apparently the prentices' meeting had gone off without any particular excitement. Nobody said much about it, but, on the other hand, everyone was ready to listen to Dickon's story of the *Katharine*. Things were going well for Dickon. He was good friends with the boys at Cripplegate and he was really interested in all that he was learning. He did not see Master Whittington nor receive the promised summons to 'Whittington's Palace' in Hart Street but as it happened he was glad; he did not particularly want to meet his godfather face to face at present.

The June sun blazed down. Working days were long, for dawn was early and sunset late, and everyone was expected to make full use of the daylight because in the winter there was so little of it. But Mother Church, determined that her children should not waste all the fine weather in toil, had bespattered the summer months with holy-days. After Ascension came Corpus Christi; after Corpus Christi, St. John the Baptist—Midsummer

Day; and less than a week after midsummer, the double feast of St. Peter and St. Paul.

So far as enjoyment went St. John's day was the peak of the whole year. There were bonfires on every open space, and all the houses were decorated with garlands and illuminated at night. People set tables outside their doors and offered cakes and ale to all comers. As a climax there was the Marching Watch, a great torchlight procession through the city streets which took place on the eve of St. John and again, the next night, on the feast itself. All the Companies and Crafts took part, and the fortunate people chosen to march with banners and torches were the envy of their fellows. Grub Street was thrown into a ferment because tall Robert was picked to carry a flaming cresset in the Mercers' contingent.

Dickon was counting the days to the feast of St. John because he was to be allowed to go home. He planned that he and Adam would fight their way to some point of vantage and watch the procession. There were plenty of places to choose from, for it started from the gate of St. Paul's and went all the way to Aldgate and back again by another route. There was no procession in the whole year to be compared with the Marching Watch. The Mayor and Sheriffs rode in it and there were about a thousand blazing torches and cressets moving like a great glittering serpent through the streets.

Very little work was done at Grub Street on the morning of June the 23rd. Dickon was supposed to be entering in the ledger a consignment of blankets from Witney which Owen and Toby were unpacking. But who could possibly attend to blankets on a blazing Midsummer Eve? They were all three listening intently for the noon bell when Robert suddenly appeared, hot and vexed. He looked straight at Dickon.

'Would you like to walk with me in the procession?' he asked. 'I have to bring an attendant to keep my cresset filled and the fellow who was to have done it is ill with the summer sickness.'

Dickon's exclamation of delight was drowned in the burst of protest from the other two. Robert held up his hand.

'I know, I know, he's new; he's only just come. But neither of you two could do it. It's no light task, I can assure you. Owen is not strong enough and Toby is too short. He'd never reach the torch.'

The grumbling died down, and after dinner Dickon was fitted out with a cloak of the Mercers' livery, and was shown by Robert what he had to do.

He could hardly believe his good luck. For years he had looked on at the Marching Watch, but he'd never dreamed that he would actually walk in it so soon. He set out from Grub Street with Robert, delighted to remember that Grandfather and Aunt Isabel and Nan had been invited to see the show from the window of a house in Cheapside.

The procession was to form up in the streets round St. Paul's. When Robert and Dickon arrived everything was pandemonium and it seemed as if it could never get into order. The City watchmen themselves numbered several hundreds, and there were pikemen in shining breastplates, trumpeters on horseback, drummers, pipers, archers in white tunics blazoned with the City arms, never to mention the parade of the Crafts and Companies with their banners and torches.

Robert had his orders and they found the Mercers' contingent without much difficulty. As dusk fell the word went round for cressets to be kindled. Dickon carried a bag containing tow, and a tinder box with smouldering shreds of linen in it, ready in an instant to replenish Robert's cresset. The smell and the smoke were suffocating as all the torches were lighted. Everybody was coughing and spluttering, but at last the order to march was passed along the line, and as the cressets were lifted high the smoke began to rise and the lights to break into flame.

The columns moved slowly at first, till they were all marshalled in their right order. At St. Paul's gate they were joined by the Mayor's special pageant—the Mayor himself riding with his sword-bearer in full armour before him, the constables in scarlet cloaks, and a following of minstrels and mummers and morris dancers which delighted the crowds.

When they turned into Cheap with pipes and trumpets, handbells and drums, all rending the air, Dickon felt a thrill of excitement. But as they passed up Cornhill, he began to find, as Robert had said, that it was no light task. The hundreds of flaring torches and cressets made the narrow streets as hot as furnaces. The crowds pressed. The noise was deafening. His livery cloak half strangled him and it was a struggle to reach up to Robert's cresset with relays of fuel. Before they reached Aldgate he was nearly dead with heat, but Robert's mouth was set in a hard line and Robert's light was still borne bravely aloft, so he determined that if Robert could hold out to the end so could he.

By the time they got back to Cheap, where the crowd was the largest and noisiest of all, he could not even raise his eyes to look for his family, and when it was all over he sat down on the nearest doorstep as if he would never move again.

'Well,' said Robert, wiping the sweat from his brow, 'I warned you, didn't I? You'll get trodden on if you sit there. I should recommend you to make for the Standard in Cheap and stick your head under the splash.'

It was good advice, particularly as Dickon was going home to sleep at Grantham's Inn and did not have to hurry back to Cripplegate. Robert good-naturedly offered to take the livery cloak for him and they arranged to meet for the second night's procession at the same time and place.

Free of his load, Dickon felt much better already. It was very exciting to be out in Cheap on such a night. He stopped to look at a party of mummers who had cleared a place for themselves close to Cheap Cross. There was another show, tumblers this time, doing their acrobatics on an improvised stage of uprooted market stalls.

When he eventually reached the Standard he found that he could not get near the spout. Obviously he was not the only apprentice who was hot and thirsty. Two boys had climbed to the top of the tank and were splashing the water about so that cascades poured down the sides. Dickon elbowed his way in among the others, cupped his hands, and deluged his head and face, as they were doing.

It was gloriously cool and refreshing. Satisfied at last, he shook the water out of his eyes and raised his head.

Next to him, wet face to wet face, was Kurt Bladebone.

They stared at one another blankly. For a second Dickon hoped that Kurt did not know him; but the hope was vain. The red-haired apprentice made a sudden grab, but Dickon was too quick for him. He turned and dived into the crowd.

To try and force a way through such a throng was like a nightmare. He had only gained a few yards when, above all the noise, he heard Kurt's yell. 'Hey, *Clubs*! Mercers! Clubs! stop that knave! Mercers!'

The sound shook him. It wasn't as if it were a good honest

Glancing behind him

prentice battle. He was alone, with nobody to stand by him, and he knew the methods of Kurt Bladebone. He jostled and pushed and dived under elbows. People looked at him angrily. One man tried to trip him. Then he caught a glimpse of the top of Cheap Cross, steered to the left and found himself at the entrance to Friday Street.

Glancing behind him he saw a red head bobbing into view. They were still on his track then! With a terrific effort he squeezed his way through the crowd at the top of the street and started to run down it.

Friday Street was brightly lighted, for people had stuck up cressets and hung lanterns out of their doors. At the cross-roads of Watling Street he again looked back. There were three of them after him. He decided to make for the river. It would be dark. Probably he knew the network of lanes down there better than they did and could make his way home. As he pounded on down the hill, tired and breathless after the strain of the procession, it dawned on him that history was repeating itself. Would they catch him on a wharf, as they had caught Lob?

Suddenly he spotted a dim alley on his left; he knew it, Five Foot Lane; it was a short cut to Thames Street. He turned down it, nearly blinded with sweat and with the sudden darkness. He bumped and slipped his way along, cannoning first off one wall, then off the other. Had they seen him turn? He dared not wait to look round. Just ahead a solitary lantern with a rushlight in it hung from a swinging sign. It made the shadows blacker than ever. As he plunged on he came to a sudden and terrifying stop, half smothered under a massive figure in a voluminous cloak.

As he fought blindly to get free, he felt himself gripped by the back of the neck.

'What's this, what's this?' roared a throaty voice, 'a cutpurse? No use struggling, my lad. I've got you.'

He was pulled into a passage and caught a glimpse of a dimly-lighted alehouse at the end of it. He did not struggle; he was glad to go, for the great cloak screened him completely, and his pursuers might run straight past without seeing him.

When they were inside the door his captor gave him a push. He staggered backwards and found himself propped against a cask.

Before he had got his breath, the gruff voice rolled out again.

'By Cock and Pie, 'tis the young Jack the giant-killer. What villainy are you up to now, my lad? *Are* you cutting purses, or have you run away from that fine master of yours?'

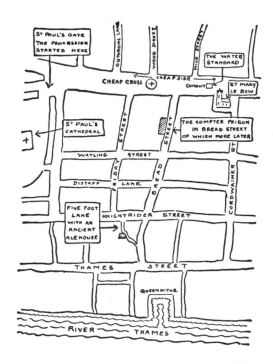

Spent as he was, it dawned on Dickon that he had run straight into the taverner from the *Green Falcon*. He still could not speak, but he nodded towards the door. Benedict Wolman followed the line of his eyes and kicked the door to.

'So, you were being pursued, were you? Well, rest you. You are safe now.' He lumbered up and looked at Dickon. 'Why, the boy *is* all but done,' he cried. 'Here, Meg, give me some ale. Sit down, lad, and get your breath. We can hear all about it presently.'

Dickon took the can that Wolman held out to him. Exhausted as he was, he realized what an amazing stroke of luck it had been. After a drink he looked about him.

The alehouse was small, hardly more than a hovel, with a hearth in the middle and a smoke hole in the roof. The mud floor, spongy with old rushes and refuse, smelt sour, and the place was lit only by a couple of rush wicks in a holder which stood upon a trestle-board.

Master Wolman pulled out a bench and straddled it, his great bulk overflowing on both sides. He patted the bench invitingly and Dickon, ill at ease, sat down and rested his mug on the board. He did not like his surroundings; he did not like the taverner; he certainly did not like the ale wife, a dirty old crone with a mountain of flesh as gross as Wolman's. But he was safe here from Kurt and the rest. He must stay, at any rate until he was sure they had gone. He took a long pull from his mug, found it comforting and drank some more.

The taverner went on talking about nothing in particular. Dickon, at rest now, took another look round. By the dim light he could just see a ladder leading up to a sleeping loft beneath the rafters, some casks standing against the wall, and, in the shadows by the casks, the shapes of two or three men.

After a while Wolman inquired what had brought him running down Five Foot Lane so desperately. Who was running after him? Dickon began to tell him; then suddenly he remembered Lob. Not for the world would he have that little rat hear that he, Dickon, his valiant rescuer, had been brought to just the same pass as himself. So he shut up abruptly. Master Wolman made no comment. He poured some more drink into Dickon's mug. Dickon protested weakly, but he sipped it all the same. It was different this time, rather thick and sweet, but it was good. He licked his lips and went on with it.

He was becoming rather confused. He thought that the taverner was asking him questions, all sorts of questions, about Grandfather's business and about Master Whittington, especially about Master Whittington. But he wasn't very sure of anything. The place seemed to be filling up with people. There were voices all round him, coming and going, and they all seemed to be saying *the net is full, the net is full, the net is full* over and over and over, like that terrible snowball that came rolling towards him in in a nightmare.

Suddenly there was a noise and he woke up, his wits for a moment quite clear. Somebody was shouting in the lane outside. Immediately the ale wife blew out the rushlights. Wolman swore at her.

'What are you doing?' he bellowed. 'Would you have us break our pates?'

'You can break them outside,' the old woman retorted. 'That was the Watch. They'll take my alehouse bush away from me. No drink after curfew on midsummer feasts, and curfew rang hours ago.'

Dickon was not aware of leaving the alehouse, but he remembered being held up along Thames Street by the taverner and somebody else, and he knew that he was singing. At Grantham's Inn there was a light in the windows of the hall. He blurted out 'Goodnight' to Wolman and went in.

Grandfather and Master Whittington were sitting together at the table, a candle between them. On Dick Whittington's shoulder crouched his Madame Eglantine, her eyes shining like emeralds. It suddenly struck Dickon as very funny that Master Whittington, the *great* Master Whittington, should be sitting with a *cat* on his shoulder. He began to laugh, and when he had once started laughing he could not stop.

The two men stared at him.

'God save us!' cried Grandfather, 'the boy is drunk.'

Dickon heard him and realized that it was true. He *was* drunk; but that was funny too, so he laughed more than ever.

'This, my friend, is a pretty point,' remarked Master Whittington. 'He is your grandson but my apprentice. Which of us two should deal with him?'

'Leave him to me,' said Grandfather grimly.

Stick passed through a finger-ring

When Dickon woke the next morning in his old bed next to Adam he was aching all over. His head ached so badly that he could hardly raise it from the pillow. As for his back, it was so sore that he could not lie in comfort. He wished now that Dick Whittington had beaten him instead of Grandfather. Grandfather's stick, he was certain, would never have passed through Master Whittington's finger-ring.

Still, it was good to be at home rather than in the garret at Grub Street, and though Grandfather beat hard he never kept up his anger afterwards. Dickon knew for certain that the subject of his coming home drunk would not be referred to again. One more punishment had been imposed. Grandfather and Dick Whittington had decided that he was not to walk in the procession again on the second night. Someone else would be found to serve Robert in his place. To Dickon this was secretly no punishment at all but an enormous relief. One dose of that heat and discomfort was quite enough, and in any case he did not want to risk parading in public lest he should again be recognized by Kurt.

The day on the whole was rather a dreary one. He went to the High Mass of the Feast with all the family; the sun shone; the streets were decorated and thronged with merrymakers; there were lots of good things to eat. But his head ached too much for him to enjoy any of it and he spent most of the time sitting on the wharf.

Adam sat with him and he told Adam all about meeting Kurt Bladebone and being chased by him. He also told him of the strange encounter with Master Wolman, and admitted that the taverner had been very good to him. He felt that he owed it to Adam to say this because the last time they met they had almost quarrelled about Adam's friends at the *Green Falcon*. But of the alehouse he said little, chiefly because he could not remember much about it. He knew that he had been there and that he had drunk too much, but beyond that it was all rather like a bad dream.

Presently Nan joined them on the wharf, full of solicitude for Dickon's headache. She had a story which she poured out eagerly to amuse him. It was all about Dick Whittington and Madame Eglantine and Bow Bells, and it was such arrant nonsense that after a bit he told her to hold her peace. Nan retorted that it was true; Master Whittington had told it to her himself. Dickon, on edge, snapped back that if she told lies she must confess them and be shriven. At that Nan wept and the peace of the afternoon was shattered.

At length Adam decided that he would walk up to St.

Bartholomew's Hospital. He had recently helped to knock a man senseless by sandbagging him so that the chirurgeon could operate on him, and he wanted to hear if the man had lived through it. Dickon said he would go too. He had no stomach for the sights and smells of the hospital, but in his present mood it was better than staying where he was and bickering with Nan. When he get there he filled in the time piously attending Vespers in the Priory Church while Adam busied himself in the hospital.

On their return to Grantham's Inn they found Nan waiting for them in the forecourt.

'Adam, you are to come quickly,' she cried. 'Master Whittington is asking for you.'

They hurried in, and found Master Whittington in the hall with Grandfather. Beside them sat a well-set-up young man in a leather doublet and long riding-boots, one of which was rolled down below a knee heavily swathed in bandages.

When the boys had made their reverence to their grandsire, Master Whittington beckoned Adam.

'This is my nephew Guy,' he said. 'He has ridden all the way from Gloucester with an open wound. He is a headstrong young fool and he will not let me call the chirurgeon. I would have you look at it and tell me what you think. You see I have not forgotten your skill with the pantry steward.'

'Go to it, my boy,' nodded Grandfather approvingly. 'Show us what you can do.'

Guy Whittington pushed his cap to the back of his head and grinned at Adam.

'My uncle would lay me by the heels when all I want is to get to horse again,' he said. 'My father and I have been set upon by cut-throats and suffered a wrong which only the King can right. I have hastened to London and now I hear that the King has gone to Winchester. I must go after him without delay. If I consulted a saw-bones, as my uncle wishes, he would likely enough cut off my leg.'

'You talk too much,' interrupted Master Whittington. 'You can tell your story to your heart's content when I have had my way. Adam, I charge you, say truly what you think of his wound.'

Cool and composed Adam brought forward a stool for the injured limb. He sent Nan running to fetch clean water and some linen rags, and Dickon to the warehouse to bring certain herbs.

When they got back he had already unwound the bandage from an ugly gash in a badly swollen leg. He folded some herbs in linen and with this pad started to wash it gently. Guy Whittington embarked upon his tale, though he broke off at times to curse the pain.

'You will remember that my father has a manor in Herefordshire called Solers Hope,' he began. 'We had been staying there and were just riding back to Pauntley, near Gloucester. You know Pauntley, I think, sir?'

'I should know it,' returned his uncle shortly. 'I was reared there.'

'A thousand pardons. You left home so long ago that I forgot—oh! a plague upon you, boy; that hurts!'

'Go on,' commanded Master Whittington mercilessly, as much to Adam as to his nephew.

'We were in lonely country and there were but six of us, my father and I and four servants. Suddenly a band of ruffians quite thirty strong rushed out from a wood. We were soon overwhelmed. They bound us and carried us off to Dymore Hill, a wild spot where there is a ruined chapel, some old hermitage, I believe. There they robbed us of everything we had and locked us in the ruin for the night.' Once again he broke into a yell. 'Curse you, how much of this must I endure?'

'Had you not best call an apothecary?' growled Grandfather. 'Adam is but an apprentice.'

'Let him alone; his head is on his shoulders,' said Master Whittington firmly. 'Nephew, you are holding back the plum of the story. Who do you think these robbers were, friend John?'

'How should I tell?' returned Grandfather testily. 'I know not Hereford.'

'You know one Hereford name I warrant. Go on, Guy. I cannot hold my peace much longer.'

'The robbers were of the following of Richard Oldcastle,' said Guy Whittington briefly.

'*Oldcastle!*' cried Grandfather, while Master Whittington chuckled with delight. 'Not Sir John Oldcastle?'

'Not Sir John himself but his kinsman, Richard Oldcastle,' said Master Whittington, taking charge of the story. 'They are a Herefordshire family. Do you remember I told you that they were neighbours of my forebears. It is known that Sir John

is in hiding somewhere in the west, for he has induced the Prior of
Wenlock to mint counterfeit coins for him. He wants money so
badly that he is quite likely to make his kinsmen take to robbery
to raise it.'

'But surely,' said Grandfather to Guy, 'you did not travel with
much treasure if you had only four servants with you?'

'It was not treasure they were after, it was ransom. Either we
agreed to pay a ransom of six hundred pounds or we could choose
which way we preferred to die—there and then by the sword, or
else slowly by being left bound without food on the wild Welsh
mountains.'

A murmur ran round the room. Dickon, all agog with
excitement, could not keep quiet.

'What did you choose?' he asked breathlessly.

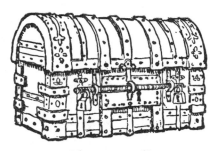

The money coffer

Guy Whittington grinned at him. 'What would you choose
in like case, young man? Personally I value life at more than six
hundred pounds, vast sum though that is. Of course we could
not lay hands on the money so easily, but on my swearing solemnly not to betray them, the rascals let me ride to Solers Hope
and bring all that was in the coffers there. When I returned with
it my father signed a covenant that we would pay the rest of the
six hundred shortly, and then we were set free.'

'Of course a covenant signed under force is not binding,'
said Master Whittington. 'Nevertheless he has ridden to London
to beg the King to declare it null and void. I'll warrant that the
King will repay everything when he hears this about Oldcastle.'

'I did not ride for that alone,' interrupted his nephew.
'When we reached Pauntley we found the Commissioners of
Array with the King's claim for fighting men. I brought fou

archers and two hoblers with me. They have gone straight to Southampton.'

'And doubtless you expect to join them, eh? But that leg does not look to me as though you could ride. What say you, Adam?'

Adam shook his head. It was a festering sore, he said. Master Guy should go in a litter either to St. Bartholomew's or to the Hospital of our Lady outside Bishopsgate.

Master Guy declared immediately that no power on earth would persuade him to go to a hospital. They would surely cut off his leg and he would rather die in the saddle with his leg on him than live without it.

Master Whittington looked at Adam and smiled. 'What shall we do with him? Shall we sandbag him and take him like a log? I hear you are good at sandbagging patients. Nay, it is a shame to make a jest of you. I tell you what we will do, nephew. We will keep you for a day or two and Adam shall tend you. If in that time you die, you shall have a magnificent requiem. If you are worse you shall go to hospital. But if you are better you shall ride to join the King.'

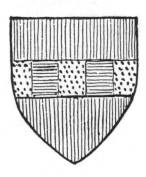

Arms of Dick Whittington

Adam departed with his grandsire's blessing

Chapter Thirteen

ADAM FOR FRANCE

DICKON went back to Cripplegate the next morning at the first
glimmer of daylight, secretly in fear of what his reception might
be. Would the news about him have been spread by Kurt
Bladebone, and how would his fellow apprentices take it?

Grandfather had wanted to send him back before the second
night's procession but he still looked so worn out that Aunt
Isabel interceded for him and he was allowed to go to his bed
when the others set off for the window in Cheapside.

But when he reached Grub Street in the morning everything
seemed to be as usual. Apparently a message had been sent to
say that he was sick and unable to march again, and Robert
simply asked him if he was better and confided that he was lucky
to have missed the second night. It was even hotter than the first.

So life settled down again quietly enough and gradually
Dickon ceased to expect Kurt Bladebone to appear round every
corner. After a few days Guy Whittington, his leg almost
healed, rode away to Winchester.

The hot July days dragged by. The town lacked rain and the
conduits ran so sluggishly that water was restricted to one
bucketful daily for each family. Goodwives gathered to do their

washing in the Thames or in the trickle of the Turnmill Brook
where it joined the Fleet at Holborn Bridge.

Where they gathered rumours spread. The place was full of
rumours. It was fairly general knowledge that the King, who
was at Winchester, had received envoys from France and that he
might marry the French king's daughter and war be avoided.
In London the idea was not popular, for the French princess was
the younger sister of that unhappy little child of eight who had
been married to Richard the Second—an ill-omened match if
ever there was one.

But there were also darker rumours, spread only in whispers;
rumours about Oldcastle, said to have been seen in many places at
once, and about risings in Wales and risings in Kent, and—a very
furtive whisper this—about Richard the Second being still alive
and ready to march on London as soon as the King's back was
turned.

One Sunday towards the end of the month, Will Appleyard
called Dickon and told him to go and see Master Whittington at
his house in The Royal. He would not say what it was about and
Dickon, who had not set eyes on his godfather since St. John's
Day, searched his conscience for any crime which might have
come to light. Could it have anything to do with the *Green
Falcon* or the taverner? He sometimes worried himself trying to
remember what had happened that night in the ale house. It was
all so shadowy, but he was sure that there had been a lot of
questions and that Master Whittington's name had come into it in
some way.

This idea, that the trouble had something to do with the
Green Falcon, was strengthened when, after rapping on the door
of Master Whittington's parlour, he went in and found Adam
already there. So he had been sent for too.

Dickon looked sharply at his brother, wishing that he knew if
Adam had already answered any questions and if so what he had
said. He twiddled his fingers together behind his back and said a
hasty prayer for help in skating over thin ice.

Richard Whittington looked tired and worried, but he did not
look stern. He greeted Dickon with a smile and a nod and
indicated a joint stool at Adam's side. He had sent for them, he
said, because he wanted their help. Did they remember that
many weeks ago he had asked them both to keep their eyes open
for any signs of Lollardy or sedition among the apprentices of

their crafts? He did not want to turn them into spies, informing against their companions, but the times were dangerous. Trouble was brewing and it was his duty to leave no stone unturned.

Dickon did some quick thinking. Thank goodness they were asked only about apprentices, so there was no need to mention his suspicions about the *Green Falcon*, though he wished with all his heart that Adam would speak of it himself. But Adam only said that he saw no apprentices except Grandfather's, who were all honest lads.

Master Whittington did not seem astonished. He turned to Dickon.

'And how about the Mercers?' he inquired. 'Have you come across anything suspicious among our boys?'

'No, sir,' said Dickon promptly. It was true. Of course Owen had used the *loaves and fishes* oath, but anyone might do that. He'd done it himself, and it was better not to raise the question.

'I'm glad and I'm sorry,' said Master Whittington with a sigh. 'Keep your eyes open, both of you. There is much going on underground. To prove to you that I am not making a parade about nothing I will show you *this*.'

'This', which he took from a coffer on his table, proved to be a roll of calfskin such as the heralds and the sheriffs carried when they gave out a proclamation.

'I don't know if you can read it,' said Master Whittington, flattening it out. 'There are only a few lines and they are indifferently written. It is addressed to the people of London and it advises them to arise and avenge their wrongs now that the King —"the prince of priests" is what it calls him—now that the King is gone.'

Startled and shocked, both boys craned their necks to look at the parchment.

'*This*,' said Master Whittington tapping it, '*This* was found at daybreak, fastened to the door of St. Magnus by the Bridge. It is the second time. There was a similar notice two nights ago, at St. Mildred's in Bread Street. Of course the writer is mistaken. The King has not yet sailed for France, but it shows what we may expect when he does go.'

He dismissed them after one more warning that they should look out for anything that struck them as suspicious. Dickon followed Adam, determined to beg him once more to have done with the *Green Falcon*, even if he did not report the place to Master Whittington. But before the door was quite closed he heard his name called. He returned to the parlour. His godfather smiled at him.

'I hear good accounts of your skill as a clerk,' he said. 'Will Appleyard tells me that you keep the ledgers very well. Would you care to stay and copy some letters for me? Some of them are business and some are private matters. I have no time to attend to them and I would prefer not to put them into the hands of a stranger.'

Flattered and delighted Dickon settled himself at the counter board by the window of Master Whittington's parlour, with a newly-sharpened quill, and got to work. He made the copies in his very best script. Master Whittington was pleased with them and gave him more. He stayed there writing until it was so late that he had to hurry to be home by curfew time. There was no chance, after all, to speak to Adam, but already he had almost forgotten what he was going to say. Master Whittington's letters had been full of dealings in foreign markets by the Merchant Adventurers. And Master Whittington had praised his work and said that he was to come again.

A few days later, just as Dickon was beginning his breakfast, Will Appleyard handed him a letter. A messenger from his grandfather had brought it the moment that Cripplegate was open.

Dickon was struck dumb. He had never in his life received a letter. He broke the seal quickly and unrolled the sheet. It was not from his grandfather but from Adam.

'Good brother [it ran], I greet you in the name of the Trinity and write to tell you that I am to go to France with the King's army. Our grandsire has given his consent to this and also that I should bid you come home at once that I may see you before I ride. Your godsire, the most worshipful Master Whittington, directs that you should show this letter to Master Appleyard that he may suffer you to come with all speed. God and His angels keep you. Your brother.'

All the way home to Grantham's Inn Dickon was in a fever of excitement. How could it have happened that Adam was going to France? He must have completed his Panacea and won instant fame and fortune as the alchemist had promised. He turned it all over in his mind as he pushed his way through the streets which were just beginning to fill up with busy morning crowds. Shopkeepers were pulling down their shutters to serve as counters. Prentices carried water to sluice the cobbles in front of their masters' shops. In every church there were bells ringing, and busy merchants came hastening out after an early mass while fine ladies strolled unhurried to a later one.

At Grantham's Inn Nan was looking out for him.

'Have you heard?' she called as soon as he was within earshot. 'Adam is going to France with Master Whittington.'

He stared at her, not able to believe his ears. 'With Dick Whittington?' he cried, half sick with rage and jealousy.

'Not *Dick* Whittington, you addle-pate; *Guy* Whittington. He came back last night. There is an uproar. Someone has tried to kill the King. Come inside. Everybody is within.'

It was certainly true that everybody was within. The hall was full of people. It seemed as if all the great men of the City were gathered under Grandfather's roof. Little groups of Aldermen stood clustered together, all wearing their rich fur-edged *houppelandes* because the morning was still fresh. Dickon peeped between them and saw the Mayor himself sitting at the high table with Grandfather and Master Whittington, while Guy Whittington, standing up, was telling the company some tremendous story. He stayed where he was to listen.

It was not easy to pick up the thread, but after a few moments he gathered that three lords, the Earl of Cambridge, Sir Thomas Grey and Lord Scrope of Masham had plotted to murder the King at Southampton. Someone had betrayed them and now they were to die. Grandfather and all the great men round the table were wagging their heads and looking very solemn. The Mayor said that without doubt the French were at the back of it; somebody else blamed the Scots, and Grandfather maintained that it was probably Sir John Oldcastle. Master Whittington, in his practical way, suggested that the first thing to do was to arrange for a solemn Mass of Thanksgiving, and then to make sure that there were no traitors in their own city. Everybody applauded and the meeting began to break up.

Dickon slipped away in search of Adam. He found him standing by the screen ready to bring more wine if Grandfather should call for it.

'What is going on?' demanded Dickon in a loud whisper. 'I know about the plot to kill the King, but what are they all doing *here*? And where did Guy Whittington come from?'

'S-sh!' Adam held up a finger. "Tis a meeting of the Mayor's Council. Master Guy brought the news from Southampton. He came here because Master Whittington was supping with Grandfather. He'd ridden without a stop and was half dead, so they summoned the Mayor rather than make him move again. They have been conferring half the night.'

Dickon went on to the point that was really absorbing him. 'But why are you going to France? What has it to do with all this?'

'Nothing,' said Adam simply. 'I am going only because Master Guy asked for me.'

Dickon frowned. That sounded nonsense. 'Is it the Panacea then?'

'No; the Panacea is not finished. The Silver Steel has not come. I tell you, 'tis Master Guy has arranged it. You see his leg is quite cured and he vows that it was I who cured it. He thinks that I could be useful with the King's army, so I am to go with him.'

Dickon heaved a great sigh. How could Adam take it all so calmly?

'When do you start?' he inquired.

'Tomorrow at dawn. Hark! There is Grandfather calling.' He picked up his flagons and hurried away.

At length the Mayor and the Aldermen departed. Last of all Master Whittington took his nephew home. As he passed Dickon on his way out, he paused and gave Dickon's elbow a friendly pinch, whispering that he might remain at home until Adam had gone. Dickon felt a warm glow as he thanked him. He could swear that, in spite of all his many cares, Dick Whittington understood what he was feeling.

Of course it was good to be at home, but all the same he did not see much of Adam, who was claimed first by Aunt Isabel fussing about what must be packed in his saddle-bags and later by Grandfather who bore him off to the armourer's and the hosier's and the cordwainer's to see that he was properly equipped. Dickon hung about with Nan with nothing to do, feeling so depressed that he almost wished he was back at work.

Adam returned at dinner-time and suggested to Dickon that in the afternoon they might both go to the Bridge. He wanted to say good-bye to Goody.

'Can I come too?' cried Nan immediately.

Adam said yes, she might, if Aunt Isabel gave leave. So when dinner was done and Grandfather had finished all he had to say, the three of them set off together, Nan very delighted that she was allowed to go without Joanna as she had both her brothers to look after her.

When they were well out of earshot of Grantham's Inn, Dickon was at last able to ask a question.

'What are you going to do about the Panacea?'

'I don't know,' said Adam. 'As a matter of fact I thought that I might go on to Southwark after I have seen Goody. You can come if you like, or you can wait at Goody's with Nan, and I will call for you on the way back.'

Dickon said very decidedly that he would stay on the Bridge. Adam continued without comment:

'Perhaps Master Gross will finish the Panacea for me. It lacks only the Silver Steel. The difficulty is that I do not know how to get the stuff to him when it comes. Maybe *you* could manage it?'

Dickon frowned. It was all very fine for Adam to slip out of things like that. '*I* cannot take it,' he said irritably. 'Remember that I am just an apprentice working on the other side of the City.'

'I'll do it,' Nan broke in eagerly. 'I'll see that Master Gross gets it.'

Adam laughed. 'You're a good little maid, but you couldn't do that. I'll tell Master Gross that he must fetch it himself.'

There was no more to be said because the noise on the Bridge made further talking impossible.

Goody was overjoyed to see them, but the news of Adam's departure was a shock. She wept a little and had to be told every detail. She was so deaf that Adam had to bellow it all into her ear. Dickon amused himself by hanging out of the kitchen window to look down on the river racing underneath. Nan, just behind him, was playing with Goody's little grandchildren and telling them stories. The name Whittington caught his attention. It was that silly tale about Dick Whittington and his cat. It made him so cross that he left the window and moved to the front of the house to watch the traffic. He realized that he was bad-tempered and he felt ashamed, because he knew the cause. He was jealous, madly jealous, of Adam's good fortune.

Presently Adam tapped him on the shoulder.

'I'm going to see Master Gross,' he said. 'I suppose you would rather wait here?'

Dickon hesitated. 'I don't want to come,' he said, 'but I'll walk with you as far as the end of the Bridge.' He felt suddenly that he could not endure shouting little bits of gossip into Goody's ear or listening to Nan's stories.

The Bridge

They walked along almost in silence. To avoid the question of coming any farther, Dickon pretended an interest in some wooden granaries built over the last arch of the Bridge, and went to have a look at them. They were used to store corn brought down the river by barge, and he examined carefully the tackle of ropes and pulleys for lifting the sacks until Adam turned the corner and headed along Bankside.

When he was out of sight Dickon turned back to the Bridge. He decided that he would explore it thoroughly. He had never had a chance before, for shopkeepers invariably chased away little boys who loitered. Now that he was a full-fledged apprentice he could take his time without anybody ordering him off.

The first thing that faced him as he turned back from Southwark was the Stone Gate which blocked the way into London. It was one of the main gates of the City and was closed at curfew like all the others.

A string of country carts in front of it were waiting their turn to pay their toll and cross the Bridge. Dickon discovered that one carried baskets of Kentish cherries. They looked good. He dived into his pouch to find a coin but he had none. The goodwife was grinning at him; he suspected that she had seen him search for money, so he touched his cap to her and asked her how she fared. Then he led the horse while she paid up her farthing toll, and when they were through the arch she invited him to fill his cap with cherries. That was just what he wanted. He waved good-bye to her, his ill-temper completely banished.

There was a gap in the houses beyond the Stone Gate, so he leaned on the parapet and watched the shipping for a while before he strolled along the narrow street of shops. They were mostly small shops belonging to craftsmen who worked on the premises, glovers and pouchmakers and a couple of mercers, which he passed in a hurry in case he should be recognized by any of the apprentices. But it was rather fun to peer into the other workshops and see everybody hard at work while he was enjoying a day off.

At the end of this group of shops he emerged on to the next open space, the Drawbridge. Here he stopped again and propping himself against a wall settled down to wait for Adam.

This was for him the real centre of the Bridge, the spot to which his eye always flew with a horrible fascination even when he saw it from a distance. For on the top of the big old wooden Drawbridge Gate stood a row of pikestaffs, each one of them crowned by a human head, the heads of rebels executed for treason against the King. He wondered suddenly if those three new traitors would be brought here. The last time there had been fresh heads was after Oldcastle's rebellion more than a year ago.

At first he did not look up, but leaned back in the sun and stared at the Drawbridge itself while he ate his cherries. He wished that a ship would come through so that he could watch the deck of the Bridge raised by those great chains. But it was low tide, so it was no good hoping. He threw the cherry stones into the water and wiped his hands on his hose.

Then he braced himself against the wall and forced himself to gaze up at the heads. He had jested about them, pointed at them, teased Nan about them, and once, out of bravado, he had even thrown a stone at them; but never until now had he dared really to look at them. He was quite relieved to find that, seen against the sky, they didn't really look human any more. They might almost be turnips stuck up for archers to practise on. They must have been much worse when they were new. Honour satisfied, he wandered across to find out exactly how the mechanism of the Drawbridge worked.

He was still examining it when Adam reappeared, looking rather out of humour. Dickon could not resist inquiring how Master Gross had taken the news.

'Like a bear,' replied Adam shortly. 'I told him I would leave him my formula but he did not seem at all pleased. His chief concern was how he was to get the Silver Steel. It's a pity, but I suppose the Panacea will have to wait until I come back.'

Dickon was relieved. He'd been feeling a little churlish, and would have liked to explain to Adam why he had refused to take the Silver Steel. But Adam really did not seem to care. All the way home he talked of other things and the Panacea was not mentioned again.

Preparations for the early morning start went on far into the night. There were a few restless hours in bed. Adam was up by candlelight to go and be housled—to confess and receive Holy Communion—before his journey. The sun was well above the roofs when the whole family went as far as Cheap to see the travellers off.

Grandfather ordered his great horse to be saddled and accompanied them for a few miles. Now that Adam had proved himself, there were no more mutterings about 'a waste of time', and Adam departed with his grandsire's blessing.

When they had vanished towards Newgate and there was no more waving to be done, Dickon found himself left with Aunt Isabel and Nan and Goody, all weeping. He was glad to take his leave and hurry back to Cripplegate.

He flung himself into his work with a will. The stay-at-home Adam was after all the first to cross the seas, but he did not intend that Adam should be ahead of him for long. That one hour copying Master Whittington's letters had opened his eyes to the doings of the Merchant Adventurers, visiting foreign fairs, sailing to strange lands to find fresh merchandise. That was the life for him and he would not be content with anything less.

One day a drover with a packhorse delivered to Grub Street a great locked and banded coffer. Will Appleyard was out and Robert with him. Neither Owen nor Toby knew anything about it, and the drover said that he could not wait as he had to be at Uxbridge by nightfall. So Dickon calculated what the man's due should be and gave him a tally for it.

The boys must take it on a barrow

But when Will Appleyard returned he was angry.

'Have you no wits between you?' he rated them. ''Tis obvious that a strong box like that contains valuables, and you must know by this time that Master Whittington's valuables do not come here. You should have made him take it on to Hart Street. It is heavy, I suppose?'

Dickon tried to lift the coffer but it was beyond his strength.

'Nevertheless to Hart Street it must go,' vowed Master Appleyard. 'I dare not trust it to a common porter, so you boys must take it on a barrow. All four of you shall go. You can take it in turns with the barrow, two at a time, while the other two stand guard with clubs.'

As soon as his back was turned Owen and Toby began to grumble because it was Saturday. Dickon secretly was delighted. At last he would see Whittington's Palace.

Will Appleyard bade them go all the way by the lane that ran along the inside of the Wall because it was quiet, but it seemed never-ending. They pushed their way through crowds of journeymen and apprentices pouring out of Aldgate on a fine Saturday afternoon, and arrived hot and weary and cross in the deep shade of Hart Street, where all the houses were so tall and projected so far that they almost shut out the sky. Robert said that many of these magnificent mansions belonged to rich merchants from Venice and Genoa, and Dickon loitered gazing open-mouthed for so long that the others, hot and resentful, made him take most of the weight for the last lap.

Whittington's Palace was at the far end of Hart Street, close to St. Olave's church. To Dickon's disappointment it was not so very much grander than its neighbours. Its beams were heavily carved and its windows glittered with glass, but he had almost expected to find it encrusted with gold. Worse still, they were received by a grumpy elderly mason who made them bring the coffer through to the courtyard, but did not invite them into the house. He gave them a pot of ale to share between them and then dismissed them with a nod.

On the way back they were free to take short cuts and Robert led them by a network of lanes that avoided most of the traffic.

As they turned a sharp corner by Fenchurch Street they bumped straight into a trio of apprentices hurrying towards Aldgate.

They were all mercers and both parties recognized each other and shouted 'How now?' and 'God save you!'

Taken by surprise Dickon realized too late that the middle one of the three was Kurt Bladebone. He tried to dodge behind Robert, but it was no good. Kurt had spotted him.

'See that knave,' he yelled pointing. 'What's he doing here? He's no mercer. He's a grocer. He's the rascal who broke my teeth.'

He lunged forward, lips curled back to show the front of his mouth. Dickon grasped his club. If he was driven to it he'd break some more teeth.

Robert seized Kurt by the shoulders and held him.

'What's all this?' he demanded. 'Was Dickon the giant who spoiled your beauty, young Bladebone? Why, you fool, he's smaller than you are.'

'Let me get at him,' cried Kurt. 'He's a traitorous cub and a coward. The last time I met him he ran for his life. He's a grocer, I tell you. We want no stinking victuallers in our craft. Ask him. Bid him deny it if he can.'

'This is not the place,' said Robert steadily. 'You had best save your breath to cool your broth. I'll have no brawling here. He's a lawfully sworn mercer apprentice and if you have a grievance you can challenge him properly at the next meeting and we'll see fair play.'

He looked round at the others, but none of them seemed keen to dispute his authority; so he made a sign to Dickon to go ahead, and when the two were well apart he let Kurt go. Grumbling under his breath Kurt and his two companions vanished round the corner and the four from Grub Street continued on their way in silence.

Dickon's mind was in a whirl. He was longing now to tell his whole story, but Robert looked cold and stern, and it wasn't until they were outside Cripplegate that he gave Dickon a chance to speak. Then, as they passed the end of St. Giles', he looked down at him and said, 'Well?'

Dickon no longer made any bones about it. There and then, in front of Owen and Toby, he told Robert everything, about his family and about the fight.

Robert let him go on until he had quite finished. Then he nodded quite kindly.

''Tis not your fault that your people are grocers,' he said. 'And Dick Whittington is your godfather; one can't ask better than that. It was a stroke of ill luck that you should have fought when you did, but I suppose you could not do otherwise. A fellow less ill-tempered than that red pate would realize it. You may have to fight him in fair contest, and I warn you that he is valiant with his fists. Time will tell. I should not lose my sleep over it if I were you.'

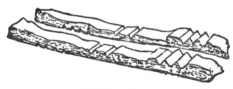

Tallysticks

The bastion of the Wall by St. Giles'

Chapter Fourteen

THE CRYPT IN BILLITER STREET

SO, for better or worse the truth was out, and in spite of whatever might lie ahead, Dickon at first was glad. At any rate he now had nothing to conceal.

Robert was as friendly as ever, and in front of Robert the other two did not dare to be hostile; but Dickon noticed that Owen avoided him, and once or twice he caught Toby humming a little song about 'St. Anthony's pig, St. Anthony's pig'. He longed to punch Toby's head but it would only have made matters worse.

He fancied that other apprentices looked askance at him, so instead of playing on Moorfields he took to going for walks by himself, or sitting on the bastion of the Wall by St. Giles', with his legs dangling, as he used to sit on the wharf when he was at home.

At Grantham's Inn Nan was lonely too. The place was so quiet with both the boys gone. Aunt Isabel, to stop her from fretting, gave her plenty to do. She inspected her needlework and pronounced it shocking. Her weaving was not much better and even her spinning was a disgrace; the thread was as coarse as rope in one place and as fine as a cobweb in another. Unless she

146

minded her ways she would never get a
husband. Even if Grandfather gave her
a dowry like a king's ransom no one
would marry such a thriftless maid.
There would be nothing for her but to
become a nun, and how would she like
that?

Nan pondered and then said that she
did not think it would be so bad, though
of course it depended what nunnery she
went into. The Poor Clares by the
Tower slept on boards and never spoke.
She would not like to be a Poor Clare.

Aunt Isabel laughed at her.

'You need not trouble yourself, my

Nan at her spinning

child. The Poor Clares are very holy
and I have seen no signs in you of such excessive holiness. But,
let me tell you, whatever nunnery you go into, you will spend
a great deal of time with a spindle or a needle, and you will find
your mistress far more strict than I am.'

Nan sighed. Aunt Isabel always won. But she settled down
and took more pains with her work.

While she was sewing and spinning she had time to think.
She went over and over all that had happened before Adam left
home and an idea began to take shape in her mind. After some
days of thought she slipped down to the wharf and looked for
Jenkyn. She saw him with his boat waiting at the end of Dowgate to pick up passengers; so, glancing quickly round to make
sure that no one was watching her, she beckoned to him.

He saw her and paddled his boat alongside.

'God save you, mistress, and what can I do for you? Would
you like a nice trip on the river?'

She shook her head. 'I wanted to ask you if you know a ship
that sailed for a Hanse merchant a little while ago? Her captain
was Master Hans Stein, but I know not the ship's name.'

'Aye! You mean the *Anna*. She sailed, if I mistake not, the
day you went to Westminster. Your brother was interested in
her, and so are others that I could mention.'

Nan nodded. 'That is the ship. You see, my brother has
gone to the wars, so I want you to tell me when the *Anna* comes
back.'

Jenkyn laughed. 'Are you doing a bit of trading too, mistress? Well, I'll let you know when she comes up the river again.'

''Tis a secret, please,' she said breathlessly. 'It is my brother's business and I want to help him. Will you keep silent that I have asked you?'

'As silent as the grave. Don't you worry, little mistress; I'll see to it for you.'

Nan tiptoed back into the house well satisfied. This was something she was going to do for Adam, and she was not going to tell anyone, not even Dickon.

In the hall she found Master Whittington, talking to Aunt Isabel. Madame Eglantine was with him. Nan picked her up and petted her, hoping to escape notice. But Master Whittington saw her at once.

'Well,' he said, pinching her cheek, 'so a little maid is missing her brothers, eh? Maybe I can help. It would do Dickon no harm to come home on Sundays, while this fine weather lasts. Adam's going was a bit of a blow to him too, I fancy. I will see if I can arrange it.'

When Will Appleyard told Dickon that he was to go to Grantham's Inn after Sunday mass and stay until nearly curfew, Dickon was thankful. He wondered why Dick Whittington had done it. When he got home he was told that it was for Nan's sake, but he did not care about that. The great thing was to be away from Grub Street for a little, not to have to pretend to be unruffled and carefree when all the time he was wondering what was going to happen next.

Then, too, at home he heard the news. On the first Sunday Grandfather told them that the King had boarded his ship and was ready to sail. A week later there were tidings that he and his army had actually landed on the coast of France and were preparing to lay siege to the town of Harfleur.

As well as going home on Sundays, Dickon also had orders to go for a couple of hours each day to Master Whittington's house and copy letters. *That* could not be for Nan's sake.

He worked alone most of the time, for Master Whittington was always busy. The King had left him much to look after. In addition to his responsibility for the work at Westminster, and his special secret charge, he was also consulted by the Mayor before any building in the City might be pulled down.

Dickon saw him only long enough to be given the work he was to do. After that he sat by himself on a high stool with parchments and ledgers piled up on the counter board in front of him.

This time most of what he had to copy was connected not with the Mercers' Company or the Merchant Adventurers, but with Master Whittington's private affairs.

Everybody knew that Dick Whittington's generosity was unbounded and that his purse strings were loosened for anyone in need. But faced with the evidence in black and white, Dickon was staggered by the extent of his master's charity.

First of all there was the work at the Greyfriars, the Franciscan

He sat on a high stool

Priory just outside Newgate. There was letter after letter about this, for Master Whittington was building a great library there, at fabulous cost; it was to be 130 feet long and filled with books to the tune of £400. Then there was much about a plan for re-building St. Bartholomew's Hospital; and another plan for pulling down the old fever-ridden prison at Newgate, where most of the prisoners died, and putting a new one in its place. At the great Guildhall, already half completed, Master Whittington was paying for all the paving and all the window glass, and he had a scheme for a library there too, a library such as had never been known in London before, where any citizen might use the books.

As well as all these great works there were smaller ones. He copied with special interest a column of figures about the college and almshouses at St. Michael's Paternoster, just outside the room where he was sitting. Then there was a letter from the Abbot of Gloucester about money for repairs in the Cathedral there; and a sheet of parchment headed 'NOTIONS', in Master Whittington's own handwriting, which made Dickon smile. It consisted of ideas dotted down for small projects here and there. There was a note about a boss for fresh water at Billingsgate, and another, with the ink still new, for a conduit outside St. Giles' Cripplegate. He remembered how Dick Whittington had asked to be reminded about that. Evidently the reminder was not needed.

One evening when Dickon returned to Cripplegate after his copying he found Robert waiting for him at the corner of Grub Street.

'I have news for you,' he called out, as Dickon came near. 'There is to be a meeting of mercers' prentices on the feast of St. Bartholomew, in the crypt at Billiter Street, just by the Abbot of Evesham's Inn. The elders have been told that you are more than two months sworn apprentice and are not yet a member. I vowed that I would bring you.'

Dickon nodded as casually as he could. He was determined not to show his feelings.

'I knew that you would come willingly,' said Robert approvingly. 'It was ordered that if you did not come you were to be bound with cords and brought by force.'

Dickon's heart pounded uncomfortably. St. Bartholomew's day was very close at hand. He kept his voice steady. 'Is it Kurt Bladebone who has done this?'

'Yes; he has informed against you. I hope that he will be content with that, but I doubt it. You may have to fight him. He has a reputation as a fighter, but after all you have beaten him once, when by your own showing he had others on his side.'

It was all very fine for Robert to say that. Now that he faced reality, Dickon's memory of the fight on the wharf became strangely vivid. He remembered those bad moments when Kurt had been pressing him back towards the wall of the warehouse. Undoubtedly he would have been punished without measure if Kurt had not put his foot on the wet straw, slimy with river mud just wiped from Dickon's shoe. That was the truth, and he had better face it.

Nevertheless he managed during the next few days to hold his head high in front of Owen and Toby, who were watching him curiously. He learned, too, something of the organization of the Prentices' Club. It was ruled by the elder boys who were elected as 'Kings' by the acclamation of the whole body. Robert was a 'King'; that was a comfort; but so was Owen, and about Owen he was not so sure.

The waiting was hard to bear and he was actually glad when the afternoon of the feast-day came and it was time for Robert to lead him to Billiter Street. Owen and Toby had gone ahead, and Robert had very little to say as they crossed Moorfields, passed

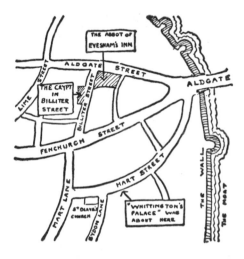

the lunatics' hospital of St. Mary Beth'lem—known to everyone simply as 'Bedlam'—and entered the City by Bishopsgate.

By himself Dickon would certainly never have found the place. Billiter Street was a quiet lane running south from Aldgate. At one corner stood the Abbot of Evesham's Inn with a plum tree peeping over the top of the fence. At the opposite corner was a garden, apparently overgrown, enclosed by a high wall. Robert turned down the lane until they reached an old stone archway sunk in the wall. Decaying oak doors hung upon great rusty hinges, and through small iron-barred windows on either side of the door, Dickon caught a glimpse of yellow torch-light flickering in the darkness below the level of the ground.

'Here we are,' said Robert, leading the way down some worn

stone steps. 'It is the crypt of an old house burned by fire hundreds of years ago.' He pushed between the ruinous doors and Dickon followed him.

At first they seemed to be almost in complete darkness. Then the yellow flame of the torches which he had noticed from outside, gave enough light for him to see that it was not a small place, but a large one, running for many yards back, with stone pillars to hold up the roof. As he grew more accustomed to the gloom he was aware of many faces peering. The torchlight picked a cheek-bone here or an ear there, and he realized that the crypt was full of apprentices.

They entered across a stone platform, like the dais of a hall. Robert's hand under his elbow guided him down the step to a place where he could stand with his back against a pillar. He drew himself as much as he could into the shadow, then turned round and faced the way they had come in.

Daylight poured through the broken doors and through the two barred windows, so that he could see on the platform a dozen or more big boys talking together in groups. Robert was there, and Owen too but he did not recognize anybody else.

The meeting began in an orderly fashion with a note on a gong, struck by a tall apprentice, even taller and broader than Robert, who seemed to be accepted as leader. The first business was the appointment of officers. The tall boy, who was addressed as Goodenough, announced that there were four vacancies among the 'Kings'. Two apprentices had finished their service and become journeymen, one had been cut down in a prentices' fight and was crippled for life, and the fourth was dead of smallpox. The meeting, with the utmost gravity, recited a prayer for the dead boy, and then broke into cheers or catcalls as names were proposed to fill his place.

Three new 'Kings' were elected without difficulty, but nobody seemed to be suggested for the fourth place. Then Owen, who had been whispering among a group at the back of the dais, stood up and submitted the name of Kurt Bladebone.

Dickon suppressed a gasp of dismay as a wave of cheering broke out. Obviously his enemy was immensely popular at the back of the crypt. Goodenough proposed Will Carpenter, prentice son of John Carpenter, the Town Clerk, but this was received in silence, and after a few minutes Bladebone was acclaimed and went up on to the dais. The light from the door caught the red of his hair as he stood there grinning. Dickon, holding his fists behind his back, clenched them tightly.

When the applause died down Goodenough rose once more.

'The next matter,' he said, 'is the swearing of a new apprentice, one who should have been sworn long since. He has been signed apprentice for more than two months. I know not why he has not been here before. Maybe there has been some error.'

He paused, and Dickon was struck instantly by the intense silence all around him. It was an ominous silence and he was thankful when Goodenough continued.

'His name is Sherwood, Dickon Sherwood. He is apprentice to Dick Whittington, who is his godfather, which should put him right with all of us. Some of you may think that he needs to be put right, for he comes of a grocer's family. Now we are all alike in having little use for victuallers, but this fellow is already made a mercer, and nothing that we can do will unmake him. I suggest that he should buy his way into our midst by a forfeit. He shall provide us with a barrel of raisins and a crate of sugar plums.'

The murmuring at the back, which had begun at the mention of the word *grocer*, changed to laughter, and there was even a little clapping. Dickon himself laughed too with sudden relief. It would be easy enough to beg the forfeit from Grandfather. But his relief was short-lived. Bladebone stepped forward.

'I'll have none of it,' he cried. 'A plague on all grocers and fishmongers and the rest of them; there is naught to choose between them. All the trouble between me and this fine grocer here began over the dirtiest stinking fish boy that ever you did see. If ever I meet the brat again I'll break every bone in his body.'

A yell of applause greeted this display of valour. Then, regardless of Goodenough, who tried to persuade him to stop, he began again, this time pointing straight at Dickon.

'As for your new apprentice, I protest that he is a treacherous knave and a coward. He knocked out my teeth by a foul trick, and when I met him on St. John's Eve he ran away, so that we had to chase him through half the streets of London and then missed him. Therefore I challenge him now to come forth in front of you all and give me my revenge.'

On the dais, with the light behind him, Bladebone looked huge. With a beating heart Dickon came out from the shadow of the pillar. It took all the strength of his will to keep his voice steady.

"'Tis you who are the coward, Kurt Bladebone,' he cried. 'Three of you set upon the fish boy that day by the river, there were three of you and I fought alone.'

He had to shout to make his voice heard above the growing uproar, but the very act of shouting gave him courage till his knees stiffened and his shoulders squared.

Bladebone lunged forward but Robert and Goodenough seized him and dragged him back.

'We'll have no bloodshed here,' thundered Goodenough at the top of his voice. 'If you would fight it out you must name a place and a time and we will all be there to see fair play.'

The murmuring grew on all sides. On the dais a whispered consultation was going on. Goodenough sounded his gong.

'Peace, you noisy fellows,' he demanded. 'Peace, and listen to what I say. We all here know that Kurt Bladebone is a valiant fighter. His adversary is unknown to us. He may be a stout fighter too; 'tis evident that he left his mark. But he is a small boy, younger than Bladebone, and to my mind it would be a hazardous contest. Now I would have you remember that you have just named Bladebone to be a "King" in the place of a boy who was all but killed in a fight. If we in this club go on allowing our fellows to kill one another we shall find ourselves tried for our lives by the Mayor's court. The Mayor has threatened it. If this new lad, Sherwood, were killed it certainly would be the worse for us, for he is Dick Whittington's apprentice—and his godson.'

Dickon took a step forward. This was more than he could stand. 'I would not shirk for that,' he cried.

'Hold your peace,' said Goodenough sharply. 'You shall prove your courage before we have done with you, never fear. But I will have no fighting. What say any of you to trial by ordeal?'

A roar echoed round the vaulted roof. Dickon felt sick. He had a sudden vision of being grilled on a gridiron like St. Laurence or dipped in boiling oil like St. Crispin.

'Then what shall the test be?' inquired Goodenough. 'I will count till two minutes are gone and then anyone who has a good idea can bring it to me.'

To Dickon the minutes seemed like a lifetime. There were

whispers all round, though he could not distinguish what they said. On the dais Kurt was the centre of a group. Dickon saw Owen join them. He seemed to have a lot to say. When Goodenough signalled that the time was up, it was Owen who went and spoke in his ear. Goodenough looked doubtful. He called to Robert and one or two of the others, and they consulted together. At last he sounded the gong and the crypt was suddenly quiet.

'Our comrade here has made a suggestion,' he began. 'He has proposed a trial which is a perilous adventure. He calls on the new apprentice to bring to us here within two weeks from now, one of the heads displayed over the gate of the Bridge. He makes no condition except this, that the challenged shall go alone and that the enterprise shall be made known to none. Kurt Bladebone, you have called him coward and challenged him. Will you accept this trial of his courage?'

Bladebone shrugged his shoulders. 'I care not what he does,' he said sulkily. 'He may as well fetch a head for those who want one as anything else.'

Goodenough turned to Dickon. 'And what say you?' he asked. 'Do you accept the challenge that you shall, alone and unaided, carry off a head now stuck on a pikestaff over London Bridge, and that the same act shall be acknowledged as proof of your courage, and that you shall then be admitted to this club? What do you say?'

Dickon squared his shoulders. 'I accept,' he declared.

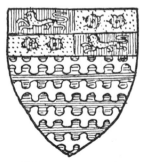

Arms of the Merchant Adventurers

The full moon over the river

Chapter Fifteen

THE DRAWBRIDGE GATE

DICKON made his way back to Grub Street alone and was in bed and pretending to be asleep by the time the others came up. But there was little sleep for him that night.

His first feeling had been one of relief that he had escaped a fight. Kurt Bladebone would certainly have set about him without mercy. He remembered the apprentice who was crippled for life, and was thankful. Having heard the threats that Kurt had uttered, he earnestly hoped that the wretched fishmonger boy, Lob, would keep well out of the way.

But the ordeal ahead appalled him. It was very strange that so short a while ago he should have stood on the Bridge and stared up at the heads. He had no illusions about the difficulty of his task. What would happen to him if he were caught he did not dare to think. But he had accepted the challenge. Somehow it had to be attempted. He rolled over on to his back and began to make plans.

Of course he had one big advantage which nobody knew about: Goody lived on the Bridge. But to make use of that advantage he would have to sleep at Goody's house, for obviously the job could only be done at night. He must play truant and go

there on Sunday night instead of returning to Cripplegate. It
would mean a beating the next day, but that could not be helped.
There would be a moon next Sunday; that would help him.
Next Sunday must be the day.

He thought and worried and schemed all night, and got up in
the morning yawning and heavy-eyed but with a definite plan in
his head.

On the following Saturday he begged leave to go and be
shriven. This was genuine enough for, although he also intended to take the opportunity of going to see Goody, he faced

A picture of St. Christopher

the fact that what he was contemplating was a dangerous business, and it would be just as well to confess his sins and be in a
state of grace.

Nevertheless he did not linger more than was necessary over
the prayers allotted to him as a penance. He lit a taper before a
picture of St. Christopher, with a confused idea that since St.
Christopher helped travellers over a river, anything to do with a
bridge would be his concern. Then he ran all the way to
Goody's to lay his plans.

It had been difficult to think of a convincing reason for invit-
ing himself to sleep at her house on the Sunday night. In the end
he had worked out an elaborate excuse about watching some ship
which was due to sail at dawn. But by a marvellous chance, as

though St. Christopher were already at work, Goody was not in the least surprised, and he did not even have to mention the ship. It would be full moon on Sunday night. Every year people crowded on to the Bridge to watch the harvest moon rise behind the Tower and see its reflection in the river. She wagged her finger at him roguishly. Master Dickon was growing up! Young men had romantic notions. She would not be astonished if there were a maiden in it somewhere. Dickon grinned. He did not mind what she thought so long as his plan prospered.

He went to Grantham's Inn for dinner on Sunday as usual, and even here fortune favoured him. Aunt Isabel and Nan went off immediately afterwards to join a party for blackberrying in Hornsey woods, and left him to his own devices. He was able to ask his grandsire's blessing and take himself off at Vespers' time without anyone so much as asking why he left so early.

He felt astonishingly calm as he walked along Thames Street to the Bridge, *too* calm considering that he was so uncertain about what lay ahead. The whole task seemed so unbelievable and so unreal that he could not imagine how he would ever come out of it alive. He only went on because it was impossible to turn back.

At Goody's the household was in a turmoil. Goody's little grandson had devoured the marchpane of almond paste and honey that Goody had made as a treat for Dickon, and was being held out of the window over the convenient torrent of the river. Simon the glover, a perky little man rather like a robin, with red cheeks and very bright eyes, beckoned Dickon to come outside.

'This is no place for us,' he said. 'What think you, Master Dickon? Shall we go and have a can of ale at the tavern?'

Dickon shook his head. 'I'd rather stay here,' he said, as casually as he could. 'Can we go up on to the Drawbridge Gate? I've never been on it. There must be a good view of the ships.'

'The view is much the same as it is from below, but we can go if you like. The Drawbridge man is a friend of mine.'

The Drawbridge man, it seemed, lived not inside the gate but in one of the adjacent houses. The doors of the gate were old and rickety and were never closed, and the gatehouse was damp and rat-infested. The Drawbridge man could easily be called to handle the gear if required and the raising of the Drawbridge itself was sufficient to bar the way.

'Is there no one here at night then?' asked Dickon, trying to suppress the eagerness in his voice.

'Not at the Drawbridge Gate. There's an armed guard at the Stone Gate, which is barred at curfew, and there's a watchman there all the time.'

The top of the Drawbridge Gate was reached by two ladders, one on the right side of the archway and the other on the left. Once they were up there Dickon looked for a while at the view,

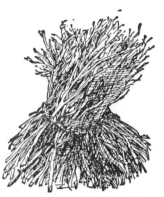

Bundles of faggots

for the benefit of Simon; after that, of course, it was perfectly natural that he should stare at the heads and listen to what Simon had to say about them while he examined the pike staves on which each one was impaled. He had no idea that pike staves were so tall. But the method by which they were secured to the roof was quite simple, so simple that Dickon could scarcely believe it. Each staff was slipped through an iron staple half-way up the wooden rampart and dropped into a groove at the bottom. The shaft was kept steady just by a rope lashing it to the parapet. If that rope were undone it should be possible to lift the pole bodily out of its socket.

He dared not appear too keen about this examination. There was the danger that afterwards Simon might remember and become suspicious. So when Simon proposed that they should go on and see the Stone Gate, he agreed cheerfully.

The Stone Gate was a far more formidable barrier than the Drawbridge Gate and Dickon was thankful that the heads were not displayed on it. To start with there was a guard of pikemen lodged there and a gatekeeper who slept in a little room close to the great doors. He was an old soldier, with one ear missing since John of Gaunt's campaign in Spain thirty years ago. He knew Simon well, and insisted that they should go and see his quarters under the arch.

The little room with a door that was never shut looked cosy enough with a bed of straw laid out in a stone recess and a small charcoal brazier to keep the place warm. At present the archway was half blocked by some bundles of faggots stacked along the inside of the arch—a silly place to leave them, Dickon reflected, as his eye took in every detail. But the gatekeeper was rather proud of the faggots. They were evidence of his own quick wits, and were left there for the Customs officer to see. He related how he had suspected them when they approached the Bridge yesterday forenoon on a wagon with ironshod wheels. Ironshod wheels had to pay a special toll to enter the City, and he had wondered why a load so light should need a heavy wagon. So he had lifted a bundle to find out, and behold every bundle concealed a butt of French wine.

"'Tis good wine too,' he said with a wink. 'I had to tap it, you see, to make sure that it was wine and not cider as the carter claimed. I sent the wagon on with a guard to the Customs house so that the wine should pay its due and the carter go to the pillory, but I unloaded a few faggots, casks and all, so that the Customs officer should not forget my hand in it. If he should forget—well, I still have the wine.'

He offered them each a cupful. Dickon made an excuse; he felt that he must keep his wits clear at all costs; but Simon pronounced it excellent, a good full-bodied wine. He drank Dickon's share as well as his own and, well mellowed, led Dickon home to supper.

Dickon went to bed in the workshop which was the general living-room of the house. He had persuaded Goody to let him sleep there because, he said, he must be off very early in the morning to reach Cripplegate by the time it opened at sunrise. Goody made a fuss about it, but Simon backed him up.

'Let the boy sleep where he wants,' he said. 'He's an apprentice and scores of apprentices sleep in workshops, under the counter very often. Can't you see that he wants to get out easily, without raising the whole household?'

It was so true that Dickon almost laughed.

So, when the full moon was high in the sky, and all the people who had come to see it rise had gone home, Dickon undressed and to satisfy Goody, allowed her to tuck him in.

He lay for about an hour, to make sure that everybody upstairs was really asleep. He had no fear that Goody would hear anything; she was too deaf. But Simon lay just overhead, in a little room facing the river. However, lusty snoring soon relieved his anxiety about Simon. He suddenly remembered the 'good full-bodied wine' and gave thanks for it.

The moon flooded the room with light, and when he had crept into his clothes again he tiptoed round making a few preparations. First of all he oiled the door lock using a jar of neat's-foot oil and a feather, which he found on the work bench. He had brought with him a pair of tweezers belonging to Adam, which might help him to grip the rope, and a small sack in which to conceal his trophy. His plan was to smuggle it under cover of darkness to the crypt in Billiter street, where an old sack could lie safely hidden in the shadows until he handed it over.

These things done he went and stood in the corner beside the window waiting for the watchmen to pass by. He had learned by questioning that the Watch came quite early in the night to see that all lights were out and the Bridge was in no danger from fire. When they had once been it would be some time before they returned, for they had the whole of Bridge Ward to patrol.

It was not long before he heard them. They made no secret about it, but came tramping over the cobbles, regardless of sleeping citizens. There were two watchmen, one on each side of the road, peering up and down and around every nook and corner between the houses. Dickon waited until they had passed back again on their return journey, and then allowed time for them to leave the Bridge altogether on the London side. At last with a beating heart, he unlocked the door and crept out. In the street everything seemed to be quiet. Far away on his left he could still see the lanterns of the Watch mounting Fish Street Hill. He closed the door softly behind him and tiptoed towards the Drawbridge Gate.

The back of the gatehouse lay in deep shadow. He had to fumble along until he came to one of the ladders. He was so nervous that he stopped at every step to listen, but the only sound was the constant race of water underneath.

At the top he emerged into brilliant light. The moon was by now high in the heavens making everything almost as clear as day. He looked over the rampart and saw the Tower cut out in silver and all the little ships lying against a pattern of tall black-and-white houses along the riverside. He thanked his guardian angel for such a fine night. Only now did he realize how hopeless his task would have been in the dark. Anyhow up here he was hidden from sight and he could take his time.

He had decided to take the end-most head, the one on the up-river side of the Bridge. It would be easier to lift a corner pole than one in the middle. He glanced up at it and looked down again with a suppressed shudder. Whatever happened he mustn't let himself *think*.

His heart was beating wildly as he set to work on the first knot, but the rope moved quite easily in the grip of the tweezers. Working firmly and steadily he untied and unwound it. It seemed that this, his worst difficulty, was really no difficulty at all. When he had at last pulled the rope free, he took a firm stand with his feet a little apart, grasped the pikestaff in his two hands, and gently raised it a few inches.

But there was a difficulty that he had not thought of. The pikestaff was double his own height and was weighted by the head at the top. It was all he could do to balance it. As he lifted the base out of the socket, he felt the top beginning to sway unmanageably. It was pulling him towards the edge. He wrestled with it with all his strength, struggling to correct the dangerous tilt. Then quite suddenly the pole righted itself. The weight became less. There was a splash that sounded like a thunderclap in the still night air. The head had dropped into the river.

Appalled, Dickon strove to regain his grip. Someone shouted down on the Bridge. Panic seized him and he let go of the pikestaff. It followed the head, raising spray as high as the gatehouse. Too long to slip through the arches, it boomed and crashed as it beat upon the starlings of the Bridge.

He stood petrified. Everyone would have heard that terrible noise. Already a man near by-was stamping about and shouting. 'What was that? Who goes there? Show yourself, whoever you are.'

It must be the Drawbridge keeper. In another minute he would come up, and then, even if he did not catch Dickon immediately, he would see that a head was missing and raise the hue and cry.

A second later footsteps sounded on the ladder nearest to him, the one by which he had come up. As quick as thought he darted across the top, slid down the second ladder and dropped into the roadway.

He looked wildly first one way and then the other. In both directions lanterns were moving in the distance. Perhaps if he made a dash for it he could reach Goody's door before the Watch arrived. Hugging the dark, and half giddy with fright, he ran. He emerged into a broad strip of moonlight with no shelter at all,

He saw them run past in the moonlight

plunged across it and flung himself into the shadow of a house on the other side. Only then did it dawn on him what he had done. He had come down from the roof by the opposite ladder and therefore had turned in the wrong direction. Instead of running towards Goody's he had run away from it towards the Stone Gate.

There was a shallow nook between two houses, only a foot or so deep. He pressed himself into it and held his breath as footsteps and voices came near. It was the guard from the Stone Gate.

'Where was it, say you?'—'The noise came from the Drawbridge Gate'—'Aye, there is someone on the top.'

He saw them run past in the moonlight. Then he heard voices in the house beside him, and the sound of bolts being withdrawn. The inmates were coming out. He slipped from his niche, and flattening himself against the shadowed wall, moved along it, hoping for a space between the houses, but there was none. He reached the corner and saw the Stone Gate just in front of him across another strip of moonlight. What should he do? Just to wait in the shadow was certain ruin.

At that moment the gatekeeper came out from his little room, holding up a lantern. Dickon saw him clearly as he stood lighting up the archway. Then he went inside again; the rays of the lantern streamed from his open door.

But in that brief minute Dickon had seen something else; the faggots. If he could wriggle behind those bundles of faggots there was just a chance that he might be safely hidden.

He darted across the strip of moonlight and lay against the shadowed side of the Stone Gate. Apparently no one had noticed him. The voices and the shouting were concentrated round the Drawbridge Gate. Perhaps all the guard had gone to see what was afoot, and only the gatekeeper was left. He ventured to peep round the corner into the archway. The light still shone out from the little room. Cautiously, by inches, Dickon slipped to the ground, wriggled behind the bundle of faggots farthest from the gatekeeper's lodge, and lay flat. If they searched of course they would find him, but it gave him a breathing space. He could hear the gatekeeper moving about. Each time the footsteps came near he held his breath.

Suddenly another sound caught his attention, as he lay with his ear close to the ground. There were horses, a long way off but coming nearer. They were approaching from the Southwark side. The clip-clop grew louder and had a hollow sound. They were *on* the Bridge. They halted outside, with hoofs clattering and bits jangling. There were heavy blows on the gate and a man's voice echoed under the arch.

'Open, in the King's name!'

The gatekeeper hastened to undo a grating in the big door, and a shaft of moonlight poured in. Somebody pushed a parchment through the grill. The gatekeeper held it up to the light and peered at the seal. Then he opened one side of the doors so that the leader on his horse might ride a few steps in. They stood parleying. Dickon could not hear what was said; it was drowned in the echoes that rolled round the vaulted roof. But he could see through the door. Between the horse's legs the way lay clear. He did not stop to think. He wriggled from beneath the faggots, and, bent double, dodged under the leader's horse and out of the gate.

There were three more horsemen waiting. He ran straight past them. But there was still trouble ahead. Lanterns were moving at the Bridge foot. That way was barred too. A shout came from the Stone Gate behind him. He had been seen. There was hope only in one direction—the river. He remembered suddenly the ropes and pulleys hanging from the corn granaries on his right. The water would be quite shallow under that last arch.

He darted down a narrow passage between the granaries, tall wooden buildings, black with pitch. He had chosen the right spot. A rope dangled conveniently from a projecting beam. He grasped it, said a quick prayer and dropped.

For a moment he hung in space—then fell, not into water but into mud.

Dickon was ferried across by Jenkyn

Chapter Sixteen

PORT IN A STORM

HE floundered about flat on his front with his mouth full of muddy water. Then his outstretched hand found something firm, an iron ring stuck in a buttress. He dragged himself up on to one of the great starlings on which the Bridge was built. At any rate he was hidden in the shadows and if he wriggled round he would be able to step on to a firm beach. Next he would have to find a boat, complete with oars, and row himself back to Grantham's wharf.

Not daring to waste time he ventured out into the moonlight. The lights were still moving about near the Bridge foot and he could hear people shouting overhead by the Stone Gate. If anyone peeped down between the houses they might see him, but he had to risk it. Once daylight came he would never get home, all plastered with mud as he was. Looking down he realized suddenly that he had lost a shoe. It was one of his best red ones which he had put on because they were soft and made no noise. Probably it had come off in the mud.

He moved along the water's edge, jog-trotting when he could. He had never before seen the river so far down. It must be just low tide, and a spring tide too, with the full moon.

He realized with horror that the boats were all high and dry, far up the beach. When he had put sufficient distance between himself and the Bridge he chose one that looked light and tugged at it, but it was stuck fast in the mud. He tried another, and yet a third, but they were all equally hopeless. Even by pulling with all his strength he could not move one a single inch.

He straightened himself, panting. The mud was drying on his face and his hose were sodden. He saw to his horror that two lanterns had moved down to the shore. They were circling about just where he had dropped from the Bridge. Then one of them began to come steadily nearer. To cross the river now was impossible. He must find somewhere to hide. There was only one place he knew in Southwark—the *Green Falcon*. After all, why not? The taverner had been a good friend when he was in trouble before.

Dodging among the shadows of the boats he turned inland. The moonlight showed him the way without much difficulty. He went cautiously round corners, earnestly praying that his memory would not fail him, and that all the watchmen of South-wark were down by the Bridge. At last with a sigh of relief he saw the sign he was looking for, and turned into the yard of the tavern. All the windows were dark and there was no sign of life until a dog began to bark. A chain rattled; thank goodness the dog was tied up. Dickon stood in the shadow uncertain what to do next. Then a door at the top of the outside stairs opened and the taverner came out, a sheet wrapped round his bulky form.

'Who's there?' he demanded loudly. 'Declare yourself, whoever you be, or I'll loose the dog on you.'

'It's me,' said Dickon croakily. 'It's Dickon—the one you called the giant killer.'

'By cock and pie, what do you at this hour?' cried the taverner. 'Is aught amiss?'

'I've been in the river and the Watch are after me. For the love of Heaven let me in.'

'The Watch? Come up quickly then, and keep your voice low.'

Dickon was already half-way up the stairs. Master Wolman reached out a hand and pulled him in through a creaky door which he closed carefully behind them. At the same moment the alchemist, clad in a nightcap and a long black *houppelande* over his bony legs, appeared bearing a lighted taper. He asked peevishly

An ale slipper

what was the matter and his mouth fell open with astonishment as he spied Dickon.

'He has been in the river and the Watch are after him,' repeated the taverner. 'Strip off your clothes, boy. Here is a cloak to wrap you. We'll have you into bed and feign illness if needs be.'

The three of them stood listening for some minutes. As nothing happened, Wolman led the way down by a steep ladder stair within the house into a kitchen place where the embers still glowed. He threw on some sticks and blew until they kindled. Then he hastened to the window and put up the wooden shutters.

Safe for the present, Dickon suddenly felt too tired even to lift his head. His teeth began to chatter. Wolman poured some ale into an iron ale slipper, threw in some spice and thrust it among the ashes to warm. Then he and the alchemist retired into a corner and talked together in a low voice. Presently Wolman returned, tested the ale and handed it to Dickon.

'Drink that; 'twill warm you,' he directed. 'And then tell us what you have been at this time. Fighting again?' He began to laugh. 'It seems that when you are hard pressed you flee to me as though I were your dam.'

Dickon sipped the drink cautiously. He did not want to get tipsy again. But this was only light ale, sharply spiced, not heady mead like last time. He felt the warmth creeping through him, and on the impulse he told the truth.

'I've been on the Bridge. I had to get one of the heads from the Drawbridge Gate.'

'Holy Christopher!' cried the taverner. He turned to the alchemist. 'Here, good master, pull the leather curtain across the door. Light shows through those chinks. Well may the Watch be after him. Now, my young valiant. What have you done with your prize?'

It was a great relief to speak out and Dickon told them everything. The taverner listened with his face screwed up till he looked like a large pink pig; the alchemist's eyes fixed on Dickon

Dickon told them everything

like a pair of gimlets. Once or twice they exchanged glances. When he described how the head fell into the water, Master Gross snarled with disappointment, and the taverner swore under his breath.

At the end of the story Wolman rose to his feet.

'My young Jack, I salute you,' he exclaimed. 'It was in truth a valiant venture. You did well to come here or you would of a certainty have been seized. Now rest you for a while. Your hose are drying. With the first glimmer of dawn you shall be rowed back across the river. Just one question I would ask. Who were the brains who thought of this scheme? For apprentices they were uncommon sharp. Can you tell us their names?'

Dickon immediately named Owen and Kurt Bladebone. There were others, but he did not know who they were.

''Tis no matter,' said Wolman, passing the matter off with a laugh. 'They are lads of originality; that is all.'

He moved away, pausing to turn Dickon's hose which were drying by the fire. But Master Gross did not stir. Instead he pulled his stool a little nearer and began to talk about Adam. He said how clever Adam was and what a brilliant future lay ahead of him. It was a thousand pities that he had been plucked away before he had put the finishing touches to his Panacea. If only he could have completed it, so as to use it for the benefit of the King's army, his fortune would have been made.

Dickon was pleased and tried to say so. But he was so tired that he kept nodding. Seeing this the alchemist took a lighted brand from the fire and began to play with it, twisting it round and making the sparks jump in a way that soon woke him up again.

'I have been thinking,' Master Gross went on. 'It is a sore shame that his work should be all wasted and he should lose his chance. So I have conceived a plan. There is a shipman known to Wolman here: he braves the pirates in the Channel and plies between London and the river Seine. Now the King's fleet lies in the mouth of the Seine while his Grace lays siege to Harfleur. If we could procure the Silver Steel, which is the only element we lack, I would complete your brother's Panacea—he left the formula with me. Then we could send it to him by the faithful shipman. Does it not touch your fancy, this scheme of mine?'

In spite of his weariness Dickon was stirred. It would be splendid if Adam could use his wonderful invention after all. He said so to Master Gross.

'But I doubt me if the Silver Steel has come yet,' he added. 'I have heard no mention of the Hanse ship, though I usually learn what ships come in or go out.'

'Nay, it has *not* come,' agreed Master Gross pleasantly. 'We have been watching for the Bridge to be raised. Have you any means, my friend, by which you could take charge of the precious earth when it arrives?'

Dickon was thoughtful. He had retorted sharply to Adam that he could not be responsible for the Silver Steel, but he admitted to himself that he had been jealous and cross because Adam was going to France. If it was really so urgent he could manage it. Wat, Grandfather's head journeyman, was a very good friend of his. Wat could set the stuff aside and he would bring it across to the *Green Falcon* at the first opportunity. He suggested this to Master Gross, who agreed heartily.

'Give it to Jenkyn if you cannot come yourself,' he said. 'I am delighted that there is still a chance that we may complete your brother's formula. Between us we shall do him a great service.'

It was broad daylight when Dickon was ferried across the river by Jenkyn and the tide was up enough for them to pull in to Grantham's wharf. The dried mud had brushed off his clothes fairly well, but he must get another pair of shoes. There were some old ones of Adam's which would serve nicely. So far he had been lucky, but he had been seen as he escaped from the Stone Gate and there was no telling what might have happened on the Bridge since then. If Simon and Goody should have slept right through the whole business, then they might think he had left at dawn, as it had been arranged. But if not—— He comforted himself by remembering that Goody was very deaf; and as for Simon, he had been snoring so very heavily that he might not have woken up.

At Grantham's Inn to his astonishment he found Nan in the forecourt fully dressed, giving Beauty an early morning run. He had forgotten that the night was over and it was almost time for work again.

Nan cried out when she saw him.

'Dickon! Where on earth have you come from?'

'Hush!' he whispered urgently. 'Don't make a noise. I've been out all night. There's no time to tell you now. It was for a wager. But I've lost a shoe. There's a pair of Adam's upstairs. Can you get them? But for the love of Heaven don't tell anyone you've seen me.'

She nodded and vanished. In a few minutes she was back, not only with the shoes but with some crusty bread and honey.

A skillet

He patted her on the shoulder as he devoured it. Truly she was a good thoughtful child.

Between mouthfuls he told her that Adam was going to have his Panacea after all; Master Gross had found a way to send it to France. He entrusted her with a message to Wat the journeyman asking him to take charge of the Silver Steel when the Hanse merchant brought it.

'I've changed my mind,' he said, licking the honey from his fingers. 'I *am* going to take it to Master Gross, as Adam asked me to do.'

He thought that she would be pleased, but for no apparent reason she turned very red and looked as if she were going to cry. Dickon had no idea what was the matter and no time to stop and ask. He gave her a kiss for what she had done for him, and after reminding her again that she was not to mention having seen him, no matter who it was that asked her, he hurried away.

He was running up Wood Street when Bow Bells rang for the beginning of work. Cripplegate had been open for a long time and outside it people were emerging from an early mass at St. Giles'. He mixed with them deliberately and then, with a shock, found himself walking next to Will Appleyard. He held his breath, waiting for the storm to break, but to his astonishment the mercer gave him a nod and a smile.

'You're in good time this morning,' he said. 'A good beginning for Monday morning, eh?'

With a gasp of relief Dickon understood that he had not been missed. Will Appleyard thought that he too had just been to church. He did not disillusion him.

The three other apprentices were all at breakfast in the kitchen when Will Appleyard and Dickon got home. They all stared when they saw the two come in together, but none of them, not even Toby, made the slightest sign to show that Dickon had not spent the night in their midst.

He could see that they were all longing to ask him questions, but Goodwife Appleyard was in the kitchen stirring something in a skillet so they would have no opportunity until they went to work.

Before the meal was over, Will Appleyard was called to the door to speak to a messenger.

'I am not to go to Master Whittington today,' he told his wife when he came back. 'His nephew has come home from France.'

Dickon pricked up his ears. Did that mean that Adam had returned too? Will Appleyard saw his face.

'No,' he said in answer to the unspoken question. 'Your brother is not there. Master Guy has come with a special message from the King. He arrived by the Bridge in the middle of the night.'

Dickon felt suddenly sick. It must have been Master Guy's horse that he dived under. Supposing he had been caught there and then! He was so much sobered by this news that when Owen and Toby plied him with questions, he refused to answer any of them, and took refuge by working in the counting-house within earshot of Master Appleyard.

At dinner-time Will Appleyard again produced a piece of news.

'I hear that there was a lot of excitement on the Bridge last night,' he observed. 'Some bold fellow tried to steal one of the traitors' heads. The head and the pikestaff both fell into the river and they are not sure that he did not go after them.'

Dickon choked over his meat. He did not do so deliberately, but it was a fortunate accident for it bore the blame for his crimson face.

'They did not catch the fellow then?' asked Toby, his eye upon Dickon.

'No, they did not catch him. Somebody escaped through the Gate as Master Guy was coming in, but that may only have been some Southwark cut-purse making for home.'

'Now why should anyone want to steal one of the heads, nasty things?' demanded Goodwife Appleyard with a shudder.

'Nobody knows *that*,' returned her husband, 'though they seem to think that it may have something to do with Lollardy.'

Dickon managed to keep his own counsel until bedtime. But when the four of them were safely in their garret there was nothing for it but to tell the whole story. They all listened spellbound. Robert and Toby were loud with praise for Dickon's pluck, but at the end Owen was inclined to quibble. Dickon had not answered the challenge, he insisted. The challenge was to bring back a head from the Bridge and he had not brought one. After a while Robert grew angry with him.

'You are behaving like a surly dog,' he told him. 'All the town knows that the head has been stolen. Do you want to see Dickon hanged for it to satisfy your spleen? He has proved his courage and all right men will say the same. Kurt Bladebone will have to accept the judgement and shake hands. In the meanwhile, I warn you that we had all better keep our mouths shut. This has gone far enough. Remember that it is a conspiracy, and we are all of us conspirators, and could go to Newgate for it.'

Chapter Seventeen

THE CHURCH PORCH

DICKON slept soundly and woke up lighter at heart than he had
been for weeks. Twenty-four hours had passed and no one in
authority had arrived to question him about the Bridge. He had
carried out his task and put himself right with his fellows. All
day long every mercer apprentice he met came up to him and,
without a word, either patted him on the back or shook his hand.
He fancied once that Will Appleyard looked at him a little
strangely, but nothing was said, and at Vespers' time he gave
Dickon a rolled bill and told him to take it to Master Whittington's house and copy it into the big ledger there. Dickon did not
want to go near his godfather at present; Master Whittington's
eye was shrewd and saw too much. And Guy Whittington was
there. There might be some reference to the episode at the Stone
Gate. However, there was no help for it. He accepted the roll
and dawdled on his way, for it had been a hot day and the City
streets were stifling.

But save for the servants the Whittington house was deserted.
The steward told him that his master had left London with
Master Guy. He did not know where they had gone, save that it
was on the King's business. They would not be back before
tomorrow or the day following.

Much relieved Dickon settled to his work, and took his time

about it. When it was finished he decided to go home before returning to Cripplegate. It would be cooler near the river, and there was another matter on his mind. He had to beg Grandfather for a barrel of raisins and a case of sugar plums to complete his bargain with the prentices' club.

At Grantham's Inn there was much talk. Guy Whittington had reported that Adam was doing well in France, and earning praise by his skill. The army was held up outside Harfleur. It looked like a long siege, and, said Grandfather, treating Dickon with a flattering confidence, the King needed money, and so of course he turned to Dick Whittington like a pitcher to the well. That was why Guy Whittington had been chosen as messenger. Grandfather was in a merry mood, chuckling into his beard, and Dickon seized the moment to mention the raisins and the sugar plums. John Sherwood hummed and hawed for a space about the impudence of these young mercers, who could treat a grocer civilly only when they wanted something. However, Dickon could have his plunder, for it was sheer plunder; but he must see that it did not happen again.

That was another problem solved and Dickon's spirits rose still higher. There was roasted capon for supper and he could not resist the temptation to stay and enjoy it. He lingered so late that he found he must run all the way if he was to reach Cripplegate before curfew. It was even hotter than it had been all day; thunderclouds hung over the City and people thronged the streets because houses were too hot to be endured. Wood Street was packed with citizens coming back from an airing on Moorfields. He was only half-way along it when the curfew went, and he knew, as he pushed against the returning stream, that he had little hope of reaching the gate before it closed. It had been shut and barred a good five minutes when he arrived panting to bang his fists on the gatekeeper's door.

But this time the gatekeeper was firm. 'Twas one thing, he said, to wink an eye and open a crack when his hand was still on the lock. But after the bars were once fixed nothing but an order from the King or the Mayor would open them. Dickon must just go back where he came from and wait till the morning.

Dickon looked wildly round. After his adventure on the Bridge he wondered if he could not drop over the Wall when no one was looking. But the gatekeeper was experienced in the ways of prentices.

'And 'tis no use your planning any mischief, my lad,' he warned. 'The Wall is higher than it looks and anyway the ditch is full on the other side. And I promise you an arrow in your behind and the pillory afterwards if you try any tricks.'

Disgruntled, his thumbs in his belt, Dickon slouched away. What should he do? Go home? He supposed so; but though Grandfather was in a good temper, he might get a beating all the same, and he'd no fancy for another like the one on St. John's Eve. Should he sleep out? It was warm enough, but it was not easy to dodge the Watch, and if they caught him without a light and without lawful business he'd be in the lock-up till morning. Besides there was going to be a storm. Already the thunder was growling in the distance. He decided to go slowly, so that it would be dark when he got home. Then, maybe, he could climb the buttery roof and get in by his bedchamber window without being seen.

The thunder, so obviously coming nearer, had cleared the streets. Everyone was scurrying to their homes. He crossed himself as the first flash of lightning lit up the houses. Perhaps he ought to hurry after all. He wondered which was the worse, to be out in the storm, or Grandfather's beating? Then quite suddenly there was a terrific crash, almost simultaneous with the lightning. Just ahead of him, at the corner of Huggen Lane, stood the church of St. Michael, Wood Street. It had a large porch. Sprinting the last ten yards Dickon thankfully plunged inside.

The porch was like a little stone room, perfectly dry and well sheltered from the street. It was pitch dark but Dickon groped his way to the far end, away from the entrance and propped himself in the corner. Really, if need be, he could quite well stay here for the night.

The rain was coming down in torrents, the lightning flashed and flickered and the thunder roared round and round like an angry giant. Dickon tried the door into the body of the church, but it was locked, so he returned to his corner again and said a prayer of thankfulness for his safe refuge.

He had been there a little while when he heard scurrying footsteps in the street. A slim figure flung itself into the porch and leaned back panting against the church door. Dickon's eyes had become accustomed to the darkness sufficiently for him to decide that the newcomer was a boy, smaller than himself, with some covering such as a sack thrown over his head and shoulders. He had obviously been running. Dickon did not speak, for a voice out of the darkness would startle him before he had recovered his breath. It must be some other apprentice locked out too.

Quite soon the boy began to shuffle about. He went to the entrance and Dickon could see the shape of his head and shoulders as he peered out into the street. Did he hope that the storm was passing? Well, he was wrong. It was coming up again. The last peal of thunder was a loud one, and the rain, which had slackened, was once more coming down as out of a bucket.

But the boy was not going. He was fumbling about in his tunic. The lightning flashed and Dickon caught sight of some-

One of those Lollard notices

thing pale and square in his hand, like a sheet of parchment. He watched with dawning suspicion as the boy moved to the inner church door. There was a pause and then a sound as of a nail being thumped with a muffled hammer.

Dickon realized without any doubt what was going on. The boy was putting up one of those Lollard notices. As the hammer thudded again he stepped forward and seized him by the shoulder.

The boy let out a startled scream. He wriggled like an eel, but Dickon had him fast. They wrestled, breathing hard, till the next flash of lightning showed up their faces. Dickon exclaimed aloud, for the boy he held was young Lob the fishmonger.

When they had once seen one another the struggle in the darkness was all over. Lob just stood snivelling and sobbing;

he knew that he was outmatched. Dickon held him firmly with one hand while he tore down the parchment with the other. He waited for the storm to show him that he was right. It was exactly like the sheet that he had seen with Master Whittington.

'What are you doing with this, you young fool?' he demanded. 'Don't you know that this is treason and that you can be hung for it?'

The boy's sobs increased. Shaking him in sheer exasperation Dickon thought that never had he known such a little milksop. From the snivelling he picked out something about being 'made to do it'.

'*Who* made you do it?' demanded Dickon. 'It will help you little to talk about "*they*". You'd best tell me all you know; otherwise, storm or no storm, I'll hand you straight over to the Watch. Out with it. Who are *they?*'

'You know them,' sniffed Lob. 'Wolman and Gross and all of them.'

It was the answer that Dickon expected, and the one that he least wanted to hear, for they were *all* involved—Adam and himself and perhaps even Nan.

'How did they *make* you do it? Beat you, I suppose?'

'Yes, but it wasn't only the beating. They said they would turn my mother out to starve unless I did their bidding. No one else would shelter a traitor's widow.'

Dickon frowned in the darkness. A traitor's widow? This was growing more and more complicated.

'I suppose you are all Lollards,' he said, 'the alchemist and the taverner and all the lot of you. What goes on at the *Green Falcon?* Come on, you had better tell me everything. It is your only chance.'

'I don't know what goes on,' whimpered the boy. 'Wolman took us in after my father was killed. I don't know anything save that Wolman gives me these parchments and tells me where I am to fasten them, under pain of a knotted rope and my mother thrown out into the kennels.'

'But you're a fishmonger apprentice,' argued Dickon, greatly puzzled. 'The Fishmongers are a proud Company. How came they to sign on such a little——' He had been going to say 'such a little worm' but he checked himself; apparently the boy had *some* feelings, so he said instead: 'such a little traitor?'

Lob suddenly spoke with a shadow of pride. 'They took me

for my father's sake,' he said. 'My father was a fishmonger, and a freeman of the Company. He was made prisoner after Old-castle's rising last year. He was one of Oldcastle's captains and he suffered death for it. They stuck his head over the Drawbridge Gate.'

Dickon felt as though someone had struck him a blow. He took his hands off Lob and clenched them.

'The Drawbridge Gate?' he repeated faintly. 'Is it there now?'

'It was,' said the boy bitterly. 'But someone has thrown it into the river and we know not what has become of it.'

Dickon's brain was in a whirl. This surpassed his wildest dreams. It was a tangle devised by the devil. Wolman and the alchemist both knew that *he* had stolen the head. At least they had been merciful enough not to tell Lob.

One thing was certain. His lips were now sealed. After he had done *that* to Lob and his mother, he could not send the boy to the gallows. He tried to steady himself enough to bid Lob be-gone quickly, and forget that he had ever seen him. But before he could find his voice, Lob gripped him by the arm and pulled him farther back into the darkness.

'Quiet!' he whispered. 'Someone is coming.'

Though it was still pouring with rain and the roadway was a muddy river, the storm had grown less. The newcomers were unhurried and made no attempt at silence. Two pairs of feet clumped and splashed up the street with the uneven thumping of two bill staves, and the dancing yellow light of two swinging lanterns. It was the Watch.

The watchmen were talking cheerfully together, despite the weather, and it seemed as if they would pass by. But just as they drew level with the church one of them suggested taking shelter for a while. The rain might cease presently. There were no rogues in the streets tonight. No one without webbed feet would be out of his bed in such weather.

They stepped into the porch, stood their lanterns on the ground and straightway turned and faced out to the street again, one tall man and one short, standing right in the entrance, oblivi-ous of the two boys pressed into the darkest corner.

Dickon and Lob, united by disaster, gripped one another's arms. Dickon could feel Lob trembling uncontrollably. He himself was feeling frightened. Quite apart from the beating which would be a certainty if he were caught, he hadn't yet made up his mind what he was going to do about all this treason. It was no doubt his duty to reveal it. But how about Lob? It might mean death for Lob, and he couldn't get over the horror of that business about the head on the Bridge. And how about Wolman and the alchemist? They had been good to him when he was in a tight corner. And how about Adam? Of course Adam had nothing to do with treason or Lollardy, but all the same

The Watchmen . . . taking shelter

he had been strangely secret about his visits to the *Green Falcon* and awkward questions might be asked. Turning all these things over in his mind, he held himself rigid, scarcely daring to breathe, while the two watchmen talked about cock-fighting and worked out the odds on a certain game cockerel which was to try its spurs on Michaelmas day.

One had just remarked to the other that the rain was stopping when all of a sudden Lob sneezed. The watchmen looked round.

The lantern

'By cock and pie, there's somebody there,' cried the short man. 'Hey, Giles, bring a light.'

They both grasped their staves and lifted their lanterns. There was a sudden flurry. Without a breath of warning Lob made a dash for it. Before Dickon could collect his wits the boy had slipped like a dark shadow behind the backs of the Watchmen and vanished into the street.

'Hey, what's going on here?' demanded the man called Giles, holding his light aloft. 'I can see you, my lad. Just you come out and account for yourself.'

Dickon stepped forward where the beam of the lantern fell full upon him. He realized that it was best to make no mystery of it.

'I did but shelter from the storm,' he said. 'I lodge outside Cripplegate and I was late for curfew.'

'Mercer apprentice, eh?' The watchman moved his lantern up and down to have a good look at him. 'Well, you know that to wander the City at night unlit is against the law; but still, this is no ordinary night, and doubtless your master will deal with you when you go in.'

Suddenly the smaller man stooped and picked up something from the floor.

'Hey, what's this?' he exclaimed. 'Bring the lantern nearer, Giles, that I may look.'

Dickon went suddenly cold. In the excitement of all that had happened since, he had completely forgotten the parchment. He glanced quickly round. Could he bolt for it, as Lob had done? But the watchmen stood squarely in front of him. After one glance at the notice the big man grasped him firmly by the shoulder.

'So ho! my lad,' he cried triumphantly, 'we've caught you red-handed. Late for curfew, eh? You'll be late for every curfew save one after this. This is what we've been waiting for. 'Twas truly the blessed saints who brought us here.'

Dickon panicked. 'It wasn't I,' he cried, ''Twas the other boy—the one who ran away. Did you not see him? I was sheltering here when he came, and I took it from him as he nailed it to the door.'

'Other boy?' growled the watchman. 'I saw no other boy; did you, comrade? Nay, you young villain, you won't escape that way. What other boy was it? Tell us his name.'

Dickon hesitated. Even in his own dire necessity he could not bring himself to betray Lob.

'I know not his name,' he declared. It was true. Lob was only a nickname and he knew no other.

The smaller man in the meanwhile was poking about on the floor. He straightened his back.

'See you here!' he cried. 'The oaf has condemned himself. If he had not spoken of it I should not have looked for this.'

He held something out in the light of the lantern. It was the hammer.

'That is enough,' declared his companion. 'We need no more than that. Into the Compter prison with him till morning. Then he can tell his tale to others than us.' He produced a piece of cord, with which he prepared to bind Dickon's wrists. Dickon began to struggle.

'You cannot take me,' he cried. 'This is a church. I claim Sanctuary. You cannot take me here.'

The watchman began to laugh. 'Hold him firmly, Giles. You young fool, you are a few yards out of your reckoning. The porch is not Sanctuary until you reach the church door and grasp it. And if you did get into the church what would you do? Sit like a sparrow asking to be fed for forty days till your right of Sanctuary was over, or quit the country marked with a cross? What sort of food would your kinsmen bring, think you? It would be served with a thick stick, I'll be bound. Now be a good lad and come quietly. If your story is true you'll be free soon enough.'

Without further ado they bound his arms behind him, and each taking an end of the rope, stepped out into Wood Street.

He was alone

Chapter Eighteen

'ANSWER ME THIS'

THE Compter in Bread Street where they put him for the night was a noisome prison; not so noisome as Newgate, which was so foul that few who lodged in it survived, but more filthy and evil-smelling than any place Dickon had ever seen. He passed the remaining hours of darkness in a stone cell with half a dozen poor creatures, the dregs of the gutter, whom he saw only for a second by the light of the lantern but whom he heard and smelled all night. At dawn he was taken to the beadle to give his name and the name of his master. As he hoped, the mention of Richard Whittington helped him, for instead of being thrust back into the general prison, he was put by himself in a small cell. It was cleaner and it had a barred window through which the fresh air blew. Here, a couple of hours later, Will Appleyard came to him.

The mercer was cold and suspicious. He told Dickon that the matter was far too grave to be dealt with off-hand. The beadle had ordered that Dickon should be brought before the Mayor at once, but he had begged that they might wait for the return of Master Whittington who was out of London. He asked Dickon no questions, telling him only that he must abide where he

was, in solitude, that he would
send food to him and a change
of hose. He also gave him a
string of Paternoster beads and
bade him pass his time in prayer
and penance. Dickon found
the advice frightening. He
asked if he were to be hanged,
to which Will Appleyard replied simply 'Not without trial,
and not till Master Whittington comes.'

Food sent in

For a whole day and another long night he was alone. At
first he felt that he would go mad. Surely Grandfather would
come as soon as he heard of it, and though he dreaded the conse-
quences when Grandfather found him in prison, nevertheless he
watched the door eagerly, unable to believe that nobody would
visit him.

Food arrived at intervals for him to eat, good food, sent in
from Grub Street; and a sack of straw for him to lie on. After a
while he became calmer. The man who brought his meals
informed him that Master Whittington would be back on the
morrow and then he would be brought before the Mayor.

He had plenty of time to think things out and settle upon his
story. At first he resolved to confess all, hold nothing back, but
throw himself upon Master Whittington's mercy. But presently he decided against it. He had no right to clear himself by
condemning others. There was Lob to be considered. He had a
duty to defend Lob because for his own purpose to put himself
right with Bladebone and the mercers, he had done this terrible
thing to Lob. Whatever else he said, he must stick to his story
that the parchment was carried by an unknown boy whose face he
did not see.

Then there was Adam. He had promised Adam, and Adam's
name must not be brought into it. That was more difficult still,
for he now knew for certain that the *Green Falcon* was a nest of
Lollards. But if the *Green Falcon* was once mentioned it would
never be possible to keep Adam out of it. Therefore he must
be silent about the *Green Falcon*.

On one point at least he had made up his mind. After this,
come what may, he would shun the *Green Falcon* like the plague,
and see that Adam did so too. Adam did not really care about

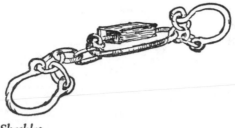

Shackles

the Panacea any more, now that he was away. If the truth were told, it was the alchemist who was so anxious about it. It was the alchemist who made such a fuss about the Silver Steel. The idea crossed his mind that perhaps the alchemist really wanted the stuff for himself and was making use of Adam to get it. Well, he should not have it. There was going to be an end to the whole business. He had sent a message to Wat, the journeyman, to keep the Silver Steel when it arrived, and it should not go to Southwark at all. As soon as he got out of here he would see to it.

As soon as he got out! That was the rub. *How* was he to get out if he could not tell the truth about anything without giving somebody away? He made good uses of Will Appleyard's Paternoster beads, and did more praying than he had ever done in his life before. He would need all the help he could get if he was to come safely out of this without betraying anybody or telling desperate lies which would endanger his own soul.

On the morning of the second day Master Appleyard came to his cell and told him to prepare himself. He would be charged in the Mayor's court, but Master Whittington was back in London and would see him first.

With his hands in shackles, a constable on one side of him and Will Appleyard on the other, Dickon was marched across Cheap, in full view of everybody, and up Milk Street to the new Guildhall.

There was a small knot of offenders gathered outside, guarded by constables with staves. One by one they vanished into the Mayor's presence and emerged again, sentenced either to the pillory or the stocks.

Dickon did not have long to wait. A beadle came and whispered to Master Appleyard, and he was led away to the side of the building, and in through a small door.

The door opened into a room where Master Whittington, alone, sat writing.

He looked up as they came in and nodded to Appleyard and the constable.

'Unshackle the prisoner and then you can leave us,' he said briefly.

For some minutes there was complete silence except for the scratching of Master Whittington's quill. Then Madame Eglantine emerged from under her master's stool, trotted across to Dickon and rubbed herself against his legs. Dickon half stooped to stroke her, but thought better of it, and Master Whittington, roused by her purring, looked up at last.

This was not Dick Whittington, as Dickon knew him. He saw instead a stern-faced man, with cold blue eyes, a set mouth tightly pressed, and all the lines of laughter and compassion changed into cold determination. For several seconds he stared Dickon straight in the face without uttering a word.

'Well,' he began at last. 'What have you to say?'

Dickon's throat felt swollen. He swallowed and tried to speak, but no sound would come.

From a small coffer on the table Master Whittington drew out the sheet of parchment that Lob had left in the church porch.

'You are charged,' he said slowly, 'with having in your possession, with intent to fasten to the door of the Church of St. Michael in Wood Street, this foul and seditious plea to the citizens of London. I know and you know that you have seen its like before. What is your answer to this charge?'

Dickon once more tried to speak. His voice sounded croaky and strange but he got the words out, and after he had made a beginning it came more easily.

'I was sheltering in the porch from the storm,' he began, 'and a strange boy came in and began to nail the parchment to the door.' He went on with his statement, slowly and carefully, just as he had rehearsed it to himself in his cell. It was all true except that he left out everything that Lob had told him, but it was so careful that even to himself it sounded thin and unreal.

Master Whittington heard him in complete silence. He continued to stare at Dickon for several seconds after the story was finished. Then he took up his pen and went on writing, while Dickon shifted his weight from one foot to the other. Surely Master Whittington did not really believe that he was guilty?

'I am not a traitor, sir,' he gulped, his voice cracking on the words.

Master Whittington heard him in silence

Still Richard Whittington did not answer. But he laid down his pen and lifted the lid of the coffer once more. From it he drew out a shoe. It was battered and dirty, but it was still red, and round the top hung the fringe of loops that had once given Dickon so much pleasure.

'If my memory serves me you wore this shoe the day I took you as apprentice,' said Master Whittington. 'Is it yours?'

He held it out to Dickon who made no effort to take it.

'Where did they find it?' he asked in a whisper.

'Nay. You shall tell me. Where did you lose it?'

Dickon let forth an enormous sigh. It was almost a relief that the truth was out.

'Was it under the Bridge?' he breathed.

This time Master Whittington did not deny him an answer. '*On* the Bridge,' he corrected. 'It was found under a bundle of faggots within the archway of the Stone Gate. It was lost there by the felon who stole the head of one of the Lollard traitors.'

'I did not know then whose head it was,' cried Dickon eagerly. 'I did not know whose it was till'—he stopped himself in time and finished tamely—'till I was told.'

'Who told you?' rapped Whittington.

'I heard it talked of afterwards. Everyone was talking of it.' That was a narrow escape.

Whittington folded his arms and leaning them on the table searched Dickon's face for several seconds before he asked the next question.

'Where is the head now?'

Dickon looked back at him in genuine astonishment. 'I know not,' he said. 'I did not take it. It fell in the river. The pole was too heavy. I could not hold it.'

'It fell, doubtless; but there was someone below to receive it.'

Dickon shook his head. 'No one. I was alone.'

Whittington banged the table with his fist. 'Don't tell lies, boy. It will be the worse for you if you do. They could not have put you to carry it out alone. Obviously there was a boat waiting underneath. I shall have the truth I promise you, so you had best tell me at once. Who bade you do this? Who was in the plot with you?'

Dickon's eyes widened. 'There was no plot,' he declared. 'There was none other but me. It was a challenge—a trial by ordeal, they called it.'

'Who called it?'

'The mercer prentices. It was because I was a grocer and I had to do it instead of fighting Kurt Bladebone. He is a big——'

'I know Kurt Bladebone,' Whittington interrupted sharply. 'Go on.'

It seemed to Dickon that the blue eyes were not quite so cold nor the thin mouth so tightly set. He told his story slowly and carefully, but careful as he was Master Whittington interrupted him repeatedly, asking rapid questions, checking every detail.

He went on steadily until he came to the part where he was lying under the faggots.

'Ah,' said Whittington triumphantly. 'That is where they found the shoe. And then the gates were opened and you escaped. Do you realize, you young blusterer, that it was my nephew whose coming saved you? The patterns that God weaves are more intricate than any of our devising, but every tiny thread is interlaced for a purpose. Neglect not to give Him thanks. Had you been taken then, red-handed, they might have strung you up forthwith.' He gave a great sigh and almost smiled at Dickon. Then he grew grave again. 'There is one more thing that I must know. Who proposed this task to you? Think carefully. What are their names? It is your duty to tell me.'

Dickon considered in silence for a moment. Beyond Owen and Bladebone he knew no names. But there had been several big boys in the group whence the idea came. He tried to describe them. While Master Whittington was writing down what he said he remembered that this was the second time that he had been asked the same question. The taverner had wanted to know too.

Master Whittington threw down his pen at last. '"Tis dumbfounding,' he said. 'But upon my soul I believe you. They have made a tool of you. There were quick wits at work among those apprentices to seize an opportunity. They might have got their head with no peril to themselves and with only you to hang for it.'

Dickon ventured a question. 'But why should they want a head? What good would it have done them?'

Whittington smiled a little grimly. 'Use your wits. Have you never walked in a procession of Holy Relics? Know you not the devotion with which the people will follow a fragment of the True Cross or the bones of one of the blessed saints? What think you then would be the value to these Lollards of the head of one whom they could claim died for their new religion? They would suppress it that the man was executed for treason against the realm. To possess a martyr, true or feigned, is the ambition of every leader of rebellion. Such a relic might easily rally the City to revolution. Well, I know now where to look; I know where the rats run in one little corner anyway. When the need comes I can spring the trap.' He stood up and for the first time looked at Dickon with his old kindliness. 'Methinks your folly has been sufficiently punished. How long were you in the Compter? Two nights? Then we will add no more to it. The charge against you shall be withdrawn. You may go home. Your grandfather, by the way, knows naught of all this. I have been at pains to keep it secret. Now we will tell him that you have been falsely accused of nailing a Lollard notice to a door. The Bridge need not be mentioned. Wait here for me a Pater-noster-while. I must report to the Mayor. Then I will come with you.'

He went out of the room leaving Dickon dazed. Madame Eglantine trotted after her master, but finding the door closed returned to Dickon. He picked her up and stroked her. Master Whittington had spoken of one miracle, but did he only know it there was also a second. His questions had ceased at the most critical point. He had inquired nothing of what had happened to Dickon after he escaped from the Bridge Gate. The truth was, of course, that he was not concerned about how Dickon got home. It was the Lollard head which was his problem. But whatever the cause the end was the same. Lob was safe and the *Green Falcon* was not mentioned.

Chapter Nineteen

SILVER STEEL

NEVERTHELESS as he walked from the Guildhall to Dowgate with Master Whittington Dickon was not happy.

He wished to goodness that he had told his godfather everything. Even now he had half a mind to do so. But once told it could not be untold. Lob might go to his death, and Adam get into serious trouble. Of course it was absurd to think that Adam really had anything to conceal, but on the whole it was better to hold his tongue.

On the way Master Whittington told him the news from France: that Harfleur was proving a harder nut to crack than the King had expected; that nephew Guy had come to arrange for money and supplies, and would still be in London for a few days more; that Adam was making quite a name for himself with his doctoring. All this Dickon knew already, but his godfather was obviously talking cheerfully to make him forget his troubles and he was grateful.

At Grantham's Inn there was a great outcry when his tale was told. Grandfather's bushy brows met in a frown and he started growling like a storm about to break. But Richard Whittington restrained him. Dickon was not to blame, he insisted. The boy had been late for curfew, but for that small crime he had received more than his measure of punishment. It had been a terrible ordeal for him to spend all that time unfriended in the Compter. So Grandfather relented and poured Dickon a cup of wine, and Aunt Isabel could not make enough fuss of him. Nan hovered on the outskirts, hopping like an eager sparrow. Dickon guessed that Nan had something she wanted to say, but he could endure no more until after dinner.

He was excused from waiting at table, and Aunt Isabel saw to it that all the titbits were put on to his plate. As a crowning grace Master Whittington told him that he might stay at home till Monday—three whole days—to recover from his adventure. When the meal was finished, he strolled down to the river feeling

The Hanse ship came through the bridge

well fed and comfortable. With a flurry of skirts and pattering feet, Nan came racing after him.

'I wanted to see you,' she panted. 'What think you has happened? The Silver Steel has come, and I have sent it to the alchemist.'

Dickon swung round. 'You have done *what*?'

'I've sent it to Master Gross. I promised Adam. Don't you remember?' She sounded triumphant. 'The Hanse ship came up on the tide yesterday. I saw her come through the Bridge. So I got Wat to go to the shipmaster and ask for the stuff Adam had ordered. There was scarce an hour's delay. It was quite a small pack, and I took it to Jenkyn. He was plying his boat at Dowgate....' Her voice tailed away as she saw Dickon's face.

'You meddlesome little lack-wit,' cried Dickon savagely. 'Did I not tell you that *I* would see to it?'

Nan stared at him, her lower lip quivering. 'Yes, but I thought you would not be home again till Sunday. You said that you were going to take it to Master Gross so that he could finish Adam's Panacea. I thought it would help.'

'I had changed my mind,' said Dickon. 'I have learned things since I said that.' He stopped. It would not be wise to trust his whole secret to Nan, so he told her only part. 'I am not sure that the alchemist is to be trusted. He may not be going to send it to Adam at all.'

'Oh, but he *is*,' Nan broke in eagerly. 'Jenkyn said that Master Gross was fairly *smitten* with joy, and he vowed that Adam should have it before the next moon.'

Dickon sighed heavily. He was tired, and this new development was quite beyond him. Perhaps it was all right after all. And anyway he was being unfair to Nan. How could she possibly know? To make up for it he changed the subject, asked questions about her doings and told her stories about some of the wonderful silks and damasks he had seen, and the great ladies who had gowns made from them. He even went so far as to let her show him her embroidery, and the linen, woven from thread of her own spinning, which was to be the beginning of her dower-chest.

On the Sunday Guy Whittington came to dinner and Dickon hung on his every word. He had plenty to tell, not only about Adam, but about the voyage, about the landing on French soil, and about the guns which the English were using to besiege Harfleur, great monsters such as the world had never seen before. They were made at the foundry by the Tower; they belched foul smoke and hurled stone cannon balls a full fifty yards. The gunners all gave their guns different names; one was called simply 'London'; a second was 'The Messenger' and another 'The King's Daughter'.

When dinner was finished and the Whittingtons, uncle and nephew, had gone home to prepare for Guy's journey back to France on the morrow, Grandfather took *The Canterbury Tales* and Aunt Isabel took the *Lives of the Saints* and withdrew each to their own bedchamber, in fact to enjoy a comfortable nap. Dickon went down as usual to the wharf and sat with his legs dangling, gazing at the ships in a happy dream of future voyages, for at dinner, in front of everybody, Master Whittington had promised him that if he settled down and worked well he might soon begin to serve his apprenticeship to the Merchant Venturers, and even go as apprentice clerk with one of the merchants visiting the Flanders cloth fair.

He remembered the day that he had sat there miserable because he was to be a mercer. So much had happened since then. He looked at the Bridge. Was it really only a week ago that he had struggled with the pole on the top of the Drawbridge Gate? He counted the little black dots stuck on their pike staves. There was still one missing from the end. How long, he wondered grimly, would the place remain empty? Master Whittington had said at dinner that everything depended on the war in France. If the King's armies covered themselves with glory the people in their joy would forget Oldcastle, and the Lollards and all the traitors working underground. But if there were disasters in France, then probably the trouble would come bubbling up, with riots and murders, just as there had been years ago, under Wat Tyler, when Master Whittington was young.

He was getting quite sleepy sitting there in the September sunshine when he heard Nan's voice behind him and looked round. She had just emerged from Grantham's lane leading by the hand a poor woman in patched and threadbare clothes, who was weeping bitterly.

'Dickon,' she cried, 'a dreadful thing has happened. Lob is at the point of death. Your mercers set upon him. They have all but killed him.'

Dickon scrambled to his feet. 'Where is he?' he cried. 'How did it happen? Who did it?'

'It was that red-haired knave again. This is Lob's mother. She came to tell us and to bring this.'

She thrust a sealed packet into Dickon's hand. He did not look at it. His mind was too full of Lob.

'Where is he?' he asked again. 'What can I do?'

The woman shook her head. 'He lies at the Domus Dei, the hospital of our Blessed Lady outside Bishopsgate. Perchance he may live. I beg you pray for him.'

Dickon spluttered with anger. 'That black villain Kurt. I'll make him pay for this.'

'Nay,' said the woman wiping her eyes on her hanging sleeve, 'you must not suffer more for Lob. You have done yourself

enough injury already to save him. He told me of it. If he is
spared I shall take him away. I was born in Oxfordshire among
the sheepfolds. We will go back there. It matters not how we
live so long as we leave this dreadful City. It took my husband
and now it is likely to take my son.' She began to cry again.

Nan patted her. 'Nay, do not cry,' she begged. 'He will
not die. We will all pray. I'm sure he will not die.'

'You are good,' said Lob's mother, 'and I would not make
you sad. I did not come for that; but he would not rest till I
promised to find you, because he was on an errand for your
brother.'

'For my brother?' repeated Dickon.

For the first time he looked down at the packet in his hand.
It was of pared sheepskin folded flat and sealed. There was

The Domus Dei outside Bishopsgate

writing on it. He read it aloud. '"To the Master Adam Sherwood in the Train of Master Guy Whittington with the King's
Grace's Army in France. By the Hand of Jean Josey, Shipman,
of Wapping."'

'What is it?' he asked, though even as he said the words he
already knew.

'I know not,' she said. 'Master Gross gave it to Lob and told
him to put it into the hands of a shipman named Josey, at the sign
of The *Crab* in Wapping. The packet was safe in his shirt when
he was attacked just inside Aldgate. He could not rest till I had
brought it to you that you may take it to Wapping in his stead.'

Dickon turned the packet over thoughtfully. 'At Wapping,'
he said softly. The word conjured up a picture of dreary mud
flats and gibbets with creaking chains. He shook his head.

'You had best take it back to Master Gross,' he said firmly.
'I can do nothing with it.'

'I cannot take it back,' she said. 'Master Gross is not there. The tavern is closed. They have all gone.'

'Gone? Where have they gone?'

'I know not,' she said. 'It all happened yesterday without warning. I was at work carrying water when they told me they were going away. Master Gross gave Lob the packet and Master Wolman gave me some money for my needs till I could get other work. They did not say

Nan's money-jar

where they were going. The *Green Falcon* is shuttered. I went there last night but I could not get in. They let me sleep at the hospital where Lob is. If I cannot lie there tonight I shall go to the Compter.'

'Nay,' cried Dickon. 'That you must not do. Nan, take her to Aunt Isabel. She will know what to do.'

Nan nodded vigorously. 'Come along,' she said, taking the woman's arm. 'I have some money saved up in my money-jar. You shall have it all.' She glanced over her shoulder at Dickon. 'You will not go till I come back?' she begged.

'You need not fear,' he replied. 'I shall not go.'

When she returned they had a hammer-and-tongs argument. Dickon declared that nothing would induce him to take the packet to Wapping. He did not like the whole business. He had never liked it. If he had got his way the Silver Steel would never have reached the alchemist at all. And now they had all fled, which made it more suspicious than ever. He would have nothing to do with it.

Nan replied hotly that he was a chicken-heart. *She* had sent the Silver Steel because Adam had wanted it to go, and she had been perfectly right. Here was the proof of it. Obviously this packet must be the Panacea, though it was very small to cause so much fuss. Master Gross had said that he would send it to Adam and here it was. What did it matter that the people at the *Green Falcon* had gone away? It was Adam who mattered.

Dickon gaped at her. Never had he heard Nan speak like this before. If she had been a boy he would have knocked her down. It was all he could do not to box her ears. Instead he became the heavy older brother, and told her that she was only a little girl and these were matters that she did not understand.

Come what may he was not going to give this packet to some
unknown pirate at Wapping. He had rather that Adam never
got it at all. Nan wept with rage. Dickon pushed the packet
into his pouch and was just about to leave the wharf when she
called him back.

'I've got an idea,' she declared a little sulkily. 'I will take it
to Master Guy. He rides tomorrow. He could carry it to
Adam.'

Dickon considered. He could have kicked himself for not
thinking of ·o simple a solution. Of course there might be
questions abou.t the *Green Falcon*; the whole business might come
out; but that could not be helped. It had all become so complicated that it would be almost a relief to be quit of it, whatever
the cost.

'If it will set your mind at rest we will *both* take it,' he said at
last, trying to sound casual. 'But, mark you, if there are any
questions *I* am going to answer them. Unless you promise to
hold your peace you shall not come.'

She became meek at once. 'I won't say a word that you don't
want me to say,' she promised, 'if you only will let me carry it.'

The steward at the house in The Royal told them that Master
Whittington and his nephew were in Master Whittington's bed-
chamber. He advised them to knock at the door.

Master Whittington's voice bade them enter.

The big bed with its testor and its curtains gaily striped stood
well away from the window, which was open into the sunny
garden. Master Whittington was throwing crumbs of manchet
bread to his white pigeons outside, while his nephew sat at his
ease on a cushioned stool, back to the wall, with Madame
Eglantine upon his knee.

Nan began forthwith by producing the package and asking
Guy Whittington if of his great goodness he would take it to
Adam.

Master Guy said yes at once, and held out his hand. He
read the address and then looked up surprised. 'This is not your
script, little mistress? Nay, I thought not. And who is Master
Josey of Wapping?'

Dick Whittington left the window and looked over his
nephew's shoulder. '"By the hand of Jean Josey, Shipman, of
Wapping,"' he read. 'What is all this, child, and who sends it?'

Nan completely forgot her promise. 'It is the cure that

Adam invented,' she babbled, before Dickon could speak. 'Lob was to carry it to Wapping but those vile mercers set on him and nearly killed him. He is in the Domus Dei about to die.'

Master Whittington frowned. 'What vile mercers and who is Lob? Speak up, my poppet; there has been too much brawling lately.'

'Lob is a poor fishmonger prentice. He is the one that Dickon saved on the wharf. And now they have nearly killed him.'

'Ah!' said Master Whittington as if he saw daylight. 'Then

Master Whittington's bed

the vile mercers are Kurt Bladebone and his friends I suppose. Upon my soul I have had enough of this. I'll have that young ruffian in the pillory this time. Now let me see this packet again. You have not told me yet who sends it?'

'It is Adam's cure,' she answered quickly. 'Master Gross the alchemist is sending it.'

'*Master Gross*,' repeated Whittington. 'Master Gross who lodges in Southwark? And what has Adam to do with Master Gross?'

Still without giving Dickon a chance to speak, Nan plunged ahead, all about the alchemist who said that Adam was wonderful and Adam who had made something called a Panacea, only it wasn't finished because some stuff hadn't come from Germany, and about herself because she had sent the stuff to Master Gross at the *Green Falcon*. . . . She stopped out of breath and Master Whittington, whose face was cold and tense, shook his head and turned to Dickon.

'Master Gross: the *Green Falcon*: the *Crab* at Wapping. I would hear more of this. Dickon, you had better make it plain. Leave nothing out, mark you. I would hear everything.'

Trying to keep his wits about him Dickon took up the story. But to pick and choose what he would say and what he would leave out was a sorry hope. His godfather's eye was upon him as it had been at the Guildhall. Question followed question till all was told—the alchemist, the Panacea, the Hanse merchant, the Silver Steel, the visits to Southwark, Wolman the taverner, even to a confession about taking refuge at the *Green Falcon* after his escape from the Bridge.

'I had suspected,' said Master Whittington grimly, 'that when I questioned you about the Bridge I heard only half the story. Now, by your leave, we will have the rest. To begin with did you tell me the truth when you said that it was for the prentices' challenge that you planned this deed, or was it for your friends at the *Green Falcon*?'

Dickon shook his head vigorously. 'Nay, they knew naught of it until I told them afterwards.'

'Ah! You told them. You know, I suppose, that they are all Lollards of the most dangerous sort?'

'I did not know then—not till I heard it from Lob.' He could have bitten out his tongue, but it was too late. Master Whittington pounced on it.

'Lob? When did Lob tell you?' Dickon, white to the roots of his hair, kept a stony silence. His godfather glared at him. 'Out with it, now. When did Lob tell you? . . . Ah, methinks I see daylight. Was it Lob by any chance who brought the notice to the church porch?'

It was hopeless to keep it up any longer. Dickon just nodded. Master Whittington looked puzzled.

'I do not understand it yet,' he said. 'You assured me that *you* were no Lollard. Is that indeed true? Then why in Heaven's name should you protect that boy who is a bare-faced young traitor? You went to the Compter because you would not reveal who he was. You might have suffered pillory or worse! Why did you shield him? What hold had he over you?'

Dickon looked at him dumbly. There was nothing for it but complete truth. 'Because it was his father's head that I threw in to the river——'

Now it was Master Whittington's turn to be struck speechless. He just stared at Dickon.

'His father's head,' he repeated at last. '*His father's head.* . . . Then he is the son of the rebel Lyte, the fishmonger, and he lives with his mother in that nest of rebels. They have made him their scapegoat. I see it all. Well, poor hapless woman, she has suffered enough. We will let the boy be. But methinks it is time that we joined issue with the *Green Falcon.*'

Dickon shook his head. 'They have all gone. Lob's mother told us. They turned her adrift and went yesterday.'

Master Whittington actually whistled. 'Nephew, do you hear that? They have sent this letter and then fled; shot their arrow and vanished before it can come to earth and reveal them.' He held up the packet. 'What think you that we shall find in here?'

Guy Whittington grinned as he scratched Madame Eglantine under the chin. 'I'd stake my life that there will be more in it than some simple remedy for the ague.'

'It will be filled with writing,' Master Whittington prophesied. 'Adam will find himself with messages to deliver, though it is hard to think that he could be such a simpleton.' He broke the seal and unfolded the soft skin. Within was another packet also sealed. There was writing on that too, small crabbed writing. He put on his spectacles to read it.

'"Deliver to Thomas Bason of the King's Guard."' He looked at his nephew. 'So it is not intended for Adam at all,' he said. 'Adam's name is but a blind. I'll admit I had not thought of that. We will examine it with all care. I warrant we will find it as full of sedition as a dog is of fleas.'

But Guy Whittington was not listening. 'Thomas Bason,' he said thoughtfully. ''Tis familiar. Where have I heard that name before? "Thomas Bason".'

'I know Thomas Bason,' Dickon volunteered timidly. 'He was the soldier at the *Green Falcon* on the day I went there first. He was from the West Country and served with my Lord

Scrope.' He stopped dead. Surely Scrope was one of those three conspirators. He had never connected it until now.

'Scrope?' barked Whittington, and stopped; for his nephew stood up suddenly, spilling Madame Eglantine on to the floor.

'I have it,' he cried and turned to Dickon. 'Is he a pockmarked knave, with a scar across his face? Ah, I am right. Good uncle, Bason is Herefordshire born, bred near Solers Hope. We were brats together. He was then *Oldcastle's* man.'

'Of a truth he picks his company,' said Master Whittington, deadly calm. 'Oldcastle and Scrope; he could hardly go further. Well, let us discover what tidings are sent to him from the *Green Falcon.*'

With great care he prised up the seal and unfolded the parchment. But within there was no sheet of writing as he had prophesied. The innermost wrapper contained only a tuft of sheep's wool. He teased it gently apart and drew from it a little metal phial which he held out in the palm of his hand.

'By all the saints, it *is* the Panacea,' exclaimed Guy Whittington.

His uncle slowly shook his head. 'I'll venture that you have not heard of this substance Silver Steel,' he said. ''Tis rare enough. As it happens Drew Barentin the goldsmith told me of it. 'Tis found in the silver mines in Saxony. Metal smiths use it. But it is perilous stuff—little crystals of arsenic in some unusually pure form.'

'All that is moonshine to me,' rejoined his nephew. 'Young Adam must be a learned fellow.'

Master Whittington carefully spread a sheet of parchment on the table and laid the phial upon it. Then, as if he had suddenly thought of something, he picked up Madame Eglantine, bore her to a coffer in the corner of the room, lifted the lid and dropped her inside. There, in spite of her muffled mewing, he left her, out of harm's way.

'Now we will see,' he said grimly.

With the utmost care he unstoppered the little phial and shook a few grains of powder on to the parchment. The others watched him, scarcely daring to breathe as he took a fragment of manchet bread, rolled it into a pellet and dipped it into the powder. Then he crossed to the window and dropped the pellet on to the sill.

Almost at once one of the white pigeons came fluttering down and gobbled it up. Hardly was the morsel swallowed than the bird gave a screech. It flung itself into the air, beat once with its wings, and fell to the ground, dead.

'Holy Saints!' cried Guy Whittington. His uncle looked at him.

'Do you mark it?' he said slowly. 'Thomas Bason *of the King's Guard.*'

Banners of the King's army

Chapter Twenty

THE TRIUMPH

SWORN to secrecy Dickon and Nan crept home in scared silence. Not a word of all this must be breathed to a soul, Master Whittington had warned them, and they scarcely spoke to each other until they reached the wharf. Then, their heads close together, they went through the whole story in awestruck whispers. Nan would not be happy till Dickon had told her everything. Feeling thoroughly humbled, he kept nothing back. Nan's little cries of wonder about his bravery on the Bridge and his nobility in going to prison in Lob's place were a salve to his wounded pride.

At Grantham's Inn they found that Aunt Isabel had not been idle. She had been to the hospital with Lob's mother and learned that Lob was better. With care he would recover. So she had visited the good nuns at St. Helen's Priory in Bishopsgate, conveniently near the hospital, and they had promised the poor woman shelter in their nunnery till her boy was fit for the journey to Oxfordshire.

At dawn on the following day Dickon went back to Cripple-gate. It seemed a lifetime since he had left there to copy a page of ledger at Master Whittington's house. All the apprentices seemed to know that Master Appleyard had been called to visit him in the Compter, and everyone crowded round to hear his story. But he told them only that he had been caught by the Watch during the thunderstorm and cast into prison upon a false charge. Very soon they all forgot about him in a wave of fresh excitement. The news spread like wildfire that Kurt Bladebone had been arrested for half killing a fishmonger brat. Kurt was

Kurt was sentenced to the pillory

sentenced to an hour in the pillory on Cornhill at the most crowded time of day, and stood raised high above the heads of the crowd to be pelted with stale fish and bad eggs by the prentice fishmongers and grocers whom he had bullied for so long. Even his fellow mercers flocked to peep at him with very little sympathy. Dickon would not go with them. He was heartily sick of the whole business.

In the prentices' club Kurt's kingship fell with his pride. One or two of his old companions stuck to him, but the younger lads rallied in a mass to Dickon's side. The Bridge episode was still on everyone's lips, though whispered behind a screen of hands, and gradually the true story of the church porch and the Compter leaked out. It even became known that Dickon had gone to prison because he would not betray Lob. Some said that Dickon was a fool to have suffered all that to save a fish boy, but they were not many. With most of his fellows he found himself a bit of a hero.

But there were questions on his mind that spoiled his enjoyment of his new popularity. He wondered what had happened about Wolman and the alchemist. How about Thomas Bason of the King's Guard? And above all how about Adam? Would there be trouble for Adam because of his dealings with the *Green Falcon*? Nan, who had spoken with Jenkyn, told him that the constables had been to examine the tavern, but it was still empty and nobody knew what had become of its late occupants.

As for Master Whittington he seldom saw him. He was not sent for to come to the house in The Royal any more and if he occasionally met his godfather at Grantham's Inn or in the street, or watched him from a distance in church, he received no more than a casual nod in answer to his eager greeting. Dickon's spirits ebbed. He had not realized how much he valued Master Whittington's confidence until, apparently, he had lost it. What a hopeless mess he had made of things. He had little chance now of rising out of the ordinary crowd of apprentices and gaining that longed-for goal, the Company of Merchant Adventurers. Would all his days be spent rolling bales of cloth and crying 'What do you lack?' to gossiping housewives on Cheapside?

A letter from Adam arrived at last, addressed to Grandfather but enclosed in a pouch of documents received by the Mayor. Grandfather summoned Dickon to Grantham's Inn to hear the news; but in truth the letter gave no news about any of the matters which were foremost in Dickon's mind. Adam sounded cheerful enough. His remedies were working wonders, he claimed; but most of them were concoctions of herbs which he had first learned from Goody. He did not mention the Panacea, or the alchemist, or Thomas Bason, or anything connected with them. It was as if his invention had never existed.

But though Adam was cheerful the war news from France was bad. The town of Harfleur stubbornly refused to yield and the King's army suffered week after week from disease and from shortage of food. It was not until a golden September was nearly over that the King himself wrote to the Mayor to announce that Harfleur had at last opened its gates.

Even then things did not improve. The summer was past and the army had not won its promised victory. Londoners who had gladly given their toil and their treasure to the dashing young King were now being asked for still more supplies to face a long winter. There were grumbles everywhere. Lollard notices continued to appear mysteriously on church doors. Whispers crept about the town. The Mayor looked grave and Master Whittington's ready smile vanished. Grandfather, in an expansive moment, confided to Dickon that if matters did not improve soon, there would be a general rising. It was said that Oldcastle was gathering his followers in the west and preparing to march on London. Elderly people who remembered the horrors of the Peasants' Revolt shook their heads.

All through October things grew worse, till all at once, as though by a given signal, a wave of rumours swept across the town. The army had met with disaster. There had been a great battle and everyone was cut to pieces. Nobody knew where these rumours started, yet everyone heard them.

"'Tis treachery that supplies such stories,' said Grandfather gloomily as, with only Dickon for company, he sat sipping his wine after the Sunday dinner. 'They are spread to ferment trouble. The Mayor has no tidings, neither has Master Whittington, nor the King's gracious mother. Yet wherever you go the people have news of disaster. When the cup of despair is full it will overflow and the streets will flow with blood. To-morrow is Mayor's Day. 'Twill be a testing time, for the crowds will be out in the streets like stubble ready for a spark. Upon my soul, boy, I think you shall remain here till the procession is over. I have not Master Whittington's leave to keep you, but I will take it on myself. Maybe I seem chicken-hearted, but I remember Wat Tyler's rabble. If we should have to hold Grantham's Inn against a mob you could be very useful.'

Dickon went to bed with mixed feelings. To stay at home for Mayor's Day was an unexpected joy. The new Mayor, Master Nicholas Wotton, draper, had been chosen two weeks ago with great solemnity after a Mass of the Holy Spirit to beg the guidance of Heaven. Tomorrow, the feast of St. Simon and St. Jude, October 28th, he would take the oath, and later ride in procession to Westminster to visit the shrine of St. Edward the Confessor, with the clergy and the monks and the friars of London's great churches going ahead of him, and all the companies and crafts of the City following after. Mayor's Day procession was one of the best of the year, second only to the torchlight march on St. John's Day.

He was also proud and flattered because Grandfather needed

him for the defence of Grantham's Inn. But the picture of streets running with blood was just a little bit too vivid, and he tossed all night, restless with bad dreams. He woke from a nightmare in which the angry roar of a besieging mob mingled with a mad clatter of bells, and sprang out of bed in a panic. It was true. The bells *were* ringing. It was barely daylight, and yet the whole air was filled with jangling and clanging.

He tore a coverlet from the bed, threw it round his naked body and flung himself down the ladder stair from his attic room. He arrived in the hall at the same time as Aunt Isabel and Nan, both of them wrapped in night-gowns. At the other end the servants with frightened faces huddled together peeping through the screen.

'Your grandsire has gone to see what it is all about,' Aunt Isabel declared, trying to appear very calm and undisturbed. 'Nan, child, your teeth are chattering. Put a cloak about you. There is no need to be frightened. The bells are pealing, not tolling, mark you. Say a prayer that it may be good tidings, not bad.'

It was perfectly true. The bells were ringing a joyful peal, though heard all together they sounded so strange and wild.

Suddenly there were footsteps on the threshold. Grandfather came in, followed by Master Whittington. They were both breathless as though they had been running and each tried to push the other forward, like a pair of schoolboys. In the end it was Master Whittington who spoke first.

'Good people, there is news,' he cried. 'A message has come from our lord the King. By God's grace he has won a great victory on the field of Agincourt.'

The cheering within the hall almost drowned the clatter of the bells. Grandfather stilled it presently with his great booming voice to tell that, by order of the Mayor, the events of the day were to be altered. First the priests in every church, with all who were lettered, would say the *Te Deum* in thanksgiving; and later instead of the usual ride to Westminster, the Mayor and his procession would go on foot to St. Paul's, then on to the Abbey, to show in humility their thanks to God for His mercy.

Sobered by this statement the family began to discuss plans. Dickon, gathering the coverlet more closely round him, tried to slip away and put on some clothes. But suddenly Master Whittington spotted him.

'Hey, boy,' he cried. 'What are you doing here? Who gave you leave to be away from your place of work?'

Neither Dickon nor his grandfather noticed the twinkle in Master Whittington's eye. They both began to offer explanations. He shook his head at them.

'Fret not yourselves. I did but jest,' he laughed, giving Dickon a sharp pinch where the coverlet had slipped. 'A thought has struck me. Since we are to go afoot in procession, I shall need a page to hold up my livery gown. He must of course be a mercer. It is fortunate that Dickon is here. Go you and clothe your nakedness quickly, my boy. You shall be my page.'

On a bright November morning nearly four weeks later, Nan hung out of the first-floor window of Goody's house on the Bridge. Pressed close to her were Goody's grandchildren, with Aunt Isabel and Goody both leaning over them from the back to get as good a view as they could. Every window up and down the Bridge was packed. Men and boys straddled the gables of the roofs. The doors of the houses stood open and people swarmed in and out like bees from a hive, though constables of the Watch with their staves paraded the narrow street ready to drive stragglers back on to their doorsteps when the trumpets sounded for the way to be cleared.

It was the most wonderful morning in the whole of Nan's life. She was there to watch the Lord King ride in triumph into London after his glorious victory at Agincourt. The sun shone from a clear sky making brighter still the bright coloured cloths and tapestries, the garlanded branches of berries and evergreens with which every house was hung. Outside the Stone Gate two wooden giants supported a triumphal arch and offered to the King the keys of the City. At the London end of the Bridge were pillars surmounted by the lion and the antelope, and a figure of St. George carried a scroll which bore the King's motto, *Soli Deo Honor et Gloria*—To God alone be Honour and Glory.

All the way through the City the decorations were marvellous to behold. Pavilions and canopies were raised in the streets. The conduits ran with wine instead of water. A tower was built round Cheap Cross from which a company of lovely maidens would issue to dance before the King; a flock of white birds would be loosed to flutter round him; and as he passed, choirs of boys dressed as angels would burst into the Song of Agincourt, a hymn of triumph written specially for the occasion. It ran:

> Our King went forth to Normandy
> With grace and might of chivalry;
> And God for him wrought marvellously,
> Wherefore England may call and cry
> 'Deo gracias Anglia redde pro victoria'.

It had a rousing tune and the chorus '*Deo gracias Anglia*' was being hummed and whistled all over the town.

Nan had been with Grandfather to see the decorations but though the grandest display was in Cheap, not for anything would she have exchanged her place in Goody's window. For here the way was so narrow that she would be almost able to touch the King as he passed.

She had another reason for delighting in her close-up view. Not only Grandfather but both her brothers were riding in the triumphal procession. Probably, Aunt Isabel reminded her, there was not another little girl in London who was so much honoured. Dickon was acting as page to Master Whittington, and Adam had come with Guy Whittington in the King's following from France.

It had been a month of feverish preparation, ever since that morning of Mayor's Day when the news arrived. Like a rain-cloud vanishing at sunrise all the misery and unrest had gone. Nobody had time to worry about grumblers and malcontents and Lollards, and such-like trouble-makers. There was too much to be done. Besides all the preparations in the streets, there was food and wine to be prepared for the feasting, and every citizen wanted new clothes. Mercers and haberdashers and glovers and cordwainers and merchant tailors were all worked off their feet. The liveries of the Mayor and Aldermen and the Companies and Craft Guilds needed hundreds of yards of cloth in scarlet and white, for it had been decided that everyone in the procession should wear the colours of the shield of St. George. Like everybody else Dickon had been working night and day, helping to produce these huge supplies. Nan had hardly set eyes on him. But it was clear that Dickon had changed. He was carefree and gay as he had not been since the day of the fight on the wharf, the day that he learned that he was to be a mercer. Already he talked as if he had been a freeman of the Mercers' Company for years, and cheerfully promised Nan a host of wonderful gifts from Bruges and Antwerp when he went there. Nan tried to question him about what had happened to Thomas Bason and the Silver Steel. Had he been caught? She was a-tiptoe to know. But Dickon could not tell her. He had ventured to ask Master Whittington, but the only answer he could get was that Thomas Bason had died in France. Whether he had died in battle or died as a traitor, Master Whittington was not prepared to say.

It seemed as if they had been waiting for ever by the window. The children complained noisily and even Nan began to tire of staring at the crowds. The Mayor and Sheriffs and the Aldermen and all the heads of the City Companies had ridden away hours ago to meet the King on Blackheath. It had been exciting to watch them. Just after the Mayor rode the Prior of Christchurch who was always first Alderman of the City; next came Master Whittington who had been Mayor three times. He raised his hand and saluted Nan as he passed and she waved joyfully back. She tried to wave to Dickon too, but Dickon stared straight in front of him and would not even smile. Grandfather came next, among the other Aldermen, and then the rest of the principal citizens in red cloaks and red-and-white hoods and hose half-red half-white. It was a wonderful sight, but it had been gone now for nearly two hours and even Aunt Isabel wished that it would hurry up. They all left the window for a while and refreshed themselves with milk and manchet bread.

Suddenly Nan cried, 'Listen!' From the Surrey side of the river came the joyful sound of bells. They all rushed back to the window and Nan leaned out so far that Goody had to grip her firmly by the legs. Now the ringing began in the belfry of the Bridge Chapel, close beside them, and immediately, as though this were a signal, all the bells of London burst forth together. Even the noise on Mayor's Day morning was as nothing to it.

It rolled backwards and forwards across the river and seemed to fill the very sky. The Triumph had begun.

First came the Mayor and Aldermen, proud to lead their hero into the City; then a company of men-at-arms, their helms and breastplates shining; next a group of heralds gorgeously blazoned; then the banner of England, and after it, riding alone, came Harry the King.

Nan held her breath, unable for a moment to believe her eyes. She had expected to see him in full armour, his crown on top of his helmet, his sword drawn and the pennon flying from his lance. But he wore no armour. He did not even wear his crown. He was dressed in a plain gown of purple cloth—purple, the colour of Lent, the colour of mourning. No jewels hung round his neck and his head was bare. What a strange way for a victorious king to ride.

As he went slowly by, looking neither to right nor to left, the people, awed by the absence of pomp, ceased to cheer. Instead they took up the chorus of the Song of Agincourt—'*Deo gracias Anglia redde pro victoria*'. The tune swelled and echoed through the narrow passage of the Bridge till it swept like a wave ahead of the King as he rode into London.

Aunt Isabel, leaning over Nan, explained in a whisper that it was his Grace's own wish that he should come without personal grandeur. He would not even allow his battered helmet or his dented sword to be carried before him. No songs were to be sung in his praise, but only in praise to God. Nor would he tarry for any speechmaking till he had been to St. Paul's for a *Te Deum*.

Nan listened gravely, but in her secret heart she wished that the King had at least worn his crown. The group of lords, his trusted friends, riding immediately behind him, were as soberly clad as he was. But after they had passed the procession again became gorgeous with colour.

A strong guard of soldiers in armour came next, some on horseback, some on foot, but all gay with pennons and banners and blazoned surcoats. A party of English bowmen followed, lustily cheered by the crowd, and then a display of royal splendour that made up for the King's sober gown. The banners carried by the heralds were encrusted with gold, but the arms embroidered upon them were not the leopards of England but the lilies of France. The royal princes riding in splendour were not English princes but French ones.

'They are the King's prisoners,' declared Aunt Isabel softly. 'His Grace gave orders that though he would have no pomp for himself, his royal captives were to be treated with full honours. The Mayor received the command from Dover. The Duke of Orleans and the Duke of Bourbon are somewhere among them, but with all these French nobles, I know not which they are.'

After the prisoners had passed Nan began to be a little weary. The procession seemed to be unending. The chief interest now was to watch for Adam, and for Dickon, who had not returned with Master Whittington. Adam appeared quite soon, riding behind Guy Whittington in a company of the King's Household. Dickon probably would come later, with the rest of the City Companies. She decided not to wait.

She craned her neck for one last peep, and, looking along towards London, the shining cross on the top of the Bridge Chapel caught her eye. For some reason she remembered vividly the day she had lit candles there—one for Adam and one for Dickon. She made up her mind that tomorrow she would go and light two more—just to say Thank you.

Still humming under her breath, '*Deo gracias Anglia*'—she climbed down.

The children seized her. 'Tell us a story,' they begged her.

Nan sighed. She did not feel in the mood for a story. But they had been so good.

'What story shall it be?' she asked.

They did not hesitate. Both of them spoke at once.

'Tell us the one you told us before; the one about Dick Whittington and Bow Bells.'

The arms of London

Postscript

BEFORE you put down this book I should like to tell you a little about some of the pictures and also about the fun I had hunting out the background for it. I'm sure those of you who like a good detective story would have enjoyed it as much as I did.

First of all I must introduce John Stow. He was my main guide. He lived in the reign of Elizabeth I and made a book about London in which he told the history of every street and of the most important houses and popped in many stories about the people who lived in them. He called it *A Survey of London*. You can still get it, and I took a copy with me when I set out to explore the City and to discover the landmarks of Whittington's London.

If ever you do this for yourselves, you may like to start as I did, by taking a train to Cannon Street. When you come out of the station turn sharply to your left and you will find that the street running down to the Thames is still called Dowgate and that even today there are boats tied up at the bottom. This part of the City has been almost totally destroyed by bombs; but as all the houses have been swept away, you can move about among the ruins of modern London, and find the street plan of old London there under your feet, its tiny lanes preserved as passages between what were, before the war, big City buildings.

I found Grantham's Lane without any difficulty, though it no longer appears on maps of London, and I stepped right on to the piece of ground where Grantham's Inn must once have stood. There was a bomb crater just in front of me, and as I poked about I caught sight of some squared stones which had probably been part of the very house which was to be the centre of my story—for you see Grantham's Inn was a real house. John Stow says that it was built by John Grantham, mayor of London, in the reign of Edward III. No picture of it exists, but I have drawn one to show what it was probably like.

I next went to Cripplegate, following the very route that Dickon and Nan took with Master Whittington. I crossed Thames Street and went up the hill, past the site of Master Whittington's house in The Royal. His church, St. Michael Paternoster is still there, but not as he knew it, for it was destroyed in the Great Fire of 1666 and rebuilt by Wren.

The Tower Royal which once stood at the top of the hill, vanished three centuries ago, but I paused on the pavement outside a radio shop and looked about me. A narrow passage beside it bore the name *Tower Royal*! I do not believe that Sherlock Holmes himself ever had a bigger thrill than that discovery gave me.

If you too go to Cripplegate you will find that Grub Street has become Milton Street. This is another blitzed area where only a few battered houses remain. Moorfields is once more a wide open space, and you, like Dickon, can gaze across it and see the towers of city churches over the long line of London Wall. This Wall has remained all these centuries hidden under buildings and has proved the only thing in the neighbourhood strong enough to resist bombs. Beyond the ruin of St. Giles' Church stands the corner bastion of the Wall (see the picture at the beginning of Chapter Fourteen). I made that sketch on the spot, but added the moat and the little water gate from an old picture, and drew the belfry of St. Giles as it probably was in Dickon's time.

The house in Grub Street (see page 49) survived until not so very long ago and was commonly called Whittington's House. I could find no positive proof that he really did live there, nor in the so-called Whittington's Palace in Hart Street. His only certain home was in The Royal. But Whittington was a great merchant and a very rich man, and he may well have had more than one house for the needs of his business.

The old tale of Dick Whittington and his cat is even more difficult to account for. It did not appear in print until he had been dead for a couple of centuries, and nobody knows how it started. The idea that Whittington himself made it up to amuse a little girl is only a joke on my part. But it is at least in keeping with the character of a man so generous and so dearly loved that, after five hundred years, he is remembered less as the greatest merchant of his age than as Dick Whittington, the hero of a favourite nursery story.

John Stow was not my only guide. I relied also on the work of Anthony van der Wyngaerde, who was an artist commissioned by Philip II of Spain, about 1550, to do a series of views of London. There is an air of truth about his drawings which suggests that he used his eyes and drew what he saw, and did not merely make formal maps, as some other artists did. The bird's eye view of London Bridge on page 140 is taken directly from his, except for a small alteration to the Drawbridge Gate. The great stone gate that Wyngaerde drew was not built until a dozen years after the time of my story. It replaced a timber one of which no picture exists.

There is one other view of the Bridge a good deal earlier than Wyngaerde's. I have made use of it for the chapter heading of Chapter Six and also for the design of the jacket. It is taken from an illuminated manuscript in the British Museum, of poems written by Charles, Duke of Orleans who was taken prisoner at Agincourt, rode into London among King Harry's captives, and languished for years in the Tower.

I will only mention a few of the smaller drawings. The seal illustrated on page 45 is copied from an impression of Dick Whittington's own seal on a parchment in the Guildhall Museum, and I have to thank the curator for allowing me to make use of his drawing. The bed on page 199 is taken from a very old print showing the death of Richard Whittington. The picture of Adam repairing the dislocated arm (page 18) comes from another manuscript in the British Museum which has pictures of many astonishing operations by thirteenth- and fourteenth-century doctors. The original ale slipper, shown on page 168, is in the West Gate Museum at Winchester, and the shackles that locked Dickon's wrists can be seen in the London Museum. The original of the Song of Agincourt is in the possession of Trinity College, Cambridge, but it is here modernized sufficiently for you to be able to pick out the notes for yourselves.

Finally, in the heading of the last chapter I have enjoyed myself by making a picture puzzle. I had intended to do a long strip showing Henry V and all his warriors, but I soon realized that it was too big a task if the book was ever to be finished. So I thought of another idea. Do you remember the speech in Shakespeare's *Henry V* which begins:

'What's he that wishes so? My cousin Westmorland?'

This chapter heading illustrates the banners of all the nobles mentioned in that speech and, for good measure, recalls the challenge 'Cry "God for Harry! England and Saint George!"' They represent (1) The banner of St. George; (2) Nevill, Earl of Westmorland; (3) The royal arms of England; (4) Humphrey, Duke of Gloucester; (5) The personal standard of Henry V; (6) Gilbert, Lord Talbot; (7) Beauchamp, Earl of Warwick; (8) John, Duke of Bedford; (9) Montacute, Earl of Salisbury; (10) Thomas, Duke of Exeter.

Before I end this Postscript I must make a confession. I have altered the date of one historical event to make it fit in to the story. Guy Whittington and his father were attacked by the followers of Oldcastle, just as described, but the attack took place a year later, in 1416, not in 1415. It must have been after Guy's return from France for he was present at Agincourt. There is no evidence that it was he who acted as messenger between the King and Whittington, but he might easily have done so, for Whittington did actually send extra money to the King during the siege of Harfleur. There is no record in history of the alchemist or his plot; but one Benedict Wolman, hosteler, was executed in 1416 for complicity in a plot to bring the bogus Richard II from Scotland, and his head was displayed on the Drawbridge Gate of London Bridge.

LONDON *in the time of* King Henry V

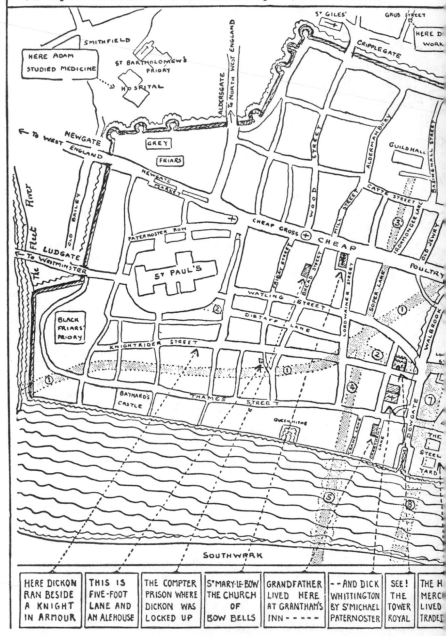

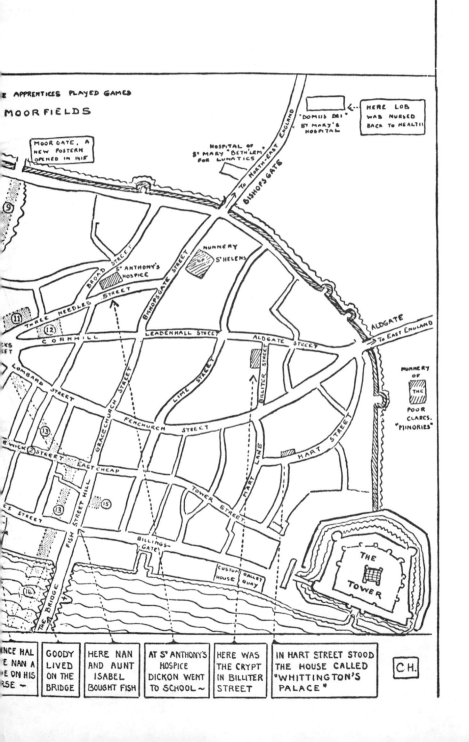

RE APPRENTICES PLAYED GAMES

MOORFIELDS

HERE LOB WAS NURSED BACK TO HEALTH!!

"DOMUS DEI" ST MARY'S HOSPITAL

MOOR GATE, A NEW POSTERN OPENED IN 1415

HOSPITAL OF ST MARY "BETH'LEM" FOR LUNATICS

TO NORTH-EAST ENGLAND

BISHOPSGATE

⑨

BROAD STREET

ST ANTHONY'S HOSPICE

NUNNERY OF ST HELENS

BISHOPSGATE STREET

THREE NEEDLES STREET

⑪

⑫

CORNHILL

LEADENHALL STREET

ALDGATE STREET

ALDGATE

TO EAST ENGLAND

LOMBARD STREET

GRACECHURCH STREET

LIME STREET

BILLITER STREET

NUNNERY OF THE POOR CLARES. "MINORIES"

CKS KET

⑬

SWICK STREET

FENCHURCH STREET

EASTCHEAP

HART STREET

CS STREET

⑬

FISH STREET HILL

⑮

TOWER STREET

HART LANE

THE TOWER

BILLINGS- GATE

THE BRIDGE

⑭

CUSTUM HOUSE

GALLEY QUAY

INCE HAL E NAN A E ON HIS RSE ~

GOODY LIVED ON THE BRIDGE

HERE NAN AND AUNT ISABEL BOUGHT FISH

AT ST ANTHONY'S HOSPICE DICKON WENT TO SCHOOL ~

HERE WAS THE CRYPT IN BILLITER STREET

IN HART STREET STOOD THE HOUSE CALLED "WHITTINGTON'S PALACE"

C.H.